Aaron Elkins is an Edgar Award winner, and lives with his wife, Charlotte, on Washington's Olympic Peninsula.

GOOD BLOOD

Professor of anthropology Gideon Oliver, and his wife Julie, take a much-needed holiday in Italy. Their friend Phil has invited them to his family's island in Lake Maggiore. But the breathtaking view and sumptuous food come at a price . . . When some bones are unearthed in the locality, Colonel Caravale of the *carabinieri* calls on Gideon's expertise. Knowing that his host's son has been kidnapped, Gideon sets out to identify the bones. But along the way, he exposes some deceptions that lay bare the malignant, long-hidden secrets at the dark heart of a highborn family.

Books by Aaron Elkins
Published by The House of Ulverscroft:

TURNCOAT
WHERE THERE'S A WILL

AARON ELKINS

GOOD BLOOD

Complete and Unabridged

ULVERSCROFT
Leicester

First published in Great Britain in 2004 by
Robert Hale Limited
London

First Large Print Edition
published 2006
by arrangement with
Robert Hale Limited
London

British Library CIP Data

Elkins, Aaron J.
   Good blood.—Large print ed.—
   Ulverscroft large print series: general fiction
   1. Anthropologists—Fiction
   2. Murder—Investigation—Italy—Fiction
   3. Detective and mystery stories
   4. Large type books
   I. Title
   813.5′4 [F]

   ISBN 1–84617–440–6

Published by
F. A. Thorpe (Publishing)
Anstey, Leicestershire

Set by Words & Graphics Ltd.
Anstey, Leicestershire
Printed and bound in Great Britain by
T. J. International Ltd., Padstow, Cornwall

This book is printed on acid-free paper

Acknowledgments

As usual, Gideon Oliver has had to turn for advice to his real-life forensic colleagues. I am happy to thank two of America's most eminent forensic anthropologists, Stanley J. Rhine and Walter Birkby, for making the Skeleton Detective look smarter than he would have otherwise.

My dear old friend Harvey Sherman of Salomon Smith Barney, who is probably the world's most honest and industrious stockbroker, cheerfully instructed me in the ins and outs of funny-money-finagling. Jean Blaurock of Bank America filled me in on wire-transfer details.

My new friend Paola Lucentini was a treasure house of information on Italian language and culture.

The Hotel Primavera that is described in the book is real, and I owe my thanks to its friendly staff for helping to make my research time in Stresa a pleasure.

Prologue

The Village of Stresa, Lake Maggiore, Italy, September 7, 1960

Domenico de Grazia was a gentleman of the old school, a refined and courtly patrician, a man of breeding, poised and self-assured. Many of the simpler folk, out of respect for his lineage and his impeccable bearing, still spoke of him as *il conte*, the count, although the nobility had been abolished more than fifteen years before. And some took their hats off when he passed, but this was a practice he gently discouraged.

Despite his reputation, Domenico knew himself to be a shy man, uncomfortable with intimacy and easily embarrassed. At this moment he was finding it impossibly hard to make the proposal that had brought him to the modest apartment of Franco and Emma Ungaretti. For half an hour he had sat in their living room making stilted small talk, while they plainly wondered, with many glances between them, what had brought him there. Emma was his niece, his brother Cosimo's only child. Franco was her husband, whom

1

Domenico employed, out of an admittedly grudging charity, as a part-time gamekeeper on the de Grazia estate.

It was not often that Domenico visited them, although once upon a time, and not so long ago at that, he had doted on Emma. But Franco Ungaretti he could barely force himself to tolerate. Emma was such a pretty, good-natured girl too; to think of the husbands from whom she might have had her choice . . . but that was neither here nor there.

With his second glass of Amaretto (which he detested) came the resolve he needed. He put down the glass and took a deep breath. 'My children,' he said — and immediately regretted the choice of words, given the strange proposition he was about to make — 'as you know, my wife has recently suffered a second miscarriage — '

Emma began to murmur something, but Domenico, determined to carry on now that he had gotten started, talked over her. ' — and Dr Luzzatto has told us she can risk no further pregnancies.'

More sympathetic murmurs, from both of them.

'Thank you, please let me finish. As you also know, the de Grazia family has maintained its holdings and its place in the life of our beloved Italy for over six hundred years, from the days of the Dukes of Piedmont.'

'Yes, Uncle,' Emma said.

'Good.' He patted her hand, but quickly drew his own back as if he'd touched a flame. That had been another bad idea. 'I am sure you will both agree that there must always be a de Grazia to continue the heritage of our family, and to — and so forth.' He was already losing them. Emma looked confused and Franco was alternating between smirking at what he no doubt considered empty platitudes, and watching a bicycle race on the muted television set in a far corner. The set had been Domenico's second-anniversary present to them a year earlier.

He decided to skip the middle paragraphs of his prepared speech. 'I must have an heir,' he blurted. 'In that regard I come to you — '

'But you have an heir, Uncle,' Emma said. 'Your daughter. Francesca.'

Emma had many fine traits, but a piercing intelligence was not among them. 'Francesca is the dearest of children, the darling of my heart,' Domenico explained kindly, 'but I must have a male heir; someone to take my place someday, someone to carry on the name.'

'Oh. But you could adopt someone, couldn't you?'

3

'I could, yes, and I've given the idea a great deal of thought.'

At this, Franco's head swiveled from the television. Bored and noncommittal till now, his face suddenly shone with . . . anticipation? Hope? Did this parasite think Domenico was going to make him his heir? What, adopt him? The mere thought was enough to make Domenico shudder.

Franco Ungaretti had been an Olympic silver medalist, a famous skier of breathtaking speed and daring, and as handsome as a movie star to boot. *Il Valangone*, the Avalanche, they had called him. But this Avalanche had also been an uneducated lout, the son of a laborer who was the son of a laborer: an ignorant, self-centered womanizer blessed with a native ability to manufacture a smooth, superficial patter that the media had been in love with. Emma, like so many other innocent young girls, had fallen under the spell of his shallow charms, and it had been her everlasting misfortune to be with him the night that he got drunk enough to decide to make an honest woman of her and get married.

Less than three months later he had been struck by an automobile. Several vertebrae in his neck had been crushed, and his sports career — and all the fame and endorsements

4

that came with it — was over. Most athletes, so Domenico understood, put on weight when their athletic careers came to an end. But Franco had lost it. At thirty-three, with his neck now permanently askew, he was a wizened, bitter old man, all sinews and grinding tendons, and the smooth patter was a thing of the past. All that was left from before was the selfish, narrow lout that was, and had always been, the essential Franco Ungaretti. And still, Emma adored him. Love, the old proverb said, was like food or music; there was no accounting for taste.

'But adoption is of no interest to me,' Domenico continued. 'What good is an heir without the splendid genes of our family? It isn't only the de Grazia name that must go on, but the good de Grazia blood that runs through our veins and has made us what we are.'

'Good blood,' Franco echoed, looking interested. 'That's very important.' Beef-brained he might be, but there was a streak of cunning in him; even if he didn't know what was going on, he could smell advantage to himself at five kilometers. Well, he was right enough about that.

'Therefore,' Domenico said, 'I have a proposition to make to you.' This was the part that he had rehearsed again and again, but

5

now he rushed clumsily through it, addressing neither of them in particular, with his eyes fixed on the coffee table. 'I would like Emma's consent, with Franco's approval, of course, to be the bearer of my child' — his face was burning — 'by means of a process — very impersonal, very proper, performed by a qualified physician — of . . . of artificial insemination. This would, it goes without saying, involve no contact between us. I would, of course, expect to repay you — both of you — generously — for the inconvenience it would cause.'

Emma, shocked, covered her mouth and stared at him. Franco's eyes narrowed. The congealed gears of his mind were beginning to move, however slushily.

'The child would be brought up as my own, my own and Stefania's,' Domenico said hurriedly, speaking to Emma. 'No one but Stefania and I and the two of you would know the truth.'

'Uncle! I, I — ' She was blushing furiously.

'How would that work?' Franco asked. 'That no one would ever know the truth?'

How perfectly Domenico understood Franco's mind, so true to its owner's class. If there was profit in it, he was interested, but first he needed assurance that his own cherished manhood — his most prized possession — would suffer no slurs. Domenico was ready with his answers. 'Emma would go to a small village up in the mountains. Gignese, a pleasant place with a good climate. I have contacts there, and Dr Luzzatto would always be within easy reach. She would have a fine villa and be cared for in luxury, anything she wished. A maid, a cook. Franco, you could go with her. A nice vacation, why not? Only after the baby was born would she return to Stresa. People would be told that she had become ill with tuberculosis and had gone to a sanatorium in Switzerland. No one would know, I promise you.'

'That's all very fine,' Franco said. 'But what about your wife, what about Stefania? Suddenly, without a pregnancy, she has a baby? How could that be explained?'

'That will present no problem. No one knows about my wife's latest . . . ' He faltered. Answering this oaf's rude questions about the most intimate details of his life took more willpower than he'd anticipated, but what choice did he have? ' . . . about her latest miscarriage,' he continued. 'However, everyone — the family, our friends, the servants — knows about the first one. So, like Emma, Stefania will go away for a while. It will be explained that, in order to insure against a recurrence of her difficulties, she has gone to a maternity rest home near Venice, where she can be professionally cared for at all times while she awaits the arrival of her baby. When she returns home, she will have the infant with her.'

Franco shrugged his approval. 'And what about my job? If I went with Emma to Gignese.'

'Naturally, you would be given a leave with full pay.' That, Domenico thought, would be no hardship to himself. With Franco not acting as gamekeeper, he expected a considerable reduction in poaching, not that it mattered one way or the other. The animals on the de Grazia lands had never been a source of income. There had been no gamekeeper before Franco, and there would be none after, unless, God forbid, another girl in the family brought home a husband equally worthless.

'In addition, I would hope you would indulge me by accepting a gift of, say, ten thousand dollars — American dollars — as a small token of my gratitude, my sincere gratitude, to both of you.'

Franco darted a quick look at Emma, who responded with an uncertain shake of her head. But Domenico could see that she was thinking about it.

'Also,' he added silkily, 'I couldn't help but notice that your Lancia is showing its age, Franco. I was thinking it would be a pleasure to see you with a new one, perhaps a larger model?' The Lancia, too, had been his gift: a wedding present.

He was ashamed of himself for dealing so baldly with Franco Ungaretti instead of with his own niece. It should have been Emma's decision to make. Indulging Franco's puerile cravings should have had nothing to do with it. But he had to have a 'yes'; there were no other options. And he knew his chances were best with Franco.

Franco shrugged. His animal instincts sensed a shift in the balance of power. 'A Lancia? I don't know.' He studied his extended left foot. 'It's a nice car, I suppose. But a Ferrari . . . now there's an automobile for you.'

Domenico held in his anger. This animal was haggling over the use of his wife's body. Not as a question of principle, of 'yes' or 'no,' but of price.

'A Ferrari,' he said through compressed lips. 'Yes, all right, that would also be possible.'

'What if she has a miscarriage? What if the child is a girl?'

Domenico shivered. On their own, his fingers traced the sign of the cross. These things must not, would not, happen. 'I would still consider that you had fulfilled your part of the bargain. What do you say?'

'Uncle — ' Emma said, and Domenico held his breath. 'What does Aunt Stefania . . . how does Aunt Stefania . . . ' She bit her lip and was silent.

She had hit on a sore point, and Domenico was honest, if halting, about it. 'Your aunt is not entirely . . . comfortable with the arrangement. Naturally enough, she would prefer that it not be necessary. But she understands the need. She will love the child as her own, you should have no fear on that score. And . . . ' he hesitated, hoping he was still telling the truth, ' . . . and she will love you none the less for it.'

'I see.' Emma didn't look much comforted.

Franco patted her shoulder. 'Give us time to think it over,' he said. 'We'll talk about it and let you know our decision tomorrow.' He gave Emma a remnant of the old, oily smile. 'All right, sweetheart?'

Emma nodded, looking at neither of them.

Domenico reached for his cane and stood up. Franco had made up his mind. He would wheedle or browbeat her into it. It was as good as done.

'I'll see myself out,' he said, unable to meet Emma's eyes.

10

★ ★ ★

Every Thursday afternoon without exception, throughout the long winter, Domenico would have Clemente drive him up the mountain to Gignese for his two o'clock visit with the Ungarettis to assure himself that things were well. At first these visits were awkward. They would sit stiffly in the beautifully furnished parlor, the three of them, over china cups of tea or coffee, and comment on the unusually fine weather, or the health-giving mountain air, or the lovely view from the windows. As for the subject on everyone's mind, the subject of Emma's pregnancy, Domenico would scrupulously avoid it. (Stefania wasn't the only one 'not entirely comfortable' with the situation.) And so it would hang between them like an immovable, impenetrable curtain around which they were forced to talk.

Domenico would ask if there was anything they wanted. The answer was always no, although Franco would sometimes have some additional requirement concerning the promised Ferrari. At precisely three o'clock Domenico would rise, Emma would offer her cheek to be kissed, he would nod to Franco — for some time he had preferred not to shake hands with him — and he would leave, feeling guilty and unfulfilled, as if there was something he had come to do, and he hadn't done it. Emma was so quiet now, so pale and resigned. With time his old affection for her had blossomed again, and his heart ached to see her as she was.

But after a month Franco's interest in these weekly calls waned and he began finding other things to do: coffee and newspapers with his friends at the café; bocce on the court beside the village square. He would spend days at a time back in Stresa, doing God knew what — cavorting with his mistresses, Domenico assumed. But it was all to the good. Emma began to blossom. She became talkative again, and laughed often, with that merry little hiccup at the end, a sweet sound Domenico hadn't heard for years. With the swelling of her abdomen she seemed to become contented and happy, and Domenico along with her. His weekly visits, far from being a chore, became something he looked impatiently forward to.

Most important, Dr Luzzatto pronounced her health, and that of the developing child, excellent. And it was his opinion, from the way she was carrying the baby, that it was indeed a boy.

There were only two things to mar his happiness. First — and this was something that Dr Luzzatto had warned him about more than once — he worried that there would be a problem later, when it was time for her to turn the child over to Stefania and him. The hormones that flowed through a new mother's body, Luzzatto had said, often exerted a power that no man could understand. Emma was likely to experience depression, even despair, when the baby was taken from her. Domenico should prepare himself for it. It was natural and expectable, and there was nothing to be done about it. Given time, it would pass. Still, it hurt him to think of her unhappiness to come.

The other worm in the apple was a thing he learned from Caterina, the live-in servant he'd hired to look after Emma. Emma had become friends with the young laundress who came once a week to bring the washed and pressed linens and to take away the dirty ones. This Gia, according to Caterina, was a sluttish, independent creature with loose morals and brutish manners. At first the friendship between two women of such different classes had been inexplicable, but then one day Caterina had heard them whispering and giggling about pregnancy and childbirth. Gia was also pregnant, and there lay the source of their closeness. But — and here the housekeeper lowered her voice to a whisper — Gia could not even say for sure who the father was. The dreadful girl spoke laughingly — laughingly! of giving the child up for adoption if there was money to be made from it. Even in jest, it wasn't right, it wasn't natural. Caterina wrung her hands beneath her apron. This Gia was not a fit companion for a woman of Emma's class.

In his thoughts Domenico agreed with her and might easily have seen to it that there was no further contact between them. But he hesitated to interfere. Whom else did Emma have to giggle with and confide her girlish secrets in? Franco? Besides, once she returned to Stresa and was with her own kind, time and distance would necessarily put an end to their closeness. The problem would take care of itself.

★ ★ ★

But the other problem, the problem of Emma's maternal hormones, did not take care of itself.

Emma gave birth at the villa in Gignese. Her labor, attended only by a midwife and her assistant (Dr Luzzatto had been with a patient in Belgirate and had not made it back in time) was difficult and extremely hard on her. The baby, a strapping, squalling boy, was healthy — everything Domenico could have wished for — but Emma's condition troubled him. When he arrived a few days later (she had asked that he permit her time to recover, which was what gave him the first real inkling that all was not as well as it might have been), she remained secluded in her bedroom, and it was the nurse who brought him the beautiful infant. Dr Luzzatto prevented Domenico from seeing her until the following day. It was not her physical condition that was cause for concern, Luzzatto warned gravely, but her mental state. It was more precarious than he'd expected. Four days now, and still her spirits were dangerously low.

The following day, when Domenico was permitted to call on her — Stefania was not with him, having preferred to remain at home — Emma was on a regimen of tranquilizers that Luzzatto had prescribed. It was like talking to some cleverly made mannequin, an automaton controlled by gears and pulleys, but ultimately lifeless. Her hair had been combed and her face had been made up to hide her pallor. She smiled, she nodded, she replied to questions, but there was no emotion, no human connection. Her eyes were enough to make one weep. For Domenico, all the joy had been squeezed from the occasion. It was the tranquilizers that were making her so spiritless, Luzzatto said, but both men knew there was more to it than that.

Even Franco, for once in his life, had been genuinely worried about his wife's state of mind for the last month. Responding to the stress in true Franco fashion, he had run off to be with his family in Caprera for the final two weeks of Emma's pregnancy, claiming that his presence only added to her nervous tension.

Domenico, who had considered his absence God-sent, had said nothing about this desertion, but he was blunt with Franco at dinner that night, while Emma stayed in her bed. She had so far refused even to look at the infant, which was being cared for by a wet nurse.

'What she needs is a baby of her own,' Domenico told him.

Franco shook his head. 'Sure, that's what I told her. But she doesn't want to go through it again. I'll tell you the truth, neither do I.' He puffed his cheeks and blew air from his mouth. It had been a few days since he'd shaved. 'So what's to be done?'

Domenico pushed away his untouched plate of pasta and let his chin fall to his chest. 'I don't know.'

But later that night, sitting in his darkened room, unable to sleep, he had an idea, and the next morning it was Domenico de Grazia who carried Emma's breakfast of caffè latte, focaccia, and marmalade to her. He set the tray on the bed for her, pulled a chair up next to her, and got quickly to the point.

'Emma, my dear, your friend Gia — has she had her child?'

'I don't know, Uncle. Any day now.'

'And what will happen to it? Is it true that she plans to give it up for adoption?'

'I don't know, Uncle. I think maybe that was just talk.' She offered up a listless smile that wrung his heart. 'And you feel different once you've had it.'

'But can she afford to keep it? A single woman? A laundress?'

Emma had picked up a wedge of focaccia but put it down again. 'It will be hard. She has no father. Her mother no longer speaks to her. She has no money . . . It won't be easy.'

But her face said it all: she would happily have traded places.

Domenico laid his hand on hers and tried to keep the building excitement out of his voice. 'Emma, I have an idea. Now don't say no until you hear me out . . . '

★   ★   ★

17

And so the arrangements were made. With the help of a generous financial settlement from Domenico, Gia agreed to part with her baby (a little too readily for Domenico's taste), and when Emma and Franco returned to Stresa a few days later, after their absence of six months, they, too, had a newborn baby boy to show off to the world. And the glowing Emma was her happy, sweet-natured self again.

The two infants were christened a few weeks apart at the parish church in Stresa, where Domenico's great-great-great-grandfather had been christened in 1786, the year of the church's founding. Domenico's new heir was called Vincenzo Paoli de Grazia, after San Vincenzo di Paoli, the great benefactor of the poor. The Ungarettis named their baby Filiberto, after Franco's maternal grandfather, a knife grinder. It was hardly the name Domenico would have chosen, but there was no room in his heart to begrudge anyone anything. Filiberto Ungaretti it would be.

All was well.

1

The Village of Stresa, Lake Maggiore, Italy,
the Present

It was the blue Honda that had started it,
both traffic policemen agreed afterward.

The two veteran traffic officers, spruce and
natty in their crisp blue uniforms and their
caps, belts, and crisp white shirts, were just
discarding their cigarettes and pushing
through the glass doors of the Polizia
Municipale building to report for the
morning shift when the blast of noise
— squealing tires, blaring horns, warning
shouts — made them turn back toward the
street.

The little Honda was trying to do the
impossible or at the very least the idiotic — to
pass another car on the Corso Italia in the
middle of the morning rush. True, the Corso
was ample by local standards, the widest
avenue in Stresa, a beautiful concourse that
ran picturesquely along the lakefront, with
two lanes in each direction. And as rush
hours went, Stresa's wasn't anything to brag
about, but that didn't mean you could expect

to lane-change as if you were on the motorway around Rome. And certainly not with a big semitrailer truck — a Mercedes-Benz cab hauling an empty flatbed — bearing down on you in the oncoming lane and more than filling it.

There was nothing they could do but stand there and watch it happen. The driver of the truck slammed on his brakes — they could see him pulling on the wheel so hard (as if it made any difference) that he was standing up, like a wagon driver hauling back on the reins. The truck slewed to the left, veered in front of the oncoming traffic, bounced heavily up over the curb, scattering pedestrians, and went scraping and grinding across the entrance to the police parking lot until its huge left front wheel sank squarely into one of the planting beds that bordered the entrance.

The only damage to city property that they could see were a couple of bushes that had been run over, but the truck was in sorry shape. The flatbed in the rear, carried forward by its momentum, had swung around to the right, snapping or twisting something in the trailer connection, so that it ended up tilted and jackknifed, with its rear end clear on the other side of the street, almost up to the sidewalk and thoroughly eliminating any possibility of through traffic for hours to come. And as if that weren't bad enough, an oncoming French tour bus had also veered wildly to avert disaster, and had ended up directly across from the police station, drunkenly sprawled in the Piazza Matteoti, which the city hall shared with the upscale Café Bolongaro. Café tables and chairs, unused at this time of the morning (so there was one little piece of luck, at any rate), had been overturned and now littered the little square. The bus passengers sat in their seats like statues, silent and white. Below the line of stunned faces, printed in bright red letters on the side of the bus, was the tour company's slogan: LE PLAISER DE VOYAGER.

As for the blue Honda that had caused it all, it had managed to scoot out of the way back into its lane and was long gone.

The two constables were running toward the driver before the truck tire had finished sinking into the soft earth. 'Hey there, are you all right? Are you hurt?' Officer Giuseppe di Paolo called up to him.

The poorly shaven, gray-mustached man raised his head from the steering wheel, looking shell-shocked. 'All right? Yes . . . it wasn't my fault . . . there was a car . . . '

'We saw, we saw,' the officer said. 'Did you get the license plate?'

'No, I couldn't . . . it was . . . no.'

At this point Officer Gualtiero Favaretto asserted his natural authority (he was senior by four months) and took charge. 'You,' he commanded the driver, 'sit there a minute, make sure you're not injured. Then go inside at once and tell them what happened.' His tone grew more somber. 'You'd better ask for Comandante Boldini.'

The driver nodded wanly. 'Yes, sir.'

Favaretto turned to his partner. 'Giuseppe, this is going to create the mother of all snarls. Nobody's going to be able to get through town. I'll do what I can to get started cleaning up here. You better go in and tell them we need to put somebody out on the Corso up by the Regina Palace, and somebody else down at the Villa Palavicino turnoff, to divert traffic.'

Di Paolo started docilely in, then stopped and gestured vaguely in the direction of the warren of narrow, winding alleys and pedestrian streets that constituted Stresa. And in the other direction was the lake. The only avenue of any substance in the town was the Corso itself. 'Divert to where?'

'That,' Favaretto replied magisterially, 'is their problem. And Giuseppe,' he added, waving at the obstructed police lot, 'tell him they'll have to get there on foot. There will be no vehicles leaving here for some time to come.'

★ ★ ★

Enrico Dellochio saw the whole thing too; unfortunately for him, from the best seat in the house — behind the wheel of the dove-gray, perfectly kept-up 1978 Daimler limousine that had been trailing the flatbed truck. He'd been stuck in its wake for three blocks, ever since the lumbering flatbed had turned unexpectedly out of Via Prini and cut directly in front of them, forcing him to jam on his brakes and bringing a petulant complaint from Achille de Grazia in the back seat. Enrico would ordinarily have had his suspicions about a truck cutting them off like that, but an empty flatbed with nobody visible in it but the driver? Not much threat there. Still, he checked the rearview mirror to satisfy himself that no one had come up behind to hem them in. No, nothing, just some tourist on a rented moped, driving with the frozen concentration of a man who wished he was anywhere but on it.

Enrico had spotted the blue Honda coming toward them, darting in and out of traffic like a bug, apparently well before the truck driver had. By the time the big rig's brake lights flashed on, Enrico had already eased the limo to a gentle, anticipatory standstill. He watched with a mixture of satisfaction and disgust — he hated idiot drivers — as the rig made the disastrous, swerving, locked-brake attempt at a stop that would leave it splayed like a beached whale across the full breadth of the Corso Italia. Meanwhile, here came the Honda, picking up speed as it slipped by the careening flatbed and getting back into its own lane barely in time to avoid the now stationary Daimler. It scooted by, gunning its engine, its rear end shimmying, and with maybe ten inches to spare. If they'd both been standing still, he could have reached out and grabbed the Honda's driver by the neck, which he wouldn't have minded doing.

'Crazy bastard!' Enrico shouted after him, applying the appropriate finger arrangement.

'Let's not have any of that,' came the adenoidal injunction from the backseat.

Enrico muttered to himself. He still tried to think of Achille as a polite, quiet kid who respected his elders, but that had been years ago, when Enrico had first started work for the boy's father, Vincenzo de Grazia, and it had been a misapprehension at the time. Since then, he'd come to know Achille only too well as the snotty, overbearing little turd

24

he was. So much for what being born to a life of privilege could do for a kid.

'Sorry, sir,' Enrico said politely. 'I couldn't help myself.'

It had been a few months now since Achille had suggested that Enrico address him as 'sir,' even in private, and it still rankled. Enrico was fifty-one years old, for Christ's sake. What was Achille, sixteen? And age differences aside, Enrico didn't take kindly to calling someone wearing a Hootie and the Blowfish T-shirt 'sir.'

By now the boy had taken in the mess in front of them. 'Oh, no, I don't believe it. Can we squeeze around that?'

'Not a chance,' Enrico said. 'Sir.'

'Well, what are you going to do? My French class starts in twenty minutes. My father will kill me if I miss another one. You better think of something, or you're in big trouble, Enrico, I'm telling you.'

That was another thing that got to him — this empty, pointless, throwing around of his puny weight — but Enrico had lots of practice repressing the urge to give the kid a whack across the chops. 'It won't be a problem, sir. That lane on our right, that's Via Principe Tomaso. We can — '

'That's a pedestrian street, isn't it?'

'Well, yes, technically, but it's early, the

25

crowds aren't out yet, we can get away with it. There are only a couple of tight corners. Principe Tomaso takes us up a block to Via Ottolini, where we can do a short left on Via Mazzini, which — '

'All right, all right, do it. Jesus Christ.'

'I have to back up a little first.'

Enrico stuck his head and arms out the window and made pushing motions with his hands. The moped driver was slow to understand, but finally rolled back a few feet. Enrico waved his thanks, reversed for a few feet, and turned up Via Principe Tomaso, a cobblestoned alley that ran between the sides and backs of buildings that faced the Corso, and was only just wide enough for the Daimler. Instinctively he glanced up at the mirror to see if anybody was following, but there was no one. There wouldn't be many people who'd be aware that you could get back onto the Corso by circling around this way. Fifty yards up the street, he turned into the equally narrow, equally empty Via Ottolini, edged cautiously around the planter boxes set out in front of the Hotel da Cesare, jogged around the blind corner at the intersection of Via Mazzini (where a surprised grocer setting his wares out on the pavement grumblingly made room for him to pass), eased with care onto Via Garibaldi —

'Enrico, are you sure you know what you're doing?'

'Yes, I know what I'm doing.' Achille had been in a fouler mood than usual from the start this morning, and Enrico, who was supposed to have had a day off today, was starting to feel a little testy himself. 'Don't get excited, we'll be back out on the road in two minutes. All we have to do is turn left on Via Rosmini there.'

'Then why are we just sitting here?'

Then why don't you look out the damn window and see? 'There's a car in our way, sir. That Audi up ahead, it's blocking Rosmini. It just backed out of the church parking lot, and it takes a while to get straightened out in these little alleys.'

Achille said something but Enrico didn't hear. He had made another one of his automatic rearview mirror checks and this time there was something there; a gray Opel hatchback with one man in it had drawn up behind them, no more than ten yards away.

Now they were blocked front and back. An edgy little prickle slid up the nape of his neck. Not that there was anything really unusual about the situation — this kind of thing was bound to happen all the time on Stresa's constricted old streets, and often did — but it was exactly the kind of predicament that he

27

wasn't supposed to get into, the kind of predicament he was paid to avoid: a narrow, virtually windowless alley hemmed in by walls of stone and stucco, a car in front and a car behind, and no room to get by either one of them.

He tapped the horn. 'Come on, come on, let's go!' he yelled to the one in front, still jiggling its way into a position from which it could drive forward. That one, he saw now, had two men in the front seat. He got a little edgier. This had been really stupid of him. The hell with the kid's French class. He'd known better, he should have used his head. They should have waited it out with everybody else on the Corso.

'Enrico, for Christ's sake,' Achille said angrily, with his hands to his ears, 'you could at least warn me before you blow that thing. With these stone walls — '

'Shut up,' Enrico said. 'Get down on the floor.'

Achille was shocked into stuttering. 'Wh — wh — what is it? Those men — '

'Get the hell down! Now!' Enrico snapped when the boy didn't move, and Achille hurriedly dropped out of sight behind him.

Enrico's eyes were fixed dead ahead. The Audi's doors had opened. The men were clambering out, brandishing handguns, their heads covered by stocking masks, their hands gloved. His nervousness had hardened into a sort of instant, stony calm. His mind was suddenly still, focused, stripped of extraneous thought. It was an instinctive reaction that had once made him a good cop and, later, a more-than-good soldier-for-hire. And it made him good at what he did for a living now.

Acting with disciplined speed, he made sure the doors were locked, pressed the button to roll up all the windows, flicked open the snaps on his holsters, jogged the grips of the handguns to make sure they were at the ready, and hit the memory button on the cell phone to dial the *carabinieri*. The two men ran up to the limo, one on either side, looking like a couple of monster twins, their features squashed and deformed by the stocking masks.

★ ★ ★

'Put the phone down!' Ugo Fogazzaro shouted through the gauzy skin of the mask, hammering on the window with the heel of his hand. 'Put the goddamned phone down!'

They'd just begun but already things were going wrong. *If the boss was such a great planner, how come nobody had mentioned the phone?* From the first day he'd had a bad feeling about this job.

The window glass was tinted, but Ugo could see that the driver had the telephone to his ear but wasn't speaking into it yet. Whoever he was calling hadn't yet answered. The driver stared ahead, stiff faced, without moving, ignoring the guns directed at him from either side. Ugo whacked the window with the butt of his gun, a heavy, snubnosed Ruger .357 magnum. The safety glass held up. He hit it again, harder, and this time it buckled, a hole opening up in the middle. Now he could hear the driver's voice.

'I'm in a car on — '

Using the barrel of the gun, Ugo reached in and batted the phone away. A welt appeared on the driver's temple, where the muzzle had scraped it, and quickly beaded with blood. The driver didn't move. Ugo put the Ruger up against the corner of his jaw. 'Turn off the engine.'

The driver did as he was told.

'Now unlock the doors, all of them.'

'The ignition has to be on.' He was still staring stolidly ahead, his jaw muscles working. A tough guy.

'No, it doesn't. Don't mess with me!' He shoved the muzzle hard against the man's jaw and clicked back the hammer with his thumb. 'Hurry up!'

There was a soft tick as the locks unlatched. Ugo pulled open the front door. On the passenger side, Marcello did the same.

'Keys,' Ugo said.

The driver took them from the ignition and handed them to him. Ugo flung them over a stone garden wall beside the church.

'Now,' he said, 'both hands on the wheel, up at the top. OK, now use your left hand to get your gun out of the holster. Two fingers only.'

'I don't carry a — '

'Don't bullshit me! told you once.' He dug the muzzle of the pistol with its jutting front sight into the tender place where neck and jaw intersected, and twisted. He could feel ligaments grind in there, and the driver grunted and tried to pull his head away. *What do you know, not so tough after all.*

The driver's gun — one of those pretty little German 9mm semiautomatics — was withdrawn between thumb and forefinger. Ugo snatched it out of his hand, a welcome fringe benefit; the damn thing was worth three times as much as his.

He released the safety on the semiautomatic and focused both handguns on the driver. 'All right, now raise your hands. Up high, push them against the roof. Marcello, if he moves, you kill him.' He pulled open the back door and leveled the two guns — he liked this two-gun stuff — to point down at the floor. 'OK, kid, come on out of there. Hurry up.'

Achille didn't move. He was on his knees, scared to death, milk-faced and shivering. 'Just tell me what you want, I know I can — '

'All I want is you. Now don't make me — '

'My father will kill you for this. Do you know who my father is?'

'Yeah, I know who your father — '

A movement by one of the driver's hands caught his eye. 'Hey!' he said. 'What did I tell you? Marcello, you — Ai!'

His first thought was that a bee had stung him on the wrist, but then he heard a clink, and when he looked down, his own .357 magnum, which he'd thought was still in his right hand, was on the pavement, and his wrist was spouting blood, and he knew he'd been shot. Before he could tear his eyes from his shattered wrist, there was a second stinging jab — he heard the shot this time — in his abdomen, dead center, a little below the breastbone. More like a punch than a jab, and this one really hurt. That bastard driver, he'd had a second piece, some stupid little-old-lady gun, tucked down his back behind his neck. And now he'd ducked down and was rolling around on the front seat, getting off shots, twisting and coiling like a snake, almost too quick to see. Where the hell was Marcello?

Now, hardly aware of what he was doing, Ugo was shooting too, spraying bullets from the driver's semiautomatic in his left hand — *crakcrakcrakcrak* — at the writhing, whirling body. 'Bastard, you shot me!' *Crakcrakcrak*. The little pistol flew out of the driver's hand. For a moment Ugo thought he was throwing it at him, but then the man arched, gave a shuddering sigh, and lay still on his back, one foot sticking out the door on Ugo's side. There was blood all over his face and on his shirt. Next to his head, the leather seat was wet.

Ugo was shaking. He'd never been shot before. He'd never killed anyone before. He was losing a lot of blood, he saw now, rhythmic gouts from the wrist, a thick, pumping flow from his abdomen. He pressed his right hand against the hole below his breastbone and stuck his wounded left hand under his right arm, but he could still feel the blood pushing out. He struggled to make himself move, to make himself think, but he'd grown confused. He felt frozen, petrified, as if time were flowing by somewhere outside him, too blindingly fast for him to step back into it. He'd lost track of the semiautomatic. He began to worry that he wouldn't be able to make it back to the car.

'Ugo!' Marcello said, coming tremulously back into sight from where he'd been crouching behind the hood of the car. He looked terrified.

'You lousy — you lousy — ' Ugo screamed. 'You just let him — you just let me — '

Marcello was staring into the car. 'Ugo, Ugo, you shot him!'

'Yeah, I shot him! Where the hell were you?'

He was having a hard time focusing. His pant leg was blood-soaked, clinging to him; his shoe was squishy with it. 'Marcello, I'm not . . . uh . . . '

He was sitting on the pavement, his back against the jamb between the limo's front and rear doors. He didn't remember going down. 'Marcello, you better get me back to the car,' he said, only his head was rolling around on his neck and his mouth didn't work right, and all that came out was this horrible mewling, like a cat that had been run over. He could no longer move his head, but from the corner of his eye he saw Big Paolo running heavily toward them from the rear car. Paolo — big, dumb, stupid Paolo — had forgotten, in his excitement, to put on his mask.

'Paolo,' he heard Marcello say urgently from around the far side of the limo, 'the bastard kid's giving me trouble. Help me out.'

'No, please — ' It was the kid's voice, cut short by a little gasp as Paolo swatted him.

Don't forget about me, Ugo tried to say, *don't leave me here*, but this time not even the mewling sound came out. His chin was on his chest. He couldn't lift his head; it was as if someone were pushing down on the back of his neck. All he could see were his pants, black and glistening with blood, and even that small field of vision was rimmed with a darkening pink haze, as if he were looking out from a tunnel. The stocking mask was squeezing him, cutting off his air. He couldn't breathe.

'What about Ugo?' Big Paolo asked. 'We're not gonna leave him here?'

'Forget Ugo,' Marcello said. 'Look at him, he's dead.'

Am I really? Ugo wondered as the pink haze darkened and the tunnel walls squeezed slowly in.

★   ★   ★

Officer Favaretto waited in the open doorway of Comandante Boldini's office while his chief finished his not-so-polite conversation with the mayor of Stresa, who could be seen through the window, gesticulating in his own

35

office just across the Corso.

'I can't help that, Mr Mayor,' Boldini was shouting into the telephone. 'I know there's a French tour bus on your front steps, all I have to do is look out my window to see it. Have you looked at my parking lot? You don't seem to understand, we're going to have to get a crane in there, for God's sake, and police business will have to come first. We — ' He paused, fuming, holding the receiver away from his ear and rolling his eyes. 'Well, that's too bad, but you'll just have to wait,' he said abruptly and slammed down the receiver. He wiped a wadded handkerchief around the inside of his stiff, braided collar and stared blackly at the telephone. 'Some people,' he muttered. 'Does he think I'm Superman?'

Favaretto tapped gingerly at the pebbled glass pane of the door. 'Comandante?'

Boldini hauled himself up and used both hands to hitch his pants up over his spreading hips. A bad sign. Here it comes, Favaretto thought sourly. Because I tried to do something, this whole thing is going to get blamed on me. Next time I'll just pretend I never saw anything and stay the hell out of it. Sadly, it wasn't the first time he'd been driven to make such a promise to himself.

'Favaretto, I thought you told that truck driver to come and see me.'

'I did, sir. I told him — '

'Well, he never did, how do you explain that? He just left the truck sitting out there and walked off, what do you think of that? The worst traffic jam in the history of Italy, and you, you don't even bother — What, damn it?' he yelled at the telephone, which had just buzzed twice at him, the signal that his adjutant was on the other end of the line.

'You, don't go away,' Boldini commanded, leveling a finger at Favaretto, who had indeed been thinking about making his exit. 'I want to talk to you.' He turned his back, picked up the telephone, and held it to his ear. 'What?' he said roughly. '*What?*'

He fell into his leather chair as if the carpet had been jerked from under him. 'What?' he said again, but far more softly. A few moments later there was an even softer, more tremulous 'Who?' followed almost immediately by 'Oh, my God.'

The phone was falteringly replaced on its base the way an old, old man — and a blind one at that — might, and then Boldini pivoted his chair around to look at Favaretto. His face, which had been dangerous a minute before, was now a dazed, sick white.

'Favaretto,' he said weakly, 'tell Maria to get me the *carabinieri* on the telephone. Colonel Caravale. Personally.'

2

In Stresa the headquarters of the Polizia Municipale and the offices of the regional *carabinieri* are separated by only five short, pleasant blocks, but they might as well be in different universes. The Polizia's office is in the bustling, upscale heart of Stresa, on the lake-front, just off the busy, modern Corso Italia, where it shares a handsome building with the ferry company and the city's chamber of commerce. *Carabinieri* headquarters, on the other hand, are hidden away on a little-traveled backstreet, next door to the overgrown garden of an empty, moldering nineteenth-century villa, in an unappealing concrete blockhouse of a building, utterly — almost purposefully — without charm.

But in this case appearances are deceiving, for the *carabinieri* are an accomplished national police force whose simple black uniforms command universal respect, while the Polizia Municipale, despite their flashier outfits and imposing sidearms, generally (and wisely) confine themselves to matters of local traffic control and minor crimes. They are quick to hand off any hot potatoes to their *carabinieri* colleagues who are, fortunately, only a telephone call away.

And when the phone call was made person-to-person, on a secure line, from Comandante Boldini of the Polizia to his *carabinieri* counterpart, Colonnello Tullio Caravale — an event that had occurred but five times in six years — Caravale knew even as he picked up the receiver that it wasn't just another hot potato, but one of which Comandante Boldini was more than usually anxious to wash his hands and to do it in a hurry.

He was right. The longer he listened, the worse it got. The extraordinary accident that had completely stopped downtown traffic for the last hour, it was now clear, had been a meticulously planned ruse, a clever kidnapping plan that had kept the police cars helpless in their lot, while at the same time forcing their quarry to detour into the narrow, deserted side streets. There the object of it all — a vintage Daimler limousine, no less — had been hemmed in and trapped on Via Garibaldi by two cars with armed hoodlums in them. The kidnapping had been successful but there had been a shootout that had left two men dead: the uniformed driver of the limo, who was sprawled on his back on the blood-smeared front seat, and one of the attackers, apparently left to bleed to death by his accomplices. Still wearing his stocking mask, he had been found mumbling beside the car but had died before the medics could get to him.

'Has anything been moved?' Caravale asked.

'No, no, Caravale, nothing's been touched. I thought you would want your people to examine the scene.'

'Very good, Boldini, that's exactly what I want.'

In his mind's eye, he could imagine Boldini's grimace of disapproval. In a meaningless ceremony a few years ago, the city council had made the *comandante* an honorary *maresciallo* of Stresa in recognition of his 'invaluable service commanding the extensive traffic reorganization necessitated by the repaving of the Strada Statale del Sempione.' And in Boldini's eyes, since marshals outranked colonels, he was entitled to call Caravale by nothing more than his last name — but not the other way around — and he was patently miffed when Caravale didn't see it that way. And so, of course, Caravale called him 'Boldini' every chance he got.

'All right, Boldini, I'm on my way, then,' he said. He began to hang up, then spoke again. 'As to who was kidnapped — I take it you don't know yet?'

Boldini hesitated. 'Actually, we do. It was, ah, Achille de Grazia.' His voice was as somber and reverent as a muffled church bell.

'I see.'

'Sixteen years old, the son of Vincenzo de Grazia.'

'Yes, all right.'

'You do know Vincenzo de Grazia . . . ?'

'Yes, Boldini, I know Vincenzo de Grazia. The son, was he hurt?'

'That we don't know for certain. There is a witness, Carlo Muccia, a grocer — my men are holding him for you — he says the boy was definitely alive, but they had to drag him to their car — it took two of them — so, yes, it appears he may have been injured.'

Or it could be that he just preferred not to go. 'Thank you, Boldini, we'll take over from here. You've informed de Grazia?'

'Ah, no, as a matter of fact. As you may know, Signor de Grazia has honored me by making it clear that he does prefer to conduct any local police business through my office. However, in this case, I think the nature of the circumstances, the regrettable nature of the circumstances, ah, suggests that you be the one to inform him, don't you agree?'

So. That accounted for the person-to-person call. Now we were getting down to it. It wasn't the shooting, it wasn't the two dead

41

men, it wasn't even the kidnapping, per se. Boldini just didn't want to be the one to tell Vincenzo de Grazia that his son had been taken. Well, his attitude, weak-kneed as it was, was understandable. The *comandante* served at the pleasure of the Stresa city council, after all, and Vincenzo, as everyone knew, was one of the powers behind that august group.

As a colonel in the federal police, however, Caravale didn't have to worry about local 'powers.' True, Vincenzo had a long reach; no doubt he could put in a good — or bad — word for him in Rome and significantly affect his chances for advancement in the force. But that didn't make any difference either. Caravale was that rare thing — a man not interested in advancing. No ambition burned in his belly, no resentment at the progression of friends and enemies through the ranks stuck in his craw. He was exactly where he wanted to be. When he'd been a boy of ten, he had sometimes accompanied his sainted grandfather on his ice wagon runs in Stresa, sitting with him up in the driver's box and working the reins if the traffic wasn't too bad. And one rainy day *Nonno* Fortunato, his words whistling through the gap where other people's front teeth were, had said, out of nowhere: 'Tell me, Tullio, what do you want to be when you grow up?'

Out of nowhere, Caravale had answered, 'A policeman, Grandfather.'

'A policeman!' the old man had said, beaming. He'd raised his arm, stood up in the driver's box, and pretended to make an announcement to the world at large. 'Honored ladies and gentlemen, you see this little fellow sitting next to me? This is my grandson, Tullio Caravale. Remember his name, because someday he is going to be the *comandante*' — he'd pointed to a building they were passing — 'right there.'

The building was *carabinieri* headquarters, and for Caravale, that had been that. Dreams of being an actor, a pilot, an international soccer star, were gone from his mind. Despite his father's often-voiced reservations about the police, he knew from that time on exactly what he wanted to do, and where he wanted to do it.

And here he was.

'All right,' he said, 'I'll take care of telling de Grazia. I'll go see him.'

'Now?'

'Give me a chance to look at the scene and see what's what first. Then I'll talk to him. His company's up in Ghiffa, isn't it?'

'Yes, Aurora Construction, but these days he'll be at his field office in Intra. It's on

43

Corso Mameli, a block north of the old port, right across — '

'I know where it is. You'll release no information before I see him?'

'No, no, not until you tell me. Do you . . . did you want me to accompany you?'

'That's not necessary. It will be simpler if I do it myself.'

'Well . . . all right, then, if you're sure that's best . . . ?'

Even over the telephone, his relief was palpable.

'Definitely,' said Caravale.

★ ★ ★

Intra, a quick ten kilometers north of Stresa, was the western shore's commercial and small-industry center. Anywhere else it would have been commonplace, but along this stretch of Lake Maggiore it stood out: a homely, workaday few blocks in the midst of the dreamlike promenades, elegant villas, and grand hotels that otherwise lined the lakeshore. Caravale felt at home here. He'd lived in nearby Caprezzo, one of the backward little villages that dotted the flanks of Mount Zeda, until he was fourteen, and he'd worked in Intra three afternoons a week from the time he was twelve.

In those days, there had been a withered, green-toothed ancient named Verrucchio who had owned a dry-cleaning shop (now a hardware store) only a block away from what was now de Grazia's field office (then a pharmacy). As a youngster, Caravale had spent a lot of after-school hours behind the counter, waiting on customers and straightening out accounts, while old Verrucchio, who could neither read nor write, sweated buckets in back and breathed in the corrosive fumes that would do him in a few years later.

On the day after Caravale's fourteenth birthday, his father, who had lived in America for five years after he got out of the Italian Army, had landed a job teaching English in Cremona and had taken the family with him. It was in Cremona a few months later that young Tullio heard about Verrucchio's death. He was shocked to learn that the shrunken old man had been only forty-seven.

The Aurora Construction Company had been a far smaller enterprise back then. The old man, Domenico de Grazia, had still been alive, and under his patriarchy the de Grazias did not willingly stoop to commerce. They had still owned untold hectares of land on the eastern shore then, and they lived like the titled aristocrats they'd been since the fifteenth century. A significant part of their income had come from timber and mining leases, but when those had begun dwindling away about twenty years ago, Domenico, looking to the future, had sold off much of the de Grazia land and put the money into several local businesses, with (so Caravale had heard) generally unfortunate results. But among them had been Aurora Costruzioni, a small construction contractor in Ghiffa that specialized in concrete work. With the help of his son, the young Vincenzo, who had been sent off to the University of Pisa and the London School of Economics for degrees in architectural design and business management, he had built Aurora into a profitable operation, with projects throughout the region.

But it had been the son, Vincenzo, who had turned it into what it was today. Gradually taking over as the old man had aged, and infusing the company with the money from continuing land sell-offs and with his own intelligence and energy, the young Vincenzo had transformed it into one of northern Italy's largest general contracting companies. After Domenico had died, Vincenzo had taken the company public and had himself installed as CEO and chairman of the board of directors. From there, things had really taken off. Aurora now had projects through-out Piedmont and Lombardy, and even, if the stories were true, consulting contracts as far away as Ireland and Gibraltar, building everything from plastic-recycling facilities to high-rise condominiums. With its fleet of heavy equipment, and its ninety permanent employees and more than two hundred seasonal and temporary workers, Aurora Costruzioni was now Ghiffa's largest employer by a factor of ten, making Vincenzo one of the area's most influential businessmen, which was the way he liked it. Unlike his aloof and courtly father, Vincenzo loved to be center stage. He was a mover and a shaker, a natural entrepreneur who relished the power plays and wheeler-dealer mentality of land acquisition and development.

'Count de Grazia,' everyone had called old Domenico as he limped about Stresa or Ghiffa. It had made Caravale's father, a socialist and a fiery antimonarchist, livid, but to young Tullio the genteel Domenico de Grazia had been the embodiment of what a storybook count should be: silver-haired and handsome, properly aloof, yes, but scrupulously courteous to all, right down to the street urchins.

Since that time, Caravale had come around to agreeing in large part with his father about the self-induced delusions of the post-war Italian 'aristocracy,' but never in regard to

Domenico de Grazia. The man had been a true, bred-in-the-bone patrician, the last of his kind. Or so it seemed in memory.

No one referred to Vincenzo as 'Count' nowadays, but his noble lineage still made some people weak in the knees, and his behind-the-scenes involvement in regional politics (useful in getting building permits and variances) had made him more widely influential than his father had ever been. None of that had any effect on Caravale. Less than nothing. To him, Vincenzo de Grazia was just another human being like him, only richer, and not one he was particularly fond of at that. His relentless terracing of the foothills of Caravale's beloved Mount Zeda into 'Residenze This' and 'Ville That' had chewed at him for years. Who needed all those developments? Who could afford them? Not the people who lived and worked here, that was for sure.

Beyond that, these new walled, gated communities of de Grazia's represented something else, something essentially un-Italian to his way of thinking. When Caravale had been growing up, the rich and the poor had lived together. People didn't believe it now anymore, but it was true. Oh, there were great villas and humble cottages, but they'd existed side by side on the same streets and alleys, as they had for centuries, sharing the same neighborhood concerns. In Caprezzo, the best drinking water had come from a centuries-old stone fountain in the courtyard of the village's wealthiest landowner, and every afternoon, as they had since Caravale's grandmother had been a girl, and probably long before, the housewives and peasant women would come to fill their jugs and bottles, and to gossip, on essentially equal terms, with the family of the *padrone*. Or if not on equal terms, then at least one could say they understood and appreciated one another. How was that going to happen when all the rich had walled themselves off behind the locked gates of these new 'California-style' communities? It wasn't, and something that made Italy what it was was being lost.

All the same, de Grazia was a father, and the news that was about to descend on him was almost as dreadful as anything a father could hear. Caravale's heart went out to him. Getting out of his car, he found himself thinking that it would be nice if there were someone else he could hand this task off to, the way Boldini had handed it off to him. But the *comandante* was right; it was Caravale who was going to be running the investigation, and the task properly fell to him.

De Grazia was not in the office, a pretty secretary, dark as a gypsy, told him, but at the site of the new golf course and residential community that the company had just begun to excavate. Did the colonel know where it was?

He did not.

'You can't miss it,' he was told. 'Take the road up Mount Zeda, and right after the turnoff to Caprezzo — you know Caprezzo?'

'That's where I was born,' he said with a smile.

'Really?' She looked as if she didn't know whether or not he was joking. 'Well, right after the turnoff, before you get to the village, you'll see an area where they're clearing the trees — lots of bulldozers at work. You'll find him there.'

'Right after the turnoff? Do you mean the big pasture below the village? He's putting in a development there? Another development?'

She laughed. 'Well, I don't know what it was before, but it's not a pasture anymore.'

Caravale's heart was perhaps just a little less softened as he returned to his car.

3

The site was just where he'd feared it would be, on what had once been a wide ribbon of undulating meadow dotted with old flowering plum trees, which curved around the mountain's flank. When he'd been a boy, it had been his playground. He and his friends had played soccer here and badgered the resident goats, pretending to be matadors — but now backhoes and bulldozers were shoving piles of rock and naked earth from one place to another. Already it was hard to remember the meadow as it had been.

GOLF AND COUNTRY CLUB LAKE MAG-GIORE, the big, laser-embossed sign said in almost-English (which presumably gave it the trendy American tone that would attract rich Swiss and Milanese buyers), and underneath it a smaller, tacked-on placard for the benefit of the locals: *Circolo Golf del Lago Maggiore. Una Realizzazione di Aurora Costruzioni.*

Vincenzo de Grazia stood in consultation with another man, both wearing hard hats, work clothes, and work boots, and leaning over a blueprint spread out on the hood of a mud-caked cement truck. Truck, men, and everything else in sight were covered with dust. That was one thing you had to say about de Grazia: He didn't run from getting dirt under his fingernails.

Caravale approached and waited for them to look up, but they remained immersed. 'Signor de Grazia?' he said after a minute.

De Grazia glanced up, calculatedly leaving his forefinger resting on the diagram. 'Yes, Colonel, can I do something for you?'

Caravale was impressed. It was natural enough that he himself should recognize de Grazia. He had seen him about often enough, and his picture was frequently in the newspaper; once there had even been a two-page spread on him in *Oggi* ('The Aristocrat of Waste-Water Treatment Plants'). Besides, de Grazia was quite striking-looking: a tight-knit, distinctively hawkfaced man with thick, stiff, ropy gray hair brushed straight back from the hairline, and a nose that cleaved the air like the prow of a ship. Add to that an air of bottled-up, restless energy and a rarely disguised impatience to get on with things, to move along, and he was not someone who would be easy to forget. Beyond that, once you watched him for a while, you couldn't help but be aware of an ingrained sense of natural authority and entitlement that was hard to ignore, although it also tended to grate on the nerves. On Caravale's nerves, anyway.

Colonel Caravale's picture was occasionally in the papers or on local TV as well, but it was always in connection with some ceremonial affair or other, for which he'd be one of a crowd, and in dress uniform, complete with lavish gold braid and cocked hat with feather. Today he was wearing his workaday uniform, a simple, businesslike black with a white shirt and dark tie. And no one, to his knowledge, had ever called him 'striking.' He was swarthy, short, fifteen pounds overweight, and heavy-featured, with beefy jowls that rode over his collars. Adolescent acne had left his cheeks deeply pitted. His thinning hair and receding hairline were more than made up for by the thick eyebrows that met in the middle of his forehead and even dipped a little, so that he had to shave the top of his nose every Sunday.

Once, dressing before a civic affair, stripped down to undershirt and shorts, he had taken a long look at his slope-shouldered, barrel-chested, short-legged figure in the mirror and shaken his head. His wife, who had been unwrapping tissue paper from the ridiculous hat, had looked at him. 'What's the matter?'

'Ah, it's hopeless,' he had said. 'Look at

me. Without my uniform, I look as if I should be slicing salami at the corner *trattoria*.'

She had shrugged and gone back to unpacking the hat. 'With your uniform, you look as if you should be slicing salami at the corner *trattoria*.' Then, under her breath, with the slightest of smiles: 'Or holding it up.'

That was as close as anybody had ever come to calling him 'striking.' It was amazing that de Grazia, whom he'd never met, should recognize him.

'If you don't mind,' Caravale said to him now. 'I need to talk to you for a few minutes. Privately.'

'I'll take care of this for you, Vincenzo,' the other man said promptly, rolling up the blueprint and snapping a rubber band over it. 'We've caught it early enough. It shouldn't be a problem.'

De Grazia grunted and turned to Caravale. 'Yes, Colonel, is something the matter?'

'Is there someplace we can sit down?'

De Grazia waved at the chaos around them and laughed. 'In three months, I hope so. Unless you want to sit in the truck?'

'That would be a good idea.'

De Grazia nodded, invited Caravale in with a gesture, and clambered deftly up into the driver's seat. He was a fit-looking, small-waisted man who moved the way he spoke, with conciseness and efficiency. Caravale, not quite so deftly, hoisted himself in opposite him. They left the doors open.

De Grazia's expression had changed. He realizes this is something serious now, the colonel thought. Probably, he's worried that we've found out about some shady quid-pro-quo arrangement to get a variance approved. Too bad that wasn't all it was.

Best to get right to it. 'Signor de Grazia, I'm sorry to have to tell you this, but your son has been kidnapped.'

De Grazia, with his mind not totally clear of whatever the problem with the blueprint had been, nodded along with him as he spoke and then kept on nodding as if he were waiting for the punch line. Caravale paused, letting the words sink in.

After a couple of seconds de Grazia's head snapped around. 'What did you say? My son? Kidnapped? Achille de Grazia?'

'In Stresa, two hours ago. From one of your company cars.'

De Grazia frowned, blinked, and frowned again. His long fingers — manicured? — played over the steering wheel. 'No, that's wrong, someone's made a mistake. Achille is in school, he goes to a private school, up near La Sacca.'

'There's no mistake, signore. I'm sorry

about it. Can you tell me what he was doing in Stresa?'

'What he was . . . ' He smacked the steering wheel with the flat of his hand. 'Who did it? What do they want? Is he all right?'

'We don't have much information yet. Can you tell me what he was doing in Stresa?'

De Grazia made a small, impatient gesture, as if brushing away a fly. 'I just told you. He goes to school near La Sacca. In the mornings, he comes with me to work — '

'Here to Intra?'

'No, to the main office in Ghiffa. That's where I go first. We take the launch. From there, I have him driven on to school. How did — '

'So to get to his school the driver — '

'The driver goes through Stresa, yes, yes. What difference does it make why he was there?'

'Who else knew about it?'

'Who else knew?' He shook his head, exasperated, 'Tell me, how the hell would you suggest one get from Ghiffa to La Sacca? Over the mountains and down to Rome, then around the back way and up through Milan?'

Caravale didn't appreciate the sarcasm, but given the circumstances, he was willing to allow de Grazia some leeway. 'What I'm getting at, signore,' he said mildly but with a

56

shaded hint of warning, 'is whether other people knew that he was driven over this route every day at this time?'

'Ah. I see what you're getting at. I'm sorry. I'm afraid I'm a little . . . '

'I understand perfectly.'

'Many people would know, Colonel. It's not a secret. Please, tell me what happened. Is he all right?' He was staring straight ahead, through the windshield, with his hands back on the steering wheel.

'It was elaborately planned. A traffic disturbance was created on the Corso, forcing your son's limousine into a side street. There it was trapped by two cars, one in front, one behind. There was shooting — '

De Grazia's head jerked. 'Shooting!'

'Your driver was killed.'

'Killed — he was *killed*?'

'So was one of the kidnappers. The — '

'What about Achille? Was he — did they — '

'No, no, there's no reason to think he was injured.'

Not quite the truth, but what would be the point of passing on an unverified report of the boy's having been dragged from the limousine? If he was hurt, he was hurt; if he wasn't, he wasn't, and nothing was served by giving de Grazia something more to worry about.

'As far as we know, he's all right.'

De Grazia sank back against the seat.

'Does your chauffeur always carry a gun, Signor de Grazia?'

'What? Oh. No, not always. On regular trips, yes. To work, from work . . . ' He hit the steering wheel again, this time with his fist, and with considerable force. 'Bastards,' The word escaped pinched, as if hung up on something in his throat. He was breathing shallowly; Caravale could see his nostrils dilate and contract.

Why, he's angry, Caravale realized with interest. Not stunned or appalled, as he'd first supposed (those being the usual reactions), or worried, or dismayed, or fearful, but angry. For Caravale, who had handled a dozen kidnappings in his career, this was something new. Anger usually came later, after the reality of the situation had been absorbed.

'What do they want, money?' de Grazia asked.

'That's what they usually want, yes. It could be something else — some political point, maybe, but my guess is you'll get a call in the next few days; maybe a fax.'

'Days!' de Grazia exclaimed. 'I'm not waiting days!'

'Possibly longer. I believe we're dealing with professionals, and they're likely to let you stew a little first before getting in touch. It makes people more accommodating.'

'Animals,' de Grazia said under his breath. He turned his head to look at Caravale, and hesitated, as if searching for the right way to say something. 'How do I . . . what should I do?' The words came hard. Asking for help wasn't something he was comfortable with.

'First, you need to decide whether you're going to cooperate with the *carabinieri* in this. They will almost certainly warn you not to. If my experience is a guide, there may be threats, frightening threats, against your son. All the same, in my opinion, it is to your advantage, to your son's advantage, for you to work with us.'

'Why?' de Grazia asked bluntly. 'What can the *carabinieri* do for me? Can they help me get my son back sooner?'

'Probably not, but it would still be helpful if you worked with us. Otherwise the left hand doesn't know what the right hand is doing, never a good arrangement. You'll want them caught, won't you?'

De Grazia thought it over but remained skeptical. 'Would I be dealing with you personally?'

'I would be in charge, yes.'

'I'm not accustomed to dealing with corporals, with sergeants.'

Caravale took a breath before answering. 'You would deal with me,' he said quietly. He was determined not to let de Grazia rub him the wrong way.

'What would be involved? I won't agree to anything that might put my son in jeopardy. None of your famous middle-of-the-night raids with all guns blazing and the news cameras grinding, nothing like that.'

Another deep, calming slow breath. 'Agreed. Achille's safety is paramount. I'm talking only about cooperation, about sharing informa-tion for later use — after your son is safe. I'm sure you want these people caught as much as I do.'

De Grazia ran a hand over his hair. It came away coated with oily dust, which he wiped off on his pants. 'All right then, we'll share information.'

'Good. I suggest that we begin by having the telephone lines to your offices and your home tapped.'

'No.'

Caravale's eyebrows went up. 'What?'

'No. I'll share information with you — and I expect you to share it with me — but I won't take any part in trying to trap them, nor will I permit you to use me for that purpose — not until the boy is safely home. Until then nothing is to be done that might frighten or anger them.' He looked directly at Caravale, his frost-blue eyes boring in. 'Have I made myself clear?'

That did it. Deep breaths or not, de Grazia had finally gotten under his skin. Caravale was a *carabinieri* colonel, and *carabinieri* colonels weren't accustomed to being ordered around. 'Signor de Grazia,' he said in his most official manner, 'you seem to be under the illusion that this is a private matter between you and your son's kidnappers. But let me remind you that kidnapping is also a crime against the State. Moreover, two men have been shot to death. If you think I'm about to sit around and do nothing for days or weeks because it might displease you, you'd better think again.'

De Grazia's face flushed. He had stiffened dangerously as Caravale spoke. 'Now just a minute. I am not accustomed — '

'And be good enough to remember, I do not take instructions from you.' He was matching de Grazia scowl for scowl.

'You — '

'Have I made myself clear?' He sat back, anticipating some outraged sputtering, but satisfied that he had gotten his point across. He hoped not to have to do it again.

To his surprise, de Grazia didn't respond in kind. For a moment he bridled, but then the tension drained out of his posture, and with a shake of his head, he lifted his hands to massage his temples in slow circles. 'I apologize, Colonel. This is all new to me . . . I don't know how to behave. Please, do whatever you think best.'

'Thank you, signore. I promise you, nothing will be done that might endanger your son.'

De Grazia nodded and looked out at the huffing earth-moving machines for a while. 'How strange,' he said dreamily. 'Half an hour ago, I had nothing worse to worry about than drainage schemes. Now . . . ' He let the sentence die away. 'And what else?'

'I beg your pardon?'

'You said that first I should decide whether or not to cooperate with you. All right, I've agreed to cooperate. What next?'

'Next, I would strongly advise you to employ a professional negotiator to deal with them. I can put you in touch with several good ones.'

De Grazia seemed surprised. 'What is there to negotiate? Colonel, I'm not about to bargain for my son's life. 'Yes, I'll give you a million euros to spare him.' 'No, I won't give you two million, go ahead and shoot him.' Is that what you want? Absurd. I will not have it said that the boy was killed because Vincenzo de Grazia was reluctant to part with his money.'

There it was again, Caravale thought — the presence of anger, of pride; the absence of anything that came across as deep human feeling. Another man might have said, 'I won't let the boy be killed because I was reluctant to part with my money.' But Vincenzo had said, 'I will not have it said . . . ' To Vincenzo de Grazia, the big problem was what people might say about him, about the de Grazias.

'Let me understand,' Caravale said, 'whatever they ask, you're prepared to pay?'

'Well, not if they name an impossible amount, naturally. But whatever is necessary, yes, of course. And the sooner it's over with, the better.'

'They may ask a great deal. You're a rich man, you have a big company.'

De Grazia gave him a wry smile. 'I'm not as rich as you might think, Colonel. But this is Italy, and I'm like any other sensible businessman. I have kidnapping insurance. The policy is for ten million dollars — twelve million euros. I've been paying regular premiums for years, damned big ones. A Bermudian company, Argos Risk Management. Now it's their turn to live up to their obligations.'

Caravale shook his head. 'All right, I can't make you hire a negotiator, but one thing you'd better understand right now is that it's not going to be over and done in a day or two. These people don't work like that, it's not to their advantage. Three weeks, a month — that's more like it. And all kinds of unexpected things are going to happen, because they just do. Believe me, it's very much to your benefit to have someone who isn't emotionally involved representing you, someone experienced — '

'I'm not bringing some stranger into it, Colonel, someone I don't know and don't trust with my son's life. I'll deal with them myself.' The skin under his eyes tightened. 'We de Grazias are not known for being overemotional.'

Caravale shrugged. How unemotional would 'we de Grazias' be when they threatened to send him one of the boy's ears to convince him to be more forthcoming? The man was hard, but was he that hard? Well, he just might be. In any case, it was up to de Grazia, not him. Besides, he probably did have enough money to meet their demands, so the chances were that it wouldn't come to that.

'Fine,' he said. 'If you change your mind, let me know. In the meantime — '

'What about you?' de Grazia said.

'What about me?'

'Didn't you say you had some experience in these things?'

'Yes, I was assigned to the crisis management unit in Cosenza for a year. I handled a few cases.'

'All right, will you negotiate on my behalf? You, I would trust.'

Automatically, Caravale began to jerk his head no. Such a thing was out of the question. Policemen and negotiators had different goals, conflicting priorities. A negotiator was a middleman, a facilitator, a neutral. He wasn't an adversary of the kidnappers any more than he was an ally of the police. His overriding objective was to bring the situation to an end without harm coming to the abductee or to anyone else. If the prisoner was released without anyone's getting hurt, he had successfully done his job, and whether or not the kidnappers got the money or got away were distant, secondary concerns. But as a *carabinieri* officer, the priorities were necessarily reversed. These men were not only kidnappers but murderers, and his primary objective had to be their apprehension.

It was impossible to do both. In Cosenza he'd been part of an experimental unit that had been kept scrupulously independent of the *carabinieri*'s law enforcement arm. But in Stresa there was no experimental unit. There was only law enforcement.

'I'm sorry, that's impossible,' had already formed itself in his throat and was on its way to his lips, when he surprised himself by a sudden reversal of gears.

'All right, if you want,' he was amazed to hear himself say.

But on second thought, maybe not so amazed. There was no rule, after all, or at least nothing in writing, that prohibited a *carabiniere* from negotiating a kidnapping. And Silvestri, his regional commander in faraway Turin, had happily given Caravale his head in just about all matters a long time ago, so there would be no difficulty there. (Silvestri was the nephew of his older sister's husband, after all.)

Why shouldn't he try it, then, given that Vincenzo had explicitly asked him to? Serving as the contact with them would likely provide valuable information for later that he'd otherwise have to try to get second-hand. *So where was the problem?* If he didn't take it on, Vincenzo had made it clear that he would do it himself, and surely that was the most dangerous path of all.

One thing was sure. It wasn't going to get in the way of his catching the bastards.

4

Through the living room's bay window they watched the gray, red, and white Coho Ferry in the distance, pulling stern-first away from the Port Angeles dock, slowly turning, lumbering into the sunshine, and starting on its stately 5:15 P.M. run around Ediz Hook and across the Strait of San Juan de Fuca to Vancouver Island, visible through the sea haze some seventeen miles away.

'*Il battello . . .* um *. . . parte a Victoria*,' Julie said. 'No, *per Victoria*.'

'Very good,' Phil Boyajian said. 'And what about you, Gideon, my man, how's the Italian coming?'

'*Muy bien, gracias*,' Gideon said.

Phil shook his head. 'Wrong language.'

'Oh. *Sehr gut*?'

'Um, you're not quite there yet, Dr Oliver.'

'Don't let him kid you, Phil,' Julie said. 'He speaks it almost as well as you do. He has this knack with languages. It's very annoying.'

'What can I say, it's true,' Gideon said immodestly. 'I spent a couple of summers on an Etruscan dig up near Tarquinia. I guess Italian just stayed with me.'

Actually, it hadn't come that easily to him — he'd been learning Spanish not long before, and the two languages were close enough to confuse him — but he'd loved the lilt of those long, high, singing Italian vowels and he'd worked at it, continuing even after he'd gotten back to the States. He'd kept it sharp by occasionally reading Italian articles on the Web, but now, for the first time in years, he'd have a chance to put it to real use. The three of them would be flying to Italy in a couple of days; Phil was going over the details one final time.

'We arrive in Milan at six-fifty in the morning, pick up the rental car, and drive up the lake. A day and a night on our own in Stresa to get over the jet lag, and the next morning we go on back down to Milan to meet our flock at the airport. And so the merry adventure begins.'

The 'flock' were the eighteen venturesome, pennywise travelers who had signed up for the 'Italian Lakes Country Pedal and Paddle Adventure,' the week-long kayak-and-bicycle tour of Lake Maggiore and Lake Orta that was being put on by Travel on the Cheap, the thriving tour and guidebook company head-quartered in Seattle. Phil, a frequent tour leader for On the Cheap, would lead it. One of Gideon's oldest friends (he had been a fellow graduate student at the University of Wisconsin), he had sweet-talked them into helping out on the trip almost a year before. Or rather, he had talked Julie into it; for expenses, she would serve as the tour naturalist and assistant 'host.' It hadn't taken much sweet talking. A supervising park ranger at Olympic National Park's headquarters in Port Angeles, it was the kind of thing that she enjoyed doing anyway, and it gave her a chance to study the natural history of a new area.

Gideon, on the other hand, was paying his own way, being basically along for the ride, although he'd promised to help out if needed. The trip had struck him as a good idea. He'd be between spring and summer quarters at the university, he'd never seen Italy's lake country, and the kayaking sounded like fun. And of course, a week with Julie in northern Italy, even with the 'flock' in tow, sounded a lot better than a week at home without her, especially with no classes, active forensic cases, or papers in preparation to keep him engaged. The bicycling part and the overnight stays at 'clean, convenient campgrounds' were less enticing, and he'd reserved to himself the right to spend the nights in more deluxe accommodations. He'd made it clear that he intended to sleep in a clean bed in a pleasant room every night, get at least one good, hot meal a day, and shower every morning — in a private bathroom of his own.

Phil had taken good-natured offense. 'Hey, wait'll you see the camp-grounds I lined up. Platform tents already set up for us, laundry machines, delicious hot meals every night, luxurious sleeping arrangements — '

'Oh, right,' Gideon said, 'On the Cheap is well known for its attention to the finer amenities.'

'OK, maybe not exactly luxurious, but — '

And what was more, Gideon said, he intended to rent a car for himself so he could get around on his own and drive wherever he pleased in luxury while the others sweated over their bicycles during the cycling phase.

These provisos had been received with the contempt they deserved. 'And he calls himself an anthropologist,' Julie had said with withering scorn.

'I am an anthropologist. That doesn't mean I have to be a masochist.'

'Soft,' Phil had sneered. 'Pathetic. Not the man I once knew.'

But Gideon had stuck to his guns and there the matter stood. No camping out, no sweaty bicycling up and down hills. 'I'm paying my own way, I'm not on a dig, and I see no pur-pose in being uncomfortable,' was his sole and frequently repeated defense.

For their first night Phil had booked rooms for them in a three-star family-run hotel in Stresa, though he'd claimed it violated his populist principles by one star.

'Besides which,' he said, 'Stresa isn't really that great a place. It's like one big English tea shop, all cutesy and super-clean and full of flowers and doilies and things. It's a resort town.'

'Sounds wonderful to me,' said Julie, 'but if you don't like it, why are we staying there?'

'Basically because it makes it easy for me to grab the boat in the afternoon for a quick visit to my family.' He hesitated. 'Hey, I don't suppose you guys would want to come along? I don't like being alone with those people.'

Gideon stared at him. 'You have family in Italy?'

'Sure, you didn't know? Didn't you know I was Italian? Why do you think I go there every couple of years?'

'Phil, you're on the road all the time. I don't keep tabs on where you go.'

'Hell, I was born in Italy. I lived there till I was seven. You're telling me you didn't know that?'

'No, I didn't know that. Do you suppose it could be because you never mentioned it?'

'I didn't? Well, maybe I didn't,' Phil allowed.

'Amazing,' Julie said, 'truly amazing. Men and women really are different species, you know that? Two women would know that kind of thing about each other inside of twenty minutes. And you two, you've been friends for twenty years.'

'Well, how could I know if he never told me?' Gideon said defensively. 'But now that you mention it, I should have figured it out on my own. What else could somebody named Phil Boyajian be but Italian?'

'Yeah, well, see,' Phil said, 'that's because my mother's second husband was Armenian — he was a petroleum engineer, which is how come I was living in Cairo and Riyadh in my teens — '

'You lived in Cairo and Riyadh?' Julie exclaimed. 'Phil, I've known you for five years myself. How could you never have told me that?'

Phil shrugged.

'See?' said Gideon.

'Anyway,' Phil went on, 'he adopted me, and I took his name. I figured Boyajian sounded more American, you know? But no, I had a good Italian name to start with.'

He bowed. 'Filiberto Ungaretti, 'atsa me.'

★ ★ ★

Gideon just shook his head. Even after two decades, Phil was always coming up with something to surprise him. His career had been one unexpected (and entertaining) twist after another, a sort of career-in-reverse. When he'd gotten his Ph. D. in cultural anthropology, he had stepped into a coveted tenure-track position at a big state university but had found university politics more than he was willing to cope with. He'd then tried teaching at a Seattle community college, but couldn't stand the committee assignments. Next had come a period as a high school teacher (but the nonteaching, largely custodial responsibilities weren't to his liking), followed by a three-year stint teaching grade school. While he pondered his next move — kindergarten? preschool? day care? — he was offered a summer job going to Egypt to research and write *Egypt on the Cheap*, the very first On the Cheap guidebook.

It had turned his life around. With his scruffy, eager, friendly manner and his natural willingness to see the best in common people and in their customs, he had at last found the occupation he'd been made for. The book had done better than anyone expected, and Phil had been made a contributing editor for the new series, a position he still held. In addition, he also led eight or ten no-frills tours a year for the company, of which the Italian lakes trip was the latest.

Gideon, by contrast, had taken a more conventional path, beginning as an assistant professor of physical anthropology at Northern California State University, where he was promoted after a few years to associate professor and contentedly settled in for a long, rewarding career of teaching and scholarship in San Mateo, California.

But fate had a jog of its own in store for him. Almost by accident, he had begun consulting for the FBI on the side, on cases involving forensic anthropology, and eight years ago one of those cases had taken him to Washington State's Olympic rain forest, where two things had occurred that would change his life forever, one to his mild but frequent embarrassment, the other to his great and unremitting joy. The first was that a local reporter following the case had referred to him as the Skeleton Detective, and the sobriquet had stuck to him like glue, providing a rich source of not-so-subtle ragging to his colleagues at meetings and conventions ever since.

The second thing, the enormous, life-altering thing, was that he'd met a beautiful young park ranger named Julie Tendler, who had been incidentally involved in finding the human remains that had brought him to Washington. His much-loved first wife Nora had been killed in a car crash two years earlier, and Gideon had never gotten over his grief. In his case, it had slowly evolved into a terrible impassivity, a sense of deep isolation from everyone around him. For two years he had felt himself to be as cold and dead and impervious to emotion — to positive emotion — as a stone. It was Julie who had reawakened him, unthawing feelings and sensibilities that he had truly thought frozen for good.

A year after that they'd been married and he'd lucked into an associate professorship at the University of Washington's Port Angeles campus (he'd since advanced to full professor). They had bought this hillside house that was a ten-minute walk in one direction from Julie's office in the headquarters building, and a ten-minute walk in the other direction to campus. A perfect location. A perfect life. A day didn't go by that he wasn't grateful to her for bringing him to life again.

'Filiberto Ungaretti,' she said now, also shaking her head. 'That's amazing. Sure, it'd be interesting to visit your family, Phil. If you're really sure they wouldn't mind.'

'Interesting I can't promise. Weird I can guarantee.'

'Weird how?' Gideon asked. 'Weird like you?'

'No, different. They own this island, sort of, and they live in practically this palace — well, you'll see.'

'A day at the Ungarettis,' Julie mused. 'Sounds good.'

'No, Ungaretti was my father's name, the creep. I haven't seen him since I was three. This is my mother's family we'd be visiting.'

'And what's their name?'

'Their name,' said Phil, 'is de Grazia.'

5

Stresa was much as Phil had described it, a bright, clean, discreetly fading nineteenth-century resort town on Lake Maggiore, full of flowers, gardens, and romantic villas, and boasting a generous, park-like promenade, the Lungolago, that ran along the lakefront from one tip of the city to the other, bordering one side of the main street, the Corso Italia. On the other side of the Corso was an unbroken row of upscale boutiques and hotels. Away from the lakefront, Stresa was equally attractive, but in a different way: a maze of romantic piazzas and narrow, cobblestoned streets lined with picturesque restaurants and hole-in-the wall cafés. Their hotel, the Primavera, was on one of these streets, a modest, pleasant place a block inland (the four- and five-star hotels were all on the lakefront). Phil, who had slept most of the time on the fifteen-hour flight from Seattle, had, amazingly, gone to sleep in his room as soon as they'd arrived, but Julie and Gideon, who hadn't slept at all, and whose eyes by now felt glued open, were eager to get out in the fresh air.

They had strolled lazily around the town for half an hour and now they sat, loopy and jet-lagged, among families of Swiss and Italian tourists, at a sun-drenched outdoor café on the promenade, where Phil had promised to join them at nine-thirty for the visit to the de Grazias. From the boat terminal a block away, ferries carried tourists to, from, and around Stresa's big attractions, the fabulous Borromean Islands a few hundred yards offshore, with their splendid seventeenth-century gardens and palaces. Gideon was reading aloud from a guidebook description of Isola Bella, the closest and most fantastic of the three islands.

"But it is to the most ambitious and far-sighted of the Borromeos, Vitalio the Sixth, to whom we owe thanks for the Isola Bella we see today. It was Vitalio who began the prodigious earth-moving project that transformed the morphology of the land into ten superimposed garden terraces in the form of a gigantic truncated pyramid on the example of the Hanging Gardens of Babylon. The many pools and fountains were fed by pipes from an enormous cistern installed beneath . . ."

He glanced up at Julie, who had been suspiciously silent for a long time. She sat with her eyes closed and her face tipped up to the sun. 'Hello?' he said. 'Are you still with us?'

'Mm-hm,' she said, keeping her eyes closed. "It was Vitalio who something-somethinged the project that transformed the something into ten superimposed something-somethings on the example of the Hanging Gardens of Babylon.' Do go on.'

With a smile, he closed the book. 'I think maybe I've had enough too. Why don't we just sit here and soak up the sunshine and this nice, warm air? Doesn't it feel great after the spring we've had, or rather, haven't had?'

'Mmm,' she said, more a purr than a murmur. Except to recross her ankles, she didn't stir.

Given the chance, he watched her face for a while: the slightly turned-up nose; the pert chin — softening now, but all the more attractive for it — the lively mouth always on the verge of a smile; the glossy, curly black hair, cut short now, that framed the whole pretty picture. He shook his head. What did I do to get so lucky? he wondered contentedly, as he had so many times before.

'I love you,' he said.

He saw her smile, though her eyes were still closed. 'Likewise,' she murmured.

'Good, I'm glad we've gotten that out of the way.' He looked at the menu again. 'I'm having a problem figuring out what to order.'

'Hm?'

'It's because of the difference in time zones.'

'Mm.'

He put down the menu and looked at her again. 'I'm not boring you? Not keeping you awake?'

'No, not at all. I'm glued to every word. 'It's because of the difference in time zones.''

'What is?'

She thought for a moment. 'What you were talking about.'

He laughed. 'The thing is, I think I'm hungry, but I don't know what to get. It's eight-thirty in the morning here, but our internal clocks still think it's eleven-thirty at night. I don't know whether to get breakfast or a midnight snack.'

'What would you get if you ordered breakfast?'

'Bacon and eggs, probably. It's on the menu, probably for the English tourists. And coffee.'

'And what would you get for a midnight snack?'

He thought it over. 'Coffee. And bacon and eggs.'

'That's a pretty tough problem you have there, mister. I don't see how I can help you with that one.'

They had finished their bacon and eggs and were on their third cups of coffee when Phil showed up, looking greatly refreshed and highly disreputable. It seemed to be a point of honor with him when he traveled, to look as if he'd been trekking through the Arabian desert for six months, so he had let his salt-and-pepper beard come in again. He'd also skipped his last few haircuts so that his thinning hair now hung in tendrils down the back of his neck. With his hitching gait — Phil habitually walked with one side a little higher than the other — he looked like a down-and-out sailor that had jumped ship a few years back and had never managed to get himself another berth.

To complete the travel-worn image, he was attired in his professional tour leader's regalia: rumpled, faded, multipocketed khaki shorts; a tired T-shirt with sagging neckline; sockless sneakers; and an old, long-billed 'On the Cheap' baseball cap. Phil's first rule of travel for his excursion groups was 'Never take more than can go in a backpack,' of which he made himself a living example. In his pack, as Gideon knew, were two duplicates of each item he was wearing (except for the sneakers, of which he had only a single extra pair), plus a waterproof windbreaker and a few toiletries, including a roll of toilet paper, without which he never traveled (rule two). That was it. As a result, Phil seemed to spend a lot of time searching out a convenient place and time to wash and dry his underwear, but he considered that a small price to pay.

'Finish up,' he said, slipping into an empty chair at their table, 'The boat's waiting. We're off to Isola de Grazia.'

'Isola de Grazia?' Julie repeated. 'You mean your family really has its own island?' Julie asked.

'Sure, what's the big surprise? I told you that.'

'You said they 'own this island, sort of',' Gideon pointed out.

'Forgive me for using a figure of speech. What, is there a difference?'

'There's a big difference,' Gideon said. ''Sort of' connotes 'not exactly' or 'not really', doesn't it? And what does it modify, 'island' or 'owned'? 'They sort of own an island.' 'They own sort of an island.' Those are two entirely different referents, and either way — '

'You have to live with this all the time?' Phil asked Julie.

'It's a trial,' she said. 'But he has good points as well.'

'I'm only trying to introduce a little clarity into your thinking, my dear Filiberto.'

'And don't think I don't appreciate it,' Phil said, getting up with a yawn. 'What do you say we go?'

The boat was a canopied launch with three rows of seats for a dozen people, but they had it to themselves. As soon as they boarded, the captain, a bony, gray-haired woman in a Greek fisherman's cap and bib overalls, cast off, eased backward from the landing, and turned the bow toward the north. In ten minutes they had left Stresa and the busy ferry run behind, and were sliding over smooth, bright, blue water, with green mountains rising from either shore, and far ahead, over the Swiss border, the grim, granite, glacier-topped mountains of the Simplon Alps. The warm, fresh breeze felt like satin on their skin and the three of them sat quietly for a while, with their eyes closed and their faces turned into the breeze.

'Don't tell me,' Gideon said when he opened his eyes.

They looked at him. 'Tell you what?' Julie asked.

'Don't tell me that that's Isola de Grazia.'

He was gesturing at a solitary island a half-mile ahead. Roughly oval and about a quarter-mile long, the point nearest them was occupied by a pink-stuccoed villa, relatively modest in size but gracefully proportioned in the refined, austerely symmetrical Palladian style of the seventeenth century. A set of stone steps at the front of the house led up to a broad, central entrance portico with four tall, slender columns supporting a Greek-style pediment at roof level. Two elegant stories high, with chimney pots shaped like Grecian urns rising from the red tile roof, the building fronted a wide stone courtyard that extended to a quay at which two gleaming wooden launches were tied up. Behind the handsome house and covering the rest of the island were formal gardens that were smaller but almost as elaborate as those they'd seen on Isola Bella. There were fountains, terraces, colonnades, statues, mazes, rows of orange trees, mimosas, and tamarinds, and pungent aromatic shrubs that they could smell from the boat.

'Yup, that's it,' Phil said. 'Home, sweet home.'

★   ★   ★

Julie was flabbergasted. 'But it . . . it really is a palace . . . and those grounds!'

'I told you.'

'You said it was *practically* a palace. You made it sound — '

Phil rolled his eyes. 'Oh, God, now she's

starting. What is it with you people, you have something against adverbial constructions? Is it some kind of a life mission?'

'Of course not,' Julie said, laughing. 'It's just that it's a little hard to imagine the Phil Boyajian we know — '

'And love,' Gideon assured him.

' — growing up in a place like that. Oh, look, isn't that a peacock?'

'Oh, yeah. They've got monkeys too, for Christ's sake. There's a whole goddamn menagerie wandering around the gardens. And yes, I grew up there, or at least I lived there for a few years. But I was born back in Stresa.' He jerked a thumb over his shoulder. 'The house isn't there anymore. It's a parking lot for the railroad station now. My mother got my no-good father a job as some kind of a watchman or maybe a gamekeeper on the de Grazia property up north, and I lived in town till I was three. That's when my father decided he wasn't a family man after all and took off for good, never to be seen again, and my mother took me to live on the island, in the villa, till I was six or seven, which is when we came to the States and she got married again. Let me tell you, that place always spooked me,' he said, looking at the house. 'I still come here every few years, kind of in memory of my mother, I guess. And it still gives me the creeps.'

'It's gorgeous, fantastic,' Julie said. 'It must cost a fortune to take care of.'

'Oh, I think Vincenzo can afford it,' Phil said with a laugh.

'Vincenzo's the owner?'

'Well, there really isn't any 'owner'. The de Grazia family owns the estate in perpetuity. They got it in the fourteenth century — along with the titles of 'Count' and 'Countess', if you can believe it — when somebody's great-uncle-twice-removed was Holy Roman Emperor for about five minutes. But Vincenzo de Grazia is the current *padrone*. He's my cousin. Well, he's my mother's cousin, what does that make him? My uncle, I guess, but we're the same age.'

'He's your first cousin, once removed,' Gideon said, shaking his head. 'What kind of a cultural anthropologist are you, anyway? Didn't they teach you about kinship systems?'

Phil shrugged. 'Sure. You want to know about the exo-patrilocal kinship structure of the Arunta? That I understand perfectly. Ours I never got straight; too complicated. Anyway, Vincenzo's father — my uncle Domenico — was the previous *padrone*, and Vincenzo's son Achille will be the next one, and so on, yeah, into the far-distant future. So he gets this humongous inheritance and he gets to live there — he has to live there, actually;

86

that's in the covenant, if I understand it right. If he doesn't, he forfeits the inheritance.'

'Not too bad a deal.' Gideon said, more and more taken with the island's beauty as they came nearer. 'I think I could live with that.'

The boat had slowed down now and was steering toward the stone quay, which led up to the courtyard by a wide flight of stone steps with two full-size palm trees in enormous pots at their head. The fabric of the building, the windows, the worn steps themselves, the many statues and plants they could see — all looked meticulously cared for, as if cleaning and pruning crews had been out that morning.

'Yeah, but it's not all gravy,' said Phil. 'See, the deal is, anybody else in the family who wants to live there also has the right to do it, no charge, for as long as he wants, and Vincenzo has to put up with him and foot the bill unless he can come up with some kind of justification not to — moral turpitude, murder, something along those lines. So aside from the oddball, so-called relatives who come and go, Vincenzo's had . . . let me see . . . four people — no, five — who've been there just about forever and are never going to leave; not in this lifetime. And there are all kinds of rules about them: They have to dine with the *padrone* if they want to, they have to be consulted in family matters, and so on. It's all very medieval and complicated. Vincenzo tried to get it over-turned once, but no luck. It's foolproof, written in stone.'

'On second thought, maybe not such a good deal,' Gideon said.

As the boat entered the still pool between the two curving arms of the quay and worked its way around the tied-up launches, a dark, lean man in mirrored sunglasses, black suit, black T-shirt, and mirror-shined black shoes emerged from the shade of a lawn umbrella, where he had been sitting in a folding chair, apparently working a puzzle in a magazine. Never turning his head away from them, he used his heel to grind his cigarette out on the pavement, shrugged both shoulders to set his suit coat better, tugged at the cuffs of his sleeves, and sauntered toward them.

'Who's this?' Gideon whispered. 'He looks like a leftover extra from *The Godfather.*'

'You're closer than you think,' Phil told him.

The dark man reached the head of the steps as the captain leaned over the boat's prow with a boat hook, making ready to tie up. '*Proprietá privata*,' he said without expression. '*Non entrate.*'

'Cesare, how're you doing?' Phil asked in Italian.

The man pushed his sunglasses an inch down his nose and peered mistrustfully over them. Then, abruptly, he smiled, like a piano lid opening to show the keyboard. 'Fili? Hey, nobody told me you were coming.'

'Nobody knew. I thought I'd give everybody a nice surprise. So is it all right if we tie up?'

The man jogged down the steps, inspecting Julie and Gideon. 'Who are your friends?'

'Old pals. Americans. Known them for years and years.'

Cesare nodded. 'All right, go ahead and tie up,' he said to the captain, who'd been waiting with the rope in her hands. And to Phil: 'The guy, I'll have to pat down. Better tell him.'

'I understand Italian,' Gideon said.

'That's nice. Climb out and lean your hands against the wall here. No offense, I hope.'

'Help yourself,' Gideon said, following instructions, while Julie looked on with wide eyes.

'I should have mentioned it,' Phil said to her in English. 'They have to do it with strangers.'

'Not to me, I hope.'

'I don't think so.'

The pat-down was quick and professional.

Cesare was lighting another cigarette and Gideon was zipping up his windbreaker when Cesare uttered a soft curse. 'I knew it, damn it, here comes the old man. He sees everything.'

Gideon looked up to see a tall, elderly, goateed man in a too-small, old-fashioned suit, starched white shirt, and tie standing at the head of the stairs and peering down at the scene below him with obvious displeasure. Gaunt and frail-looking, he leaned on a silver-headed, metal-tipped cane but stood extraordinarily upright. Gideon thought he might be wearing a corset to keep him so straight. He was accompanied by an ancient dog, as old in dog years as the man was in human years; a fat, panting, waddling Corgi on a leather leash.

'In my brother Domenico's time,' the old man said in a thin but steady voice, 'all who wished to come were welcome on Isola de Grazia. The stranger was trusted no less than the relative.' He spoke more in sadness than in accusation, in a flowery textbook Italian that Gideon had seen in books but had never before heard spoken. It sounded beautiful.

Cesare hung his head respectfully. 'I'm sorry, signore, I'm only following orders.'

The old man sniffed. 'Vincenzo's orders.'

'These are dangerous times, signore.'

'Terrible times,' said the old man, shaking his head.

'Hello, Grandfather,' Phil said, 'it's wonderful to see you looking well.'

The old man started. 'No . . . ' He peered hard at Phil. 'Fili, is it you?'

Laughing, Phil ran up the steps. The old man opened his arms, letting the cane and the leash drop. He was trembling as Phil gently embraced him and they exchanged happy greetings.

Coming up the steps with Julie, Gideon picked up the cane, noticing that the silver knob atop it was a beautifully wrought feline paw 'holding' what appeared to be a flower bud on a stem, some of the features worn blunt from years of use. When the old man let go of Phil, Gideon handed it to him.

'I thank you, signore,' de Grazia said, then looked eloquently at Phil.

Phil looked back at him for a couple of seconds before he got the message. 'Oh. Right. Uh . . . Grandfather, may I present my good friends Dr Professor Oliver and Mrs Dr Professor Oliver. Gideon and Julie, my respected grandfather, Signor Cosimo Giustiniano de Grazia.'

De Grazia bent his head to kiss Julie's hand, then shook Gideon's. 'I'm very pleased to know you.'

'They're Americans, Grandfather,' Phil said.

'Americans!' the old man cried. He gathered himself together, and in halting, heavily accented English, said: 'You are here most welcome.'

'*Molte grazie, signor de Grazia*,' Julie said in equally deliberate Italian, and the old man mimed good-natured applause, and everyone laughed pleasantly.

'Ah,' said Cosimo. 'Well. So.' Suddenly sobering, he grasped his grandson's wrist. 'Thank you for coming in this time of crisis.'

'I felt it was my duty to come, Grandfather,' Phil said. The old man nodded his approval, then turned his attention to the dog, which now had its leash in its mouth and was uttering plaintive whimpers.

'Yes, Bacco, we'll go now,' he said, taking the leash and smiling once again. 'My dog,' he told Gideon, 'is a de Grazia through and through, a follower of tradition. At ten o'clock I am required to accompany him on his morning constitutional — twice around the villa, out to the swan fountain, and back. This I must do rain or shine, crisis or no crisis, visitors or no visitors. No variation is permitted.'

Another round of shaking hands, another graceful hand kiss for Julie, and a few more words in delightfully accented English for Julie — 'Forgive, signora, I regret I no speak so well English.' — and man and dog shuffled slowly off.

'What an old charmer!' Julie said.

Phil laughed. 'He is that, and I love the guy dearly. He pretty well raised me after my mom brought me here. That's the one thing I thank my lousy father for — if he hadn't walked out on us, I'd never have gotten to really know that great old man. Come on, let's go meet the rest of the clan.' He rolled his eyes. 'Might as well get it over with.'

They began walking toward the house. The entire courtyard, Gideon saw, was paved with smooth black, white, and rose-colored pebbles embedded in concrete in floral patterns. In the center was a circular mosaic of the same materials, sun-faded and very old, arranged into a larger version of the same feline paw and bud that was on Cosimo's cane, plus a six-pointed star on either side.

'Family crest?' Gideon asked.

Phil nodded. 'Lion's paw holding a tea bud. The de Grazias are supposed to have brought tea to Italy. I forget what the lion has to do with it. Nobody takes that heraldic crap too seriously anymore. Well, except for my grandfather, of course, God bless him.'

'What was that he said about a crisis? Did we come at a bad time?'

Phil shrugged. 'I doubt it. *Nonno* Cosimo isn't always . . . well, he kind of lives in his own world — namely the pre-1946 world, before the dissolution of the aristocracy. Anyway, he's well into his eighties, and sometimes, you know, the skylight leaks a little? In a charming way, of course. 'Time of crisis' probably means Bacco didn't take his morning dump.'

'Fili, welcome to the island, why didn't you tell me you were coming?'

It was spoken in Italian, with impatience — if not irritation — and it didn't sound like much of a welcome. They turned to see a trim, wiry, gray-headed man dressed in a perfectly tailored cashmere sport coat; tie; pale, flawlessly pressed trousers; and tasseled loafers striding, with every appearance of authority, toward them. Ah, the boss man, Gideon thought. Vincenzo de Grazia, *il padrone*.

The corners of Phil's mouth turned down just a little. 'Hello, Vincenzo. When have I ever told you I was coming?'

Vincenzo uttered a flat, one-note laugh. 'That's true enough. But at a time like this? You might have let me know.' Gideon noticed that the usual Mediterranean embrace wasn't in evidence.

'At a time like what? Is something the matter?'

'Are you serious? You didn't know? Achille — ' He stopped and peered at Gideon. 'Who are these?' he said to Phil.

'These are my friends Professor and Mrs Oliver,' Phil said.

'Americans?' Vincenzo asked, and on receiving nods, switched without comment to fluent English. 'You're welcome here, but we are having a problem. My son has been kidnapped.'

Phil gaped at him. 'Achille?'

'Do I have another son?' Vincenzo said tartly.

'I'm sorry, I only — '

'I know, I know. I apologize, I'm a little tense. It's good that you're here, Fili. We're about to hold a . . . you know, a *consiglio* . . . ' He groped for the English word.

'A council,' Gideon supplied. He didn't want to seem to be hiding from Vincenzo the fact that he had some Italian.

'A family council, that's right.' Vincenzo said, unimpressed.

'They're all waiting in the gallery. When Cesare told me you'd come, I assumed that was why.'

'I didn't know anything about it. But I'd like to sit in, if that's all right. Maybe there's something I can do.'

'Of course it's all right. You're one of the family, aren't you?' Then, after another joyless laugh: 'More than most of them, anyway.' He turned to Gideon. 'In the meantime, perhaps you and your wife would care to — '

'I'm afraid we've picked a bad time for a visit,' Gideon said. 'We're sorry for your trouble, signore. I think it'd be best if my wife and I just went back to Stresa.'

But Vincenzo wouldn't allow it. 'Certainly not. It won't take us long. Make yourselves comfortable in the breakfast garden. My man will see to refreshments. And the island is yours to explore. The animals are tame.'

'*Grazie, signore,*' Julie said.

'Jesus, Vincenzo, I really am really sorry about this,' they heard Phil saying as he was led back to the villa. 'Is he all right? When did it happen? Jesus.'

6

The Gallery, in which the *consiglio* was to be
held, was a smallish room without windows
on the ground floor, the faded, red-flocked
walls of which were covered floor-to-ceiling
with portraits of defunct de Grazias, some in
medieval armor; some in frilly seventeenth-
century courtiers' garb, some in military
uniforms or 1930s businessmen's suits, and
in one case, the reason for which was no
longer known, in a balloon-trousered Turkish
pasha's outfit complete with turban and
jeweled dagger. Furnished with the oldest,
ugliest, and least comfortable furniture in the
house — dark, slab-backed, hard-seated
wooden chairs from the Italian Gothic
(apparently a time when human anatomy was
imperfectly understood) — and with a couple
of massive, grim commodes to match, the
gallery had been Vincenzo's choice for
familial *consigli* from the day he took the
reins from his father. He frequently said it
was because it imbued their councils with the
fitting ambience of family tradition. But the
prevailing view, in which Phil shared, was that
he'd picked it because the uncomfortable

seating guaranteed that the meetings would be brief. There was even a rumor that he'd had an inch taken off the front legs of all the chairs to help speed people on their way.

On the way there, Vincenzo took Phil aside, into the music room with its two harpsichords and virginal — tuned every three months without exception and dusted weekly, but never, to Phil's knowledge, played — to fill him in on the current status of things. Achille had been taken from a company limousine the previous Thursday, four days earlier. There had been shooting and two people were dead, but Achille was believed to be all right. Nothing at all had been heard until a few hours ago, when the *carabiniere* in charge of the case, Colonel Caravale, had telephoned. It seemed that a fax from the kidnappers, with their demands, had been sent to Vincenzo's office in Ghiffa and automatically diverted, as were all faxes and telephone calls for the time being, to *carabinieri* headquarters.

'What do they want?' Phil asked.

'I don't know yet. I didn't speak with him personally. He'll be here with it at eleven o'clock.' As custom required, Vincenzo had called a *consiglio*, and the de Grazias and their kin were now gathered and awaiting the colonel's arrival.

'The usual crew?' Phil asked.

With a sigh and a barely discernible lift of his eyes, Vincenzo nodded. 'Every last one. Your 'sainted' grandfather, of course, who, in his usual way — '

'Yes, I met him outside,' Phil said, cutting him off. He didn't want to hear Vincenzo's mocking assessment of the aged Cosimo. 'Let's go in.'

'I want to wait out front for the colonel, but you go ahead and join the others,' Vincenzo said. 'I know you can't wait to see them all again.'

'Mm,' said Phil noncommittally.

★ ★ ★

The fact was, he always did look forward to seeing them. His Italian relatives were, after all, the only family he had. Between visits he would invariably forget how much they got on his nerves. That is, he knew they did, but he couldn't quite remember why. It usually took about ten minutes for it to come back to him, and today was no exception. Once the excitement and surprise at his showing up had died down, it started.

And as usual, it was Dante Galasso who was the first to get to him.

Technically speaking, Dante wasn't a

relative — that is, a blood relative — either of Phil's or of the de Grazias'. But he was married to Vincenzo's older sister Francesca, which gave him the privilege of residing with her at the villa, along with the right to participate in the *consigli* if he so chose, which he unfailingly did.

A sinewy man with a deeply lined face, a bony head atop a snakelike neck, and a thin, contemptuous twist to his lips, as if he knew all sorts of things you didn't, he had been a Marxist professor of Italian language and culture at the University of Bologna in 1984, when Francesca had been a student there. She had fallen under his spell and the following year, over the vigorous objections of her father Domenico, she had married him. This had caused Domenico enormous grief, inasmuch as Francesca, even more than his brother Cosimo or his son Vincenzo, had been his dearest confidante and had served as mistress of Isola de Grazia since the death of her mother.

A week after the wedding the married couple came to the villa to pay their respects. In a rare emotional scene, the outraged Domenico had Dante forcibly ejected, and for many months father and daughter were estranged. But when Francesca began visiting without Dante in tow, Domenico's reserve broke down, and they soon became as close as ever. As Phil understood it, the one condition the old man insisted upon was that Dante's name, or the fact of Francesca's marriage to him, never be referred to, even indirectly. Francesca, apparently, had no objections and took to spending one or two husbandless weekends a month at her old home.

In the meantime, Dante had continued to teach in Bologna, living in nearby Modena with Francesca, until Domenico had died in 1993. Then, with the old man's hostility no longer an issue and the widowed Vincenzo more than happy to have his sister on hand to reassume her old role as mistress of Isola de Grazia, he had returned with Francesca to take up residence at the villa 'for a year of reflection and renewal.'

That had been ten years ago, but here he was, still reflecting and renewing away, with no sign of letting up.

'So then, here we are,' he said when they had retaken their uncomfortable seats after greeting Phil. He sipped from a gold-rimmed teacup and gestured at the dark, sober portraits that surrounded them, 'Once again we find ourselves in the de Grazia Family Hall of Undistinguished Provincial Magistrates, Obscure Papal Sycophants, and

Second-Rate, Do-Nothing Admirals.'

This was said just as Cosimo came in from his walk with Bacco. Phil knew perfectly well that it was meant to bait the old man, and predictably, it did.

'The de Grazias have centuries of public service to their credit,' he said sternly, taking one of the remaining chairs, pointedly turning it so that he wasn't required to rest his eyes directly on Dante, and settling the old dog beside his legs, 'which is more than can be said for the Galassos. And I remind you that my sainted brother Alfredo was no 'do-nothing admiral'. He fought and died as a decorated naval officer in the Second World War.'

Dante tipped back his head and laughed. 'Sure, with the Fascists. Now there's something to be proud of, all right.'

'He despised the Fascists, as you well know. He loathed Mussolini.'

'But he fought on their side anyway. Pardon me, but I've never understood how that makes sense.'

Bacco, sensing that his master was in need of support, uttered an uncertain growl in Dante's direction. Cosimo sat very straight, stroking the furry, nervous head. 'It is to Alfredo's unending credit that he gave his life in a war he hated, obeying a leader he

102

abhorred, in a cause he distrusted. I assure you, if he didn't bear the name he did, he would not have done it, something I don't expect you to understand.'

He sat up even straighter. 'Do you know what he said to Domenico and to me the morning he left?' He was addressing the entire group now. ''This war is going to be lost, brothers, I have no doubt of that. But we must lose it as well as we can.'' He looked from face to face. 'He was a de Grazia.'

Dante shook his head, as if in incredulity, although he, like all of them, had heard the story before. 'All I can say is, let us all be grateful that such traditions are now obsolete, along with the decadent, moribund aristocracy that spawned them.'

'Decadent ... I ... you ... ' Cosimo, having run out of steam, shook his head with an old man's trembling frustration. The dog, looking up at him with concerned eyes, nuzzled his hand.

It was an old debate, and although on an intellectual level Phil had to agree with Dante, it was his grandfather's side that he instinctively took. The only thing that had kept him from publicly standing with Cosimo so far was his reluctance to begin his visit by getting into an unwinnable argument. Besides, this had been going on for years and would keep going on after he left, so what difference would it make? But he was now resolved to jump in if Dante pushed his luck in the face of Cosimo's capitulation, as he probably would.

Francesca saved him the trouble. Before Dante had gotten out another full sentence ('Once it's understood that all the tired old ideas of reactionism and imperialism have been obsolete for fifty years, and Italy comes to terms with its tawdry history of marginalization — ') her dismissive, painfully incisive voice cut him off.

'Tired old ideas is exactly right. Keep it up, Dante, and when the revolution comes, you won't have to kill all the capitalists, you'll have bored them to death long before.'

Dante glowered at her. 'How very amusing.'

'I thought it was time for someone to be amusing.'

Francesca de Grazia Galasso had been — still was — one of those classic Italian beauties, long-nosed, black-haired, flashing-eyed, and from Phil's point of view, overwhelmingly, almost frighteningly, hard-edged. Although they had never taken to each other — as a child, Francesca had preferred to keep well clear of her Ungaretti kin — he was always grateful for her presence at family affairs, which were dull things in her absence. With Francesca around, the clang of steel blades, the exciting glint of armor, was never very far away.

Well into her forties now, and more formidable than ever, she had been a textbook example of the adoring student who fulfilled her dreams by marrying the professor she idolized, only to find that his brilliant and profound observations tended to be less dazzling after she'd heard them a few dozen times. It also hadn't taken her long to figure out — correctly, in Phil's opinion — that she was smarter than he was. For many years now she had been paying little attention to anything he said, and on the few occasions she did, she was equally likely to be bored or irritated.

Over those years she had turned from the rebel against her own class that Dante had briefly made her, into as much a defender of the ancienne noblesse as Cosimo was, but of a very different sort. Caustic and exacting, she was the terror of the household staff, more than once reducing a new maid or young assistant gardener to tears. Not long before, Clemente and Genoveffa Candeloro, the married couple who had served as major domo and housekeeper since Domenico's day, had thrown an unprecedented joint tantrum and walked out. It seemed that Francesca, during one of her white-glove tours of inspection, had shut one too many French windows and said, one too many times: 'If dirt does not get in, dirt does not have to be got out.' It had taken the intervention of Vincenzo to get them to return, and relations were still on the dicey side.

Long ago, when Francesca had first started talking back to Dante, he had reacted with astonishment and indignation, neither of which had had any lasting effect on her. Now she no longer argued, but she no longer listened either, and when she casually cut him off or publicly ignored him, he still flared up once in a while, but generally did nothing worse than mutter back at her and eventually shut up. What their life might be like in private nobody knew and nobody wanted to guess.

As it was, and probably very much for the better, they spent little time together. The highly intelligent Francesca, who had gotten her accounting degree at Bologna despite the distractions provided by Dante, was Aurora's chief financial officer and Vincenzo's trusted second-in-command. In effect, it was Francesca who ran the company day-to-day, while Vincenzo was jetting around making deals or getting his clothes filthy at the building sites — an arrangement they both preferred. These duties kept her away from the villa a good forty, and sometimes fifty, hours a week (to the great relief of the household staff). Dante, on the other hand, stuck close to home, cranking out fiery manifestos for various left-wing or post-modernist antiestablishment periodicals, unbothered by the paradox of living high off the hog, in the bosom of a patrician family, while doing it.

Around the corner of the room from them, seated side-by-side, shoulders touching, like a pair of oversized nuthatches, on a heavy wooden dowry chest from the fifteenth century, were two people who were, in appearance, almost the exact opposites of the Galassos: a plump, pink-cheeked couple who were invariably protective of each other. These were the Barberos, Bella and Basilio. Bella was the daughter, by a previous marriage, of Domenico's wife, which made her Vincenzo's half-sister, which, Phil supposed, made her his own . . . what, stepaunt? Second cousin, once removed? He'd have to ask Gideon.

Or maybe not. He'd gotten along until now without knowing, after all.

As Domenico's stepdaughter, Bella had

grown up on the island, among the de Grazias, and had married Basilio when they were both twenty-four. That had been thirty-five years ago, and if they'd ever said a cross word to each other since, nobody could remember having heard it. Not that Bella had any shortage of cross words when it came to other people. Hypersensitive and short-fused, she had chafed most of her life under the humiliation of depending on the largesse of her step-family. Marriage to Basilio had come as a tremendous release, and she'd wasted no time in escaping to Milan with him. However, her husband, an ineffectual, jovial man with a diploma in human resources, had proven unequal to the task of supporting her in the style to which she'd become accustomed. After a few years of relative deprivation in Milan, she had turned for help to her stepfather.

Not unexpectedly, Domenico had come through. Following his father's instructions, Vincenzo had created a make-work job with a nice title for him at Aurora: employee salary and benefits administrator. With the appointment to this position, the Barberos had come back to the villa to live. It had been intended as a temporary measure until they found someplace nearby, but somehow it had settled into permanence.

Later, when Vincenzo had taken over the company as CEO and chairman of the board of directors, he had given the somewhat underemployed Basilio another essentially meaningless responsibility as chairman of the newly created policy advisory committee. In the decade since then, Basilio, being Basilio, had voted with Vincenzo 434 out of 435 times, the one exception being in 1996 when Basilio stood up for his principles and voted, against Vincenzo's openly expressed wishes, for installing a candy machine in the plant. There had been no similar revolt since.

While Domenico had been alive, it hadn't been so bad for Bella at the villa. Although not a de Grazia, she was, after all, the daughter of the *padrone*'s own wife and he had treated her with consideration, if not with great affection. But after the old man died, once Vincenzo had become *padrone*, the atmosphere had changed. It was nothing he'd ever said in so many words, but he made it clear, every day, in a hundred ways, that she was now nothing more than one more unwelcome ward, an unasked-for, barely noticed obligation he was honor-bound to meet. His despicable sister Francesca and even the snot-nosed young Achille had taken their cues from Vincenzo and had begun treating her accordingly. But despite the many provocations, after twenty-two years it no longer seemed conceivable to live elsewhere. Besides, the damned de Grazias owed it to her.

Basilio Barbero was very different from his wife, a nervous, always-jolly, accommodating man with thinning reddish hair and a drinker's veiny nose and cheeks. Left to his own devices, he would take whatever hand Fate dealt him without complaint. Unlike Bella, he was constitutionally averse to conflict, so that while Bella had been taking malicious pleasure at the exchange between Dante and Francesca, her husband had been getting increasingly uncomfortable.

'I can't help wondering,' he piped up as Dante arranged his all-but-lipless mouth into the most satisfactory position for a cutting retort to his wife, 'what those people' — he meant the kidnappers — 'have to say. And I certainly hope young Achille is all right. I know we're all terribly worried about him.'

'Oh, are we really?' Dante said mockingly. 'Tell me, would it be violating some primeval law of the de Grazia canon to be honest for once? Is there anyone here who really cares, one way or the other, what happens to that know-it-all brat?'

'I — ' Cosimo began indignantly.

'Except, of course, for our venerable

patriarch over there,' Dante allowed, with a half-bow in his direction.

'Come now, Dante, I know you don't mean what you said,' Basilio replied with a chuckle. 'After all, who among us did not become a know-it-all at sixteen?'

'I did not.'

'That's true enough,' Francesca muttered into her cup of espresso. 'Dante knew everything there was to know from the day he was born.'

Her husband folded his arms and turned away in his chair to make it clear that a direct reply was beneath him. 'Charming,' he said.

'*I* care about Achille,' Bella Barbero blurted, as if she'd been holding herself back only with difficulty. 'I feel very deeply for him.'

The others looked at her with skepticism — including Phil, who was aware that the family's antipathy toward Achille, with the sole exception of old Cosimo, was universal and well deserved. Kidnapped or not, there was no denying that Achille was, and always had been, a pill: demanding and disrespectful as a child; arrogant, contemptuous, and self-centered as a teenager. To his credit, Vincenzo, proud of his new son, had really tried with the boy at first, but fatherhood did not come naturally to him, and in any case,

111

nothing, neither tolerance, nor severity, seemed to make a lasting difference. Achille was simply Achille. And when Vincenzo's wife, Achille's mother, had died when the boy was eleven, Vincenzo had thrown up his hands altogether. He had turned Achille's upbringing over to the busy Francesca, who had eventually thrown up her hands in turn and more or less given him over into Genoveffa's care.

Vincenzo still tried sometimes with him for the sake of familial continuity, but it was apparent to all that their relationship had become strained and distant, and he, like the others, had been openly relieved as Achille grew older and began to spend more and more time off the island. Only Cosimo still saw the possibility (increasingly remote, although he wouldn't admit it) of the noble, truly patrician genes of the boy's grandfather someday asserting themselves in him.

'Very deeply,' Bella repeated through her teeth, while her considerable bosom swelled. She had a somewhat pneumatic appearance to begin with, and when she was angry, she gave the remarkable impression of physically expanding. 'There are good reasons for his behaving as he does. I, too, was an unloved child in this house,' she said darkly. 'I understand what he's had to go through.'

'Oh?' said Francesca. 'And how were you mistreated? Tell us, were you chained up in the cellar? Were you denied food?'

'Not all mistreatment need be physical,' Bella said, her fingers at the strand of pearls on her throat.

'That's so,' said her husband. 'Indeed, that's so. Many, many cases — '

'You're a de Grazia, Francesca,' Bella went on without pause. 'I don't expect you to comprehend. You think that because I happen not to have your noble and wondrous name, I should sit without complaint, keep my mouth closed, and be grateful for every crumb, every kind word that's thrown to me.'

Phil understood her point. To Francesca, as it had been to Domenico and as it still was to Cosimo and Vincenzo, blood counted above everything, and the blood that counted above all other blood, no matter how ancient or ennobled, was that which ran in the veins of the de Grazias. By that token, the only members of the *consiglio* whose opinions really mattered, who were there by virtue of an unassailable hereditary right, were Vincenzo himself, Cosimo, and Francesca. And Phil, too, although to a lesser degree. Although he'd been born an Ungaretti, he was nevertheless the grandson of Cosimo and great-nephew of Domenico. The blood of the

113

de Grazias flowed in his veins. But the others — Dante, Bella, Basilio — were members of the de Grazia family merely through marriage, the most technical of loopholes.

'Oh, I understand, all right,' Francesca shot back. 'I understand you hated it here so much you didn't leave until you were twenty. And you ran back soon enough with your tail between your legs; you and your husband both.'

Bella's eyes bulged. Although it seemed impossible, the great bosom distended even more. 'If you think for one minute — '

'You know what? I believe I'll stand up for a while,' Basilio announced out of the blue.

The others watched him stand up.

'There, that feels better,' he said, waggling his arms. 'It gets the circulation going. Dr Luzzatto says we should all stand up and move our limbs at least once an hour. At work, I make sure that my secretary lets me know whenever I've been sitting at my desk for more than an hour. It's very easy to lose track of time when one is constantly busy. Of course, if I'm in a conference that can't be interrupted, well, then, it simply has to wait. Work comes first. But other than that, once an hour, Basilio Barbero is up and about. By example, I try to encourage our employees to do the same thing, but I'm not always successful. One of these days, I'm going to get a conditioning room put in, so that our office employees can use their breaks for healthy, enjoyable exercise. Personally, I'd be in favor of allowing everyone twenty minutes for exercise, over and above any other breaks. Well, not the construction workers, of course; they get all the exercise they need, that goes without saying. People think that such a policy would reduce work output, but in reality the opposite is true.'

Phil was beginning to remember what it was about the essentially harmless Basilio that got on his nerves. It wasn't merely that he was too anxious to please, too quick to laugh at your jokes, too relentlessly cheery, too scatterbrained. Those were mild annoyances compared to the way he had of gabbling away like a chimp on amphetamines. Whenever he got nervous, or agitated, or anxious (all of which occurred frequently), his tongue would start flapping, and once he got started, it was impossible to shut him up.

Basilio took a breath — a quick one, not long enough to give Bella and Francesca a chance to start taking whacks at each other again. 'Look at the clock, it's fifteen minutes past eleven,' he rattled on. 'Wasn't he supposed to be here at eleven? I understand that the man is a *carabinieri* colonel with a good many responsibilities and you can't expect him to be prompt down to the minute, but aren't our responsibilities to be taken into consideration too? Ah, well, I suppose I might as well sit down again. Standing's not going to make Colonel Caravale get here any sooner, is it? Still, you would think that if he knew he was going to be as late as this, he would have had the common courtesy to have us telephoned. But common courtesy is hardly as common as it used to be, is it? It's all push and shove and go and run nowadays. People have forgotten — '

Phil shot out of his chair and ran for the pantry across the corridor, where the tea and coffee had been set up on a trestle table. 'Jeez,' he said as opened the tap of the coffee urn to fill an espresso cup, but he was laughing as he said it. 'What a — *damn!*'

'Oh, excuse me, signore!'

In turning away from the buffet he had collided with a thin, sallow, worn-looking woman with limp, mouse-brown hair and indistinct features unenhanced by makeup. He had juggled and caught the espresso cup before it hit the stone-tiled floor, but not before it splattered some of its contents over his T-shirt.

'I'm so sorry, signore. I wasn't looking where I was going . . . ' Her near-colorless eyebrows went up. 'Oh, my God, it's Fili, isn't it? What are you doing here?'

He stared at her, open-mouthed. 'Lea?'

She smiled. 'Have I changed so much then?' She wore a thin, button-up, old-womanish sweater over a nondescript collared blouse and tan pants, along with a pair of bulky, multicolored running shoes.

'You haven't changed at all. I just didn't expect to see you, that's all. You look wonderful.'

She looked, he thought, like absolute hell. Lea Pescallo, the daughter of Bella and Basilio Barbero, had been an early love. He had first known her — and then forgotten her — when they had both been children at the villa. But later, on a family visit when he was eighteen, he had fallen passionately, hopelessly in love with her. At that age, he had been pretty much a younger version of what he was now in his forties: knobbly, gangling, vaguely ill-formed. (He'd been desperately shy, too, but that, at least, he'd been able to overcome with the years.) But Lea . . . Lea had been heartbreakingly beautiful; seductive and ethereal at the same time, like something out of Botticelli.

'That one will die young. You can see it in her face,' his mother had remarked years before, but Phil had found Lea's fragile

117

beauty, her gentle, wonderfully graceful hands, her soft voice, her quiet, modest ways, heartbreakingly attractive . . . and miles beyond anything a misfit like him might conceivably hope for. Around her, he'd turned into a nitwit, blushing and perspiring after every dumb thing he'd said.

They had somehow become friends in spite of this, and had carried on a chaste, pointless, increasingly intermittent correspondence for years, until she had fallen in love with and married the impossibly dashing Raffaele Pescallo, he of the gleaming white teeth, a rising star on the European motocross circuit. As a sort of self-punishment — for what he wasn't sure — Phil had come to the wedding, a predictably flashy affair in Arona. It was the last time he'd seen her and it was clear that the intervening seventeen years had been brutally hard on her. Someone seeing her now for the first time — the defeated shoulders, the faint pink smudge of mouth, the puffy, watery eyes underscored with bruise-like streaks of fatigue — would have a hard time believing that this drab, beaten-down woman had once been beautiful, and not such a very long time ago at that.

'Are you here for the *consiglio*?' Phil asked, searching for something to say. It wasn't only her appearance that had devastated him, but

118

her question: 'Have I changed so much then?' No effort at irony, just a melancholy, rueful query — more a statement, really — to which she already knew the answer.

'The *consiglio?* Oh . . . no, I wouldn't feel comfortable at that. I don't really belong. No, I'm just . . . visiting.'

'Ah. Well. Are you still working for that hotel group?' The last he'd heard, she was some kind of consultant for a consortium of hotels that operated throughout Europe.

'Oh, yes. And you, do you still . . . the tours, the travel books?'

'Yes.' He was wildly pleased that she remembered. 'That's really why I'm in Italy now, doing a tour.'

'Ah. Well . . . ' She was getting ready to go.

'Is Raf here with you?' he asked.

'Raf? No. I've left him, didn't you know? No, why would you know? It was three months ago. I've been staying here, with my parents, until . . . well, until I can figure out where I go next.'

'I'm sorry.' He waited to see if she'd tell him anything more, and after a few seconds she did.

'I was wrong and everybody else was right about Raf,' she said humbly. As her lips pressed together, he noticed for the first time the dry, middle-aged lines that radiated from

119

their corners. It was as if a pincer squeezed his heart. 'He was never cut out to be a husband. I thought he would change. I should have known better.'

To his shame, a surge of something like vindication flowed through him. *If you had married me instead of Raf, you would still be beautiful. I would have made you happy. You should have married me.* The fact that he had never asked her to, or even hinted at it, was forgotten for the moment.

'You should have married me,' he said to his own surprise. And to his astonishment, he was blushing again, something he'd thought he'd gotten over twenty years ago.

She looked down, but he could see she was smiling. 'Maybe I should have.'

He was relieved to hear Vincenzo's rough, dismissive voice from across the corridor, at the entrance to the gallery:

'You all know Colonel Caravale. Shall we get started? Where's Fili?'

7

''We have your son','' Caravale read aloud.

''He is in good health. If you would like him back you will need to pay five million euros. Payment will be made by means of a wire transfer to our account. You will receive detailed instructions later.

''Do not try to get in touch with us at this point. As soon as the money is available, you are to place a classified advertisement in La Stampa. The advertisement is to be under Real Estate for Sale and must say 'Prestigious villa, near Oggebbio, mountain view, 5,000,000 euros. Cash only,' followed by the name, telephone number, and fax number of the person we are to contact. You have exactly one week. Do not waste our time with counteroffers, delays, or explanations, we are not interested and will not respond. If this advertisement does not appear by Monday, June 23, you will not see

your son again. His fate will be on your head.''

He laid the fax down, readjusted the glossy, white Sam Browne belt that ran diagonally down the front of his tunic, folded his hands on the small, homely table that had been provided for him, and looked around the room while he waited for the buzz to die down.

He was in a bad mood and having a hard time not showing it. This *'galleria'* was, he thought, probably the least favorite room he'd ever been in; at any rate among those that didn't have a dead body in them. All those deceased, self-satisfied, better-than-thou de Grazias looking down their noses at him. All those live, self-satisfied, better-than-thou de Grazias looking down their noses at him. This archaic *'consiglio'* business annoyed him too, more than he liked to admit, even to himself. It was irritating to let all this blue-blood nonsense get to him, but he couldn't help being put out by it. Like father like son, he supposed. An old story.

Vincenzo, to whom he'd shown the fax a few minutes before, sat scowling, resting his chin on his hand. Most of the others were talking, some of them to themselves. Having met them at a previous *consiglio* the day after

122

the kidnapping, and then talked individually with them, he was beginning to know what to expect from each of them. Old Cosimo sat removed in the far corner, gravely conferring with his dog, who listened with rapt attention. Basilio Barbero chattered excitedly to his wife Bella, who shrugged as if to say: 'What could you expect with a family like this?' Near them, Dante Galasso muttered to his wife with that smirk of his that implied he knew a great deal more than he was letting on. At the previous meeting, Caravale, briefly suspicious, had wondered if that was indeed the case with Dante, but he was soon convinced that it was merely Galasso's everyday, know-it-all expression. He was, after all, a onetime professor, and a Red one at that, so it was hardly surprising. Galasso's jet-haired wife — Francesca, was it? — stared at the ceiling, manifestly not listening to her husband.

The only person he hadn't met before was the bearded American, Filiberto — Phil — Boyajian, a cousin of some sort. Improbably enough, Caravale had taken to him almost on sight, probably because he seemed as out of place among the de Grazia clan as Caravale himself. Phil, wearing walking shorts, had sat with his hands in his pockets, saying nothing during the reading, but he was the first to speak up afterward.

'What do we do now, Colonel?'

'That's up to Signor de Grazia,' Caravale said, looking at Vincenzo, and six other pairs of eyes swung toward the *padrone*.

Vincenzo jerked his head angrily. 'It's more than I thought they'd ask, damn them. Five million.'

'Your insurance company will cover it and then some, so what's the problem?' Dante Galasso asked. 'They can afford it. They make millions every year from bilking the ignorant and the greedy.'

With a brief, lancing look at Dante ('Who asked for your opinion?' he might just as well have said), Vincenzo directed his response to Caravale. Argos, like most kidnap insurers, didn't actually pay ransom demands directly, he explained; they reimbursed you for what you paid (minus a 250,000€ deductible in Argos's case) from your own resources, and only on proof that the ransom had indeed been paid.

'But if the insurance company guarantees payment,' Phil said, 'can't you just borrow on their guarantee? Argos is a big firm, they have a good reputation.'

Unfortunately no, Vincenzo explained. As with other kidnap insurers, it was strictly against the rules, and possibly against the law,

124

to use the policy itself as collateral. Doing so would invalidate it, so he had to come up with the money on his own. His Aurora stock alone would more than provide the necessary collateral, never fear. He was surprised — angry — that they would demand so much, that was all.

He turned again to Caravale. 'What do you propose, Colonel?'

'Well . . . ' Caravale began.

He already knew what Vincenzo had just told them about Argos because he'd looked into it on his own the day after the kidnapping. He also knew that the policy explicitly required that there be cooperation with the police, which meant that Vincenzo's posturing the other day about how much he trusted him had been so much buttering up. He thought he understood the point of it too. To Vincenzo he was just another version of Comandante Boldini, a petty functionary who was supposed to swell with pride and loyalty at being brought into the confidence of the noble de Grazias. Well, not bloody likely.

In the expectant hush that followed his 'well,' he had scribbled two lines at the bottom of the sheet. 'Here is the reply that I propose. 'Prestigious villa, near Oggebbio, mountain view, 1,000,000€;. Contact signor

125

Pinzolo' — that's me, of course, how do you do? — 'telephone 032358285, fax 032358266'.'

There was a spatter of confusion and surprise.

'One million . . . '

'But they said . . . '

'How can you . . . '

Caravale raised his hand, wrist cocked, like the traffic policeman he'd once been. 'It's not a good idea to give in too quickly to their initial demands. If we do, they're likely to conclude they asked too little and come back with a higher ransom demand. Better to offer less, but to show at the same time that we're willing to negotiate.'

Vincenzo was shaking his head doubtfully. 'They were very explicit, Colonel — no counteroffers would be accepted. How much clearer could they be? I understand what you're getting at, but this is my son's life we're talking about, not some game. We de Grazias — '

'Signore,' Caravale interrupted before Vincenzo could tell him what 'we de Grazias' would or wouldn't do, 'I have to tell you that in a case like this, you can never know for sure what they will do, but I think it's safe to assume that their threats are empty. What would be the point of harming or killing their captive? What would they gain? They'd come away with nothing at all but the *carabinieri* hot on their trail. And I assure you, they do not expect to get five million euros.'

'That makes sense,' said Phil. 'Otherwise, why would they have made the amount part of the ad they want us to place? It would have said something else — it could have been anything — and not mentioned money at all. Putting in an amount must have been a way of giving us a chance to respond with a different amount.'

'Yes, I suppose that's so,' said Vincenzo, obviously impressed.

Caravale was impressed too. This rather subtle point hadn't occurred to him either. He wondered if the kidnappers realized it themselves.

'If we are in agreement, then,' he said, 'I expect matters to proceed about like this: We'll go ahead and offer the one million. They'll express outrage but make a counter-offer of, oh, four million. We'll offer two, they'll come down to something like three-fifty, and we'll probably settle for three million or thereabouts. It shouldn't take too long once the process begins.'

Dante laughed. 'If it's as cut-and-dried as all that, why not offer them the three million now and eliminate all this busy work?'

'I'm sorry you don't find the discussion

more worthwhile, Dante,' Vincenzo said. There was no love lost between those two.

'On the contrary, I'm fascinated. I can't wait to see it happen. It's like a lesson in the capitalist ethic. One party has a commodity to sell, another party wishes to buy it. They freely work out a price between themselves, without the interference of regulations or the intrusion of government. Do we not have before us the free market system at its most elemental?'

'Oh, for God's sake,' Francesca said, again lifting her eyes to the low, hammer-beamed ceiling, something she seemed to do pretty often with Dante around. She must once have been quite beautiful, Caravale realized. She still was, he supposed, but now she'd weathered into a collection of hard angles and sharp edges.

The stern, thin, measured voice of Cosimo de Grazia was heard from his corner. 'My nephew is not a commodity.'

'Certainly not, Uncle,' Vincenzo agreed. 'Colonel Caravale, when do you suggest this advertisement be placed?'

'Not until you do have the money available. It would be a mistake to mislead them on that score.'

'A million, do you mean? That's no problem. I'll go into Milan tomorrow morning and see my banker. To be completely safe, the advertisement can appear the following morning. Wednesday.'

Caravale showed his surprise in spite of himself. 'You can raise — borrow — a million euros cash in one day?'

De Grazia smiled. 'But it's not cash, Colonel, it's a wire transfer. No money actually changes hands. Very up-to-date. I assure you, it involves far less in the way of logistics than trying to collect a million euros in ten-and twenty-euro notes, or whatever you're used to.'

'Of course,' Caravale said, but the truth was that he hadn't given much thought to this aspect of the demand. All of the kidnap-ransom cases that he'd dealt with had concerned cash ransoms. And de Grazia was right about the logistical difficulties involved. As it happened, Caravale knew from personal experience exactly what one million euros in ten-euro notes involved. It took one hundred thousand ten-euro notes — no easy thing to collect — and when you had them all together, they weighed two hundred pounds and filled four garbage bags to bursting. Even the crooks in that case had been taken aback when they saw what they had to deal with.

He was going to have to get himself filled in on electronic money transfers before this went much further. He didn't like being behind the times. And he didn't like being patronized by Vincenzo do Grazia.

'I'll see that the advertisement runs Wednesday then,' he said. 'Who knows, they might even accept, although that's doubtful. But if not, it'll give you a chance to raise more while we negotiate.'

'One moment, please,' Bella Barbero said, her nail-chewed fingers playing over her pearls. 'I realize I don't know much about such things, but it seems to me you're putting quite a lot of confidence in these gangsters knowing these, these 'rules' as well as you do.'

'Yes, that's so,' exclaimed her husband Basilio. 'For all we know, we could be dealing with crazy people, or amateurs who don't know how such things are supposed to work.'

'Oh, I think we can assume that these gangsters, as you properly call them, signora, belong to the class of experienced, professional kidnappers of which Italy, unfortunately, has no shortage. The abduction of Achille was' — a work of art, he almost said — 'meticulously planned. The diversion on the Corso, the blockage of the police cars on their lot, were executed with foresight and precision. There was nothing amateurish about them.'

'That may be so, but I don't agree with

your conclusions,' Bella said, openly challenging him. 'What about the kidnapping itself? It could hardly have been more botched. All that wild shooting, two people dead. They might easily have shot . . . ' She didn't finish the sentence.

'True, signora, the execution of the plan was bungled, but that was the fault of those that were hired to do it, not of the men behind it. Kidnappers for ransom often use hired thugs for the most dangerous aspects.'

'I don't quite see how you can be so confident anybody hired anyone,' Vincenzo said irritably. 'Why is it necessary to conjure up some hidden mastermind behind it all?'

Caravale shook his head. 'I don't know about any 'mastermind', but we do have an ID on the dead one. His name is Ugo Fogazzaro, and he is — he was — a Milanese hoodlum who survived partly through his own petty crimes, and partly by making himself available, for a fee, to others who could come up with grander schemes. It seems reasonable to assume the other men involved in the actual kidnapping were of the same type. I might be wrong in this, but I don't think so. I can tell you this much: Ugo Fogazzaro didn't think this up by himself.'

Vincenzo nodded slowly. 'So you have been working on your own.'

'I told you I would.'

'Yes.' He looked as if he wanted to comment further but changed his mind. 'All right, does anyone else wish to say anything before we close?'

'Colonel,' Phil said, 'are you able to tell where the fax was sent from?'

'Yes, we know that, but unfortunately it came from the biggest, and busiest, public copy facility in Milan. I'm afraid there's no help there. No one can remember who sent it.'

'All right then, is there anything else?' Vincenzo asked. He was getting out of his chair. 'I'm sure Colonel Caravale wants to — ' He sighed and dropped back down. 'Yes, Uncle, you wish to say something?'

'A question, if it's permitted?' said Cosimo.

From Vincenzo, a resigned dip of the chin, barely this side of polite.

'What about Achille?' the old man asked. 'Is he all right? How can we be sure? How do we know these people who sent the message really have him, as they say they do?'

Well, bless the old buzzard, Caravale thought. Somebody in this room full of cold fish finally expressed some concern for the boy. And naturally, it would be Cosimo. It was strange — the old man was the snootiest of them all, the most like Caravale's idea of

132

an arrogant, time-warped aristocrat, and yet there was something about him he liked, something that reminded him, of all people, of his beloved grandfather, his loving, morally upright, steadfastly old-fashioned maternal grandfather Fortunato, who had been a humble ice-wagon driver all his life.

'That's a good question, Signor de Grazia,' he said, 'and it's the first thing that must be established. When they call, I will ask to speak to Achille myself.'

'And if they refuse?'

'I expect they will. In that case, I will have ready — with your help, ladies and gentlemen — a set of questions that no one but Achille could answer. They will have to provide me with his replies, not only then, but at each step before we proceed further. I don't expect this to come as a surprise to them. Even in a kidnapping, there are certain conventions, certain rules, that are to the advantage of all.'

'Rules again,' muttered Bella Barbero with a toss of her head.

8

While the *consiglio* met in the gallery, Gideon
and Julie sat at a wrought-iron table in the
breakfast garden, a flagstone-tiled patio
overlooking the formal plantings and classical
statuary of the three terraces that made up
the rest of the island. The crescent-shaped
terraces nestled, each one within the curve of
the one above, and descended in measured,
eighteenth-century perfection from the rear
of the villa down to the shore.

They had meant to stroll the attractive,
well-kept paths, but when Vincenzo's 'man'
Clemente appeared with a pitcher of iced
coffee, two frosted glasses, and a tray of anise
and poppy seed cookies, a pleasant, jet
lag-induced laziness got the better of them
and they stayed where they were, sitting in
the warm breeze from the lake, inhaling the
thick, lush scents of oleanders, camellias,
rhododendrons, and citrus, chatting about
nothing, and half-dozing.

A white peacock strutted up and down in
front of them, showing off its tail feathers for
a while before concluding that neither one of
them was a likely prospect for love, and at

134

one point a pint-sized monkey with a body no bigger than a fist scrambled up onto their table to balance on the edge and scowl at them like the outsiders they were. Contemptuously turning down an anise-flavored cookie but deigning to accept a poppy seed one, it briefly scolded them, stuck the sweet in its mouth for safekeeping, hopped down, and scuttled irritably off.

'Cute little fella,' Julie said, smiling. 'Kind of crabby, though.'

'Marmoset,' Gideon said. 'Family Callithricidae, genus *Callithrix*, species *jacchus flaviceps*.'

'I knew that.'

'The most primitive of the New World monkeys. They lack opposable thumbs.'

'Aw, is that why he was so crabby?'

Other than these island fauna, and the venerable, elephantine Clemente, who lumbered back twice simply to pour their coffee for them, the only sign of life they saw was a drab, narrow-shouldered woman in sneakers who came around the side of the villa from the back, smoking a cigarette and pulling her thin sweater around her despite the day's warmth. When she saw them, she turned on her heel and went quickly back around the corner.

'I'm afraid we spoiled one of the maids'

135

break times,' Julie said. 'What do you say we take that stroll after all, and leave the tables to the staff?'

'You're on,' Gideon replied. 'Just let me gather my strength for a minute.'

But they were still gathering their strength five minutes later, when Vincenzo and Phil came out to find them. Vincenzo offered a curt, pro forma invitation to the three of them to stay for dinner, but they declined and went back to Stresa with Colonel Caravale in the police launch. Squalls were dancing over the lake, so they were inside, sitting knee-to-knee on the U-shaped, cushioned bench in the tiny cabin. After a little small talk about the weather, conversation flagged. Caravale was terse and preoccupied, and his glowering, thuggish looks hardly invited socializing. With his ostentatiously decorated military headgear, grim black uniform, epaulets, Sam Browne belt, and holstered sidearm, he could have been a corrupt police chief in some tinpot republic. If nothing else, he looked as if he'd be a good man with a rubber hose or an electric prod.

'You speak English extremely well, Colonel,' Julie said, searching for something to say.

He turned from the window he'd been staring through. 'I'd better, signora. This is a tourist region. A lot of the people I have to deal with here don't speak anything but.'

'Victims or perps?' Phil asked.

Caravale gave them a brief smile. 'A little of both. There are English courses at the academy, signora.' He touched the brim of his cap and went back to looking out the window.

'But you speak it so idiomatically,' said Julie, who was hard to deter when she wanted to get someone talking. 'Where did you learn? Surely not in a class?'

'No, I learned in Connecticut.' He turned toward them again, more fully this time, and with an air of resignation. Apparently these Americans weren't going to let him think in peace.

'My father was a supply master in the Italian Army. He was captured in 1942 and spent the rest of the war at a POW camp in Colorado. He had a wonderful time, he couldn't say enough about America. So after the war, before I was born, he went back and lived in New Haven with my aunt and her family for five years, until he came back home to get married. Later, he sent me back there every summer but one from the time I was twelve until I was seventeen. I still visit with my own children every few years. And so now I speak Italian with a Connecticut accent, and Connecticut with an Italian accent. Nobody understands what the hell I'm talking about.'

It was a joke — Caravale's English was excellent — so everyone laughed, but then the conversation died again, until Phil spoke up with the air of a man who'd just come up with a terrific idea. 'You know, Colonel, I was just thinking. Dr Oliver might be able to help you out on this case.'

'Oh, really?' Caravale stiffened slightly, which Gideon, an old hand at this, correctly read as a danger sign.

Not Phil, however. 'Oh, yeah, absolutely. He's famous. They call him the Skeleton Detective, you've probably heard of him, he — '

'I'm a forensic anthropologist,' Gideon put in quickly. He knew enough about policemen to know that they did not always — well, just about never — welcome unsolicited 'help' from unknown outsiders, particularly nonpolicemen, particularly nonpolicemen who were foreigners. Even solicited help wasn't always gratefully received.

Besides, that wasn't what he was here for, and anyway, what did he know about kidnapping?

'I wouldn't be of any use to you in something like this, I'm afraid,' he said to Caravale. 'In forensic anthropology it's mostly skeletal material that we deal with. We — '

138

'I'm aware of what forensic anthropologists deal with,' Caravale said shortly. 'Believe it or not, we have them in Italy too. As a matter of fact, I myself worked with one on a case involving bones several years ago.'

'Really?' Julie prompted politely when he showed no sign of continuing.

'That's right, a local doctor came upon the headless skeleton of a little girl in the woods near Baveno and contacted us. So I called our expert — our forensic anthropologist — in Rome and talked to her before doing anything. And at the site I took pains to have my men follow her instructions to the letter. We did everything: photographs, drawings, layered excavation with trowel and brushes, sifting the soil into buckets, everything. It took us six hours, but we recovered every scrap of bone there was and sent it off, numbered, bagged, and cross-recorded, to the criminalistics lab. They said it was the most thorough job they'd ever seen.'

'Did you ever catch the killer?' Julie asked.

'Unfortunately, no, but I have good reason to believe that the perp' — a quick, wry glance at Phil — 'was a red fox that had been seen in the area.'

'A red — ?'

'The skeleton was that of a rabbit,' Caravale said impassively. 'I understand it was a source of amusement at the laboratory for some time and is now something of a legend there.'

Julie and Phil made sounds of commiseration but Gideon was annoyed at the undertone of reproach. Whose fault was it that the thick-jowled Caravale, let alone this Italian doctor of his, couldn't tell the difference between a human child and a rabbit? To be fair, though, it was far from the first time he'd run across a physician who didn't know animal bones when he saw them. It really wasn't surprising. Differentiating human from nonhuman bones wasn't part of any medical school curriculum that he knew of, and why should it be? But for cops it was a different story.

If you'd taken the session I put on at the International Conference on the Forensic Sciences when it was held in Rome a few years ago, Gideon thought but didn't say, you'd have taken one look at the pelvis, or a scapula, or any long bone, and saved yourself five hours and fifty-nine minutes of work.

'There are some fairly simple ways to differentiate animal and human bones,' he contented himself with saying. 'I can recommend a book or two if you're interested.'

'I don't think so, thanks, not today.' The

launch thudded gently against the Stresa dock and came to a stop. Caravale was the first to stand. 'However, if any further skeletons turn up, I'll be sure to call upon you.'

'Do that,' Gideon said. 'Just make sure it's sometime in the next week.'

'I'll see what I can do,' said Caravale. He made a formal little bow to the three of them, grunted his good-bye, and pulled himself up onto the pier.

'Well, that certainly went well,' Phil said brightly.

Gideon made a grumbling sound deep in his throat. 'Let's go get some lunch.'

9

The kidnappers' answer came on Thursday morning, twenty-four hours after the advertisement had appeared. It was in the form of a padded envelope that had been slipped through the after-hours courier-delivery slot at Aurora Costruzioni's field office in Intra during the night. The clerk who found it lying on the floor, seeing nothing on the front but VINCENZO DE GRAZIA in block letters — no business logo, no return address — was immediately suspicious. Following instructions from the *carabinieri*, she didn't touch it, but called them at once.

Within minutes the envelope was dusted for fingerprints (none) and opened. Inside was a one-page letter folded around a cassette tape, both of which had also been wiped clean. The letter, envelope, and tape were placed in separate plastic sleeves for further examination and taken to *carabinieri* headquarters.

Half an hour later Vincenzo, working distractedly and intermittently at home on a proposal for a waste-water treatment facility near Bergamo, received a telephone call from Caravale.

'We've heard from them.'

'What?' Vincenzo put down the proposal. 'How?'

'It came to your office in Intra. There's a letter and an audiotape that's supposed to be of Achille. Can you come in to headquarters to — '

'What do they say?'

'As far as we can tell, Achille is all right — '

'What do they say?'

Caravale took the last puff from his morning cigar and breathed out the smoke before answering. 'They say 'no'.'

★ ★ ★

Sitting opposite Caravale at *carabinieri* headquarters, Vincenzo mumbled his way through the brief message.

"We are not interested in negotiating. Five million euros only. Do not waste our time by telling us this is not within your means or that you need more time. On the upper story of your villa, directly over the front entrance, is a window that is now kept shuttered. If you intend to cooperate, you will open those shutters as a signal, and we will then give

you final instructions and tell you where to wire the money. As soon as we have the money, your son will be freed unharmed. If the shutters have not opened by noon on Friday, we will assume you do not wish to comply'.'

He looked up at Caravale. 'Friday. Tomorrow.'

The colonel nodded. 'Yes.'

Vincenzo flicked at the sheet of paper with his fingernails. 'Shutters, shutters . . . but doesn't this tell us that the kidnappers are right there, on Isola de Grazia? Either that, or they have an accomplice — '

'No, not necessarily. The front of your villa is visible from the shore here. With a pair of binoculars, they wouldn't have any trouble seeing the shutters.'

'Oh. Of course, yes.' He seemed to drift away, thinking.

'You want to finish the letter, signore.'

Stiff-faced, Vincenzo went back to it.

''In that case, your son will be killed at once. Preparations have already been made. This is our last message. You will not hear from us again'.'

144

He snorted and slid it back across the table. 'I want to hear the tape.'

They were sitting in one of the interrogation rooms. A small tape recorder lay on the table. Caravale reached out and pressed a button. Vincenzo leaned in over it, shoulders hunched, head cocked. He had rushed over without slipping on a jacket, and with his shirtsleeves folded up over hairless, smooth forearms, he seemed to be vibrating with nervous energy.

'Papa?' The voice was tentative and frightened.

'Huh!' came from Vincenzo.

In the background they heard someone mutter, 'Louder, kid.' There was a scraping sound; the recorder being moved closer.

'Papa?' Louder, much more intense.

Vincenzo nodded. 'It's him.'

'I'm all right . . . they gave me a Game Boy . . . '

They could tell Achille's throat was clogging up, and a moment later he was bawling. 'Papa, they're going to kill me if you don't pay them! I know they really mean it. I don't want to d — '

That was all. Vincenzo listened for a few seconds longer to see if there was anything more, then threw himself angrily back against his chair. 'You call that 'all right'? I don't.'

145

'What are you going to do?'

An uneven laugh. 'I'm going to pay them, what else?'

'The entire five million? You have it?'

'I've made arrangements for it. A telephone call to Milan is all that's needed.'

'Listen, Signor de Grazia . . . '

Vincenzo waved him off. 'I know what you're going to say.'

'Do you? I was going to say that Achille could already be dead.'

'The tape . . . '

'The tape could have been made days ago, right after they got him. My advice — '

'Your advice,' Vincenzo said through narrowed lips, 'was to offer them a million euros, and we see how that worked out, don't we? Will you stand in my way if I try to pay the ransom?'

'No, it's up to you. But you're operating in the dark. You're liable to be out five million euros and still not get your son back.'

'Let me be frank, Colonel. I will be out nothing but the deductible and the interest on the loan. That I can afford. It's my insurer that will be out the five million euros. Am I willing to risk Argos's money on the chance of getting my son back alive? What do you think?'

'I think — '

'What would you think if it was your son, not mine?'

'I would — ' Caravale stopped and dipped his chin. He knew what he'd think, all right.

'Good,' said Vincenzo, taking charge now. 'May we go back to your office? With your permission, I'd like to use your telephone to tell my man to open the shutters.'

The call was made to Isola de Grazia at 10:22 A.M. At 10:24, Clemente opened the shutters. At 10:55, 'Signor Pinzolo,' the name that Caravale had chosen for his role as negotiator, received his first, last, and only telephone call. The police technician who recorded it quickly ran the tape up to Colonel Caravale. 'I think the call was made on one of those throwaway phones, Colonel. That's not good.'

Vincenzo, in the act of leaving, sat down again and both men listened to the message, heads bent, ears pricked.

'Bank of Rezekne, Latvia,' the weird, gibbering voice said. 'R, E, Z, E, K, N, E.'

'Damn,' Caravale muttered. Whoever it was had used an electronic voice distorter, one of the new generation that processed the sounds through an encoded chip and put them back out in a digital format. Next to impossible to trace. Voice prints wouldn't work. Voice stress analyzers wouldn't work. Chances were, they

147

wouldn't even be able to tell if it was a man or a woman.

'Account number. One. Eight. Eight. Zero. Five. Two. Nine. Six. Two. Seven. By tomorrow.'

When it was clear that there was nothing else, Caravale turned off the machine.

Vincenzo was shaking his head laughing again, this time in perplexity. 'For God's sake — Latvia?'

★ ★ ★

Major Massimiliano d'Este, deputy chief of the *carabinieri*'s financial crimes unit, also laughed when Caravale called him after Vincenzo had left.

'Latvia?' he said over the telephone from Rome. 'A numbered account? Well, they know their business, I have to give them that.'

'It's going to be hard to trace?'

'It's going to be impossible, Tullio. Compared to Rezekne, those banks in Liechtenstein or in the Cayman Islands — they're open books.'

Latvia, he explained, was a recent entry in the anonymous banking field. In its all-out effort to attract business from persons interested in what it euphemistically referred to as 'asset protection' or 'tax optimization,' it had installed the strictest confidentiality laws in the world. The banks themselves often didn't know their clients' real identities. And unauthorized disclosure of information about accounts or account holders was a felony. Only on proof of a criminal act by the client could the records be opened up. The Latvian —

'Well, what the hell do you call kidnapping and murder?' Carvale demanded.

'I said 'proof'.'

'I have two men dead. I have a boy kidnapped and held for ransom. That's not enough proof for you?'

'For me, yes. For the Latvian Court of Justice . . . mm, no. You're out of luck, Tullio. Maybe two years from now you'll squeeze a little information from them. Even then, I doubt if they'll be able to tell you who the account holder is. Or was; I expect he'll close the account and disappear the minute he gets the money. Wouldn't you?'

Caravale shook his head. Where did he go from here? There were no leads, no voices to try to trace (except for that indistinct 'Louder, kid'), no evidence that could be physically linked to them, no vehicle to put a tracking device on . . .

He sighed. 'Well, thanks for your help, Massimiliano.'

'Next time you envy my assignment in Rome,' d'Este said, 'just remember that I have to deal with this kind of frustration every day.'

'Who said I envied your assignment in Rome?' Caravale said.

★ ★ ★

After four days spent with the travel group, Gideon was getting a little desperate. It wasn't that the Pedal and Paddle Adventure itself had been unpleasant — the leisurely days of kayaking and sightseeing from Arona at the south end of the lake up past Stresa and through the Borromean Islands had been relaxing and fun, at least until the rains had hit that morning, and the food had been decent. The bicycling was still to come, a two-day trip to and around little Lake Orta that would conclude the tour, and Gideon would probably give that a skip, especially if the rain kept up. Even the camping accommodations, truth be told, hadn't looked too bad, although the well-equipped, two-and four-person platform tents were usually set up in the midst of smelly, lumbering RVs packed with French- or German-speaking families loaded with noisy kids. And while Phil had asked Gideon to help out once or twice, the duties had hardly been onerous.

He'd been able to stick to his clean-bed, private-bath stipulations by driving out in the rented Fiat to meet the group every morning, spending the day with them, then getting a taxi back to the morning's starting point — they covered only five or six miles a day, so it was easy enough — getting back into the car, and returning to the Hotel Primavera in Stresa for a solitary, enjoyable glass of wine, usually at a sidewalk cafe, and a good meal in one of the town's many restaurants. Everything seemed to be working out just fine.

Well, almost. By day four he was feeling a bit like a fifth wheel — unneeded and maybe a little in the way. Or it could have been that he was simply getting restless. Gideon was one of that unfortunate breed who could take only a few days of pure vacation at a time before he began to get twitchy. He needed something to do. Classes had been out for almost two weeks, and it had been two months since he'd finished his last forensic case. He wished now that he'd brought a paper or a course curriculum to work on, although he knew that there would have been no way to do that without hauling a great load of research materials to Italy with him. And regardless of how much he brought, the items he would turn out to need wouldn't be among them; he'd learned that through experience. Still, that didn't prevent him from feeling vaguely guilty and at loose ends.

The tour members, by and large, were pleasant enough — mostly middle-aged, travel-experienced couples from around the United States, appreciative and undemanding. However, as he soon learned, the Prime Law of the Classroom — in every group of students, no matter how delightful otherwise, there must be one whose mere presence makes you cringe — also applied to tour groups. (This law, as all professors knew, was so immutable that even if you were lucky enough to somehow get rid of the offending member, another would invariably come forward in his or her place.)

In the case of the Italian Lakes Pedal and Paddle Adventure, the inevitable fly in the ointment, or maybe it was the straw that broke the camel's back, was Paula Ardlee-Arbogast, one of the few singles and the quietest and most retiring of the group — a stick-thin, flat-muscled woman of forty-five who kept pretty much to herself. But on the fourth day, after Gideon had helped the group stow their kayaks in the racks at the Campeggio Paradiso 'camping village' — jammed, as they all seemed to be, even on a wet, gloomy day like this — and after he'd

152

taken his now-customary 'quality time' walk alone in the rain with Julie along the lake, Paula approached him respectfully just after he'd called for a taxi from the public telephone. He was seated, soaked to the skin despite his wind-breaker, at a covered picnic table, waiting for it to arrive.

She hesitated. 'Am I bothering you?' She was wearing a plastic raincoat, but she looked as waterlogged as he was. Dripping, ginger-colored hair hung in strings beneath the brim of a transparent rain hat. 'Of course not,' he said. 'Sit down, get out of the rain.'

She sat on the bench across from him, shoulders hunched, hands clasped in her lap, screwing up her courage. 'This is fantastic!' she surprised him by gushing. 'I can't believe I'm actually here talking to you.' Her eyes were stretched wide. 'I read your book.'

'Oh, did you?' Gideon asked. He had two books to his credit: *A Structuro-functional Approach to Pleistocene Hominid Phylogeny*, a 400-page text now in its third edition; and *Bones to Pick: Wrong Turns, Dead Ends, and Popular Misconceptions in the Study of Humankind*, a popular treatment for the general reader, published last year. Whenever a stranger would come up to him and say 'I read your book,' he had a pretty good idea which one they were referring to.

153

Not that it happened often enough to do anything but please him.

'I thought it was absolutely fascinating.'

'Thank you.' *Bones to Pick*, all right. 'Fascinating' wasn't a word likely to be applied to *A Structuro-functional Approach*.

'Especially the chapter on the contribution of demographic factors to the demise of the Neanderthals. I'm very interested in the Neanderthals.'

He blinked. Amazing. The woman had actually read *A Structuro-functional Approach!* Other than graduate students and professional colleagues, this was a first. 'Well, thank you,' he said, this time with complete sincerity.

'I wanted to ask you — uh, do you have a minute?'

'Sure, I'm just waiting for a taxi to show up. What did you want to ask?' A professor through and through, he was always ready to talk about his subject with an interested audience.

'I wanted to ask your opinion of the EBE-interference theory.'

'Um . . . I'm not sure I'm familiar — '

'The theory that EBEs interfered genetically with hominid evolution seven hundred thousand years ago? You see, because wouldn't that explain why the Neanderthals

154

died out so suddenly? That they were simply a genetic experiment that didn't pan out, so that the EBEs gave up on them and replaced them with us?' She was burbling excitedly away now, rattling out more words than he'd heard her speak in all four days put together. 'I mean, couldn't it be that all we are is a kind of new, improved-model android that's doing the EBEs' work without our even being aware of it?'

'Well, now . . . '

'I'm sure you know about the briefing paper that was submitted to President Clinton from the Science Advisory Committee in 1994, that the government tried to hush up, and then there was President Eisenhower's Executive Memorandum, NSC 5410 — ' She made herself stop speaking the way a child does, clapping a hand over her mouth. 'I'm talking too much. It's just that I'm so excited. Anyway, what do you think?'

'What,' Gideon made himself ask, 'are EBEs?'

'What are — ?' She couldn't believe it. 'Extraterrestrial biological entities. EBEs.'

'Oh,' said Gideon, 'those.' He threw a glance over her shoulder, hoping for the appearance of the taxi, but no relief was in sight. 'Well, truthfully, the evidence is somewhat . . . scant.'

155

'Oh, no, we have their own word for it.'

'The Neanderthals?'

'No, of course not,' she said, laughing. 'The EBEs. I went to a talk in April — this was back in Iowa — by David Moody, who's been abducted three separate times by EBE research craft — he's written a wonderful book about it, with some amazing photographs — and he told us that Garnoth-Thoth — oh, I'm sorry, Garnoth-Thoth is their chief life-form scientist — told him that they'd interfered — that was Garnoth-Thoth's word, 'interfered' — with the proto-human genome at that time, and I just don't know whether to believe it or not, because, I mean, Garnoth-Thoth hasn't always been truthful, so that's why I wanted to know what you thought about it.' She stopped, out of breath.

'Well, frankly, Paula,' he began slowly, not wanting to offend but not wanting to give any credence to this depressing nonsense either — not wanting to have this conversation at all, in fact. 'My own view — ' He brightened. 'Oh, darn, here's my taxi. I'm afraid I have to go.'

'That's all right, Dr Oliver,' she said agreeably. 'There's plenty of time. Maybe I can catch you at lunch tomorrow? There's so much else I want to ask you.'

'I'll look forward to it,' he said miserably.

* ★ *

'This is bad,' Ignazio Calderone said.

'It's not good,' agreed Luigi Abruzzi.

The two men, field supervisor and senior foreman of Aurora Costruzioni, stood in the flooded ditch, hunched against the slanting rain. Water poured from the brims of their sou'westers and ran in braided runnels down the lengths of their slickers, much of it finding its way into the tops of their work boots.

'The ditch is wide enough,' Calderone said, his toes curling against the wet chill. 'That's not the problem. What we need is a bigger-diameter pipe through the culvert here. With all the construction up above, there's more runoff than there used to be. If this keeps up, it's going to wash out the road and make all kinds of problems for us down below. We better do something.'

'This is the biggest pipe we have on hand, boss. We'd have to order some more. It would take days.'

Calderone used his finger to brush beaded water from his glasses, then knuckled the runoff from his upper lip. He hated this wet weather with all his sunny Sicilian heart. 'I'll tell you what. Let's dig out the culvert, get another length of this pipe, the same

157

diameter, and lay it in there right alongside this one. That'll double the capacity for now. And then add some more gravel to neaten it up. It won't look bad, and later, in the dry season, we can put in a bigger pipe. Take a couple of men off the foundation work to help you. It shouldn't take any heavy equipment, just shovels.'

Abruzzi scratched the stubble on his cheek. 'You mean now?'

'What's the matter, you're afraid of getting wet?'

'No, but don't you want to check with Vincenzo first? This area here, isn't it part of the green stripe, the green band — '

'The green belt, yes, so?'

'So we're not supposed to disturb it. Remember what happened to Matteo when he took down two little trees that were in the way, without asking first? You want to get us fired too?'

What he wanted was to go back to the shed and get out of the damn rain. 'In the first place, look for yourself, it's already disturbed. And if we sit on our asses, it's going to be more disturbed. And in the second place, we're not touching any trees. We're not even widening the ditch. If you do it right, it won't even look any different.'

'Yes but — '

'And in the third place, Vincenzo's kid still hasn't shown up. He's worried, he has a lot on his mind. You want to call him to ask about a piece of drainage pipe? Be my guest.'

Abruzzi sighed. 'All right, I'll put a couple of men right on it.'

Twenty minutes later, with the rain finally beginning to tail off, two of the day laborers, having gotten their instructions from the foreman, unloaded the new length of PVC pipe next to the ditch and began to lay open a channel in the gravel beside the existing drainage pipe. They had moved no more than a half dozen spadefuls when one of them dropped his spade and crossed himself.

'Oh, Jesus, look at this.'

The other one came over to see, and to poke a little with his finger. 'Will you look at that?' he said with interest. 'Should we go get Abruzzi?'

'Abruzzi? Never mind Abruzzi, the *carabinieri* will want to see this!'

★   ★   ★

In the evening, with the rain having slackened off, Gideon had a half-carafe of local Barolo at the outdoor café across the street from the hotel, then walked the two short blocks to the cobblestoned Piazza Cadorna, to the Ristorante Nazionale, where he, Julie, and Phil had been for dinner on their first night. He sat outside, on the lively piazza, at an umbrellaed table set among potted flowering plants and ordered what he'd had before: *pizza quattro stagione*, with artichokes, ham, olives, and mushrooms, each on its own quarter; a salad; and a *limonata*. As it had been the other time, the pizza was perfectly baked in a brick, wood-fired oven, the crust was thin and tender, with just the right dusting of ash on the bottom, and the vegetables were fragrant and *al dente*. But this time the meal seemed to lack zest. He was thinking about alien abductions. He was thinking of the conversations to come in the days following.

His old teacher, Abe Goldstein, had put it well, as he had put almost everything. 'If these aliens would only keep all the people they abduct, the world would be a whole lot less crazy.'

★   ★   ★

But back at the Hotel Primavera, salvation awaited him. Angela, the kindly desk clerk who had taken a sympathetic interest in him because he was the only resident who was

160

there alone, had a message for him. Colonel Caravale of the *carabinieri* would appreciate it if Gideon called him. He would be in his office until nine.

'You're not in trouble?' she asked, handing him the message.

'Not as far as I know, Angela.'

'Because I know this Colonel Tullio Caravale, he can be a hard one. You want my advice? Better not try to bribe him.'

'I'll remember that,' Gideon said.

★ ★ ★

How long, the colonel wanted to know, does it take for a dead body to become a skeleton?

Gideon took a sip of the Vecchia Romagna — he'd developed a taste for the flinty Italian cognac on an earlier trip — which he'd poured into a bathroom glass before sitting down to return Caravale's call, and pondered. *What was this about?* Did there lurk the possibility — he hardly dared allow himself to hope — that there was something doing in this for him? A forensic case to get into? A possible escape, even if temporary, from Paula Ardlee-Arbogast, Garnoth-Thoth, and the cunning EBEs?

'That depends on a lot of things, Colonel,' he said. 'First of all, the environment

161

— whether the body was indoor or outdoors —'

'Outdoors.'

'Outdoors. OK, that speeds decomposition up. Was it buried or was it on the surface?'

'Buried.'

'Buried. All right, that slows decomposition down. Clothed or unclothed?'

'That I don't know.'

'What kind of soil is it in, what's the weather, what —'

'It's here, in the soil of Piedmont; a gravel bed. The temperature's moderate, the rainfall's — I don't know — light, I guess.' He waited.

'Look, Colonel,' Gideon said, getting a little impatient, 'how about just telling me exactly what it is you need to know?'

'Could it turn into a skeleton in one week?'

'Highly doubtful.'

Just about flat-out impossible, but he'd learned not to commit himself, especially on the basis of someone else's description of skeletal remains. Skeletonization was tricky business, depending on a lot of variables, many of which were imperfectly understood. Once he'd exhumed a Civil War burial, and the corpse had looked (and smelled) as if it had died the week before. Another time he read a police report's description of a defleshed shoulder girdle that had been fished out of Puget Sound and recklessly said (this was before he'd learned not to commit himself) that it had been in the water a week to ten days. The body had gone in the night before.

'What about eight days?' Caravale asked.

Gideon's interest quickened. He did a quick calculation. 'Eight days, did you say?' *Let me take a wild guess here.* 'Colonel, do you think you might have found the de Grazia boy, is that it?'

Caravale let loose a long, troubled sigh. 'De Grazia paid the ransom yesterday. His son was supposed to be released right away. He hasn't shown up yet. And now, this afternoon, two local workmen come upon some human bones buried in a shallow grave. So, yes, the thought that it just might be Achille de Grazia has crossed my mind.'

There was almost no chance that the skeletonized body could be that of Achille de Grazia, but bones were bones, and he could surely help. Caravale might not be the most amenable colleague in the world, but he was better than Paula Ardlee-Arbogast. 'I doubt it very much, but would you like me to look at them? I'd be happy to.'

Caravale hesitated, reluctant to ask for more assistance. 'I wouldn't want to take you away from your travel group,' he said gruffly.

'That's all right,' Gideon said. 'I don't mind at all. Are we talking about tomorrow? I could do it tomorrow.' *Say yes.*

'Tomorrow?' There was another pause, and then the colonel took the plunge. 'Tomorrow morning would be excellent, Professor. Perhaps I could pick you up at seven? Or even at six, if you don't mind getting up early. I put off the crime-scene search until daylight, so we sealed the site and left things as they are for the night, under guard, of course, but I'd like to get at it as early as possible.'

'Six is fine,' Gideon said. 'Six is perfect.'

He hung up the phone and stood looking out the window, at the iron-stained stone belltower of the old church across Via Cavour, and at the lake, rose-colored in the day's last light, and at the soft green mountains beyond. Another rich, slow sip of cognac slid warmly down.

Things were looking up.

10

How many times, Gideon mused, had he been part of this slow, solemn scenario? A quiet forest in the early morning with threads of fog still drifting among the trees, and the dew shimmering on spiders' webs that had been woven during the night, and the moist fragrance of the woods at its sweetest. And wandering over the leaf-littered forest floor, heads down, a silent group of half-a-dozen intent men, photographing, drawing, taking notes, or kneeling with tweezers to stuff some tiny crumb — a single dull black tooth from a comb, a cigarette smoked down to the filter, a plastic nubbin from some unknown gadget — into a plastic envelope or a paper bag. Considering that he had started his career with dreams of making some small but important theoretical contribution to the study of proto-hominid locomotion, it was a hell of a thing to be so intimately familiar with.

Life was funny.

They had arrived here, on the gentle lower slopes of Mount Zeda, at 6:30 A.M., both men dressed in short-sleeved knit shirts and jeans. Caravale had pulled his unmarked black Fiat up behind a slab-sided crime-scene-investigation van parked at the side of a dirt road that ran through a broad, winding grove of gnarled oaks, laurels, cypresses, and olive trees. The trees had been there a long time, probably for centuries, but there was a spanking new, walled housing development — red-tile-roofed condominiums, tennis courts, swimming pool — off to the left, among rolling meadows, and another one being built upslope around a golf course. The twenty-first century had come to Mount Zeda. For a few minutes they remained in the car, finishing the cappuccinos they'd picked up in Intra and observing the disciplined crime-scene crew go about their jobs.

'So then, are you ready?' Caravale asked, crumpling his empty cup.

'Any time.'

Getting out of the car, Caravale returned the waves of the crew and asked a quick question of the only man in uniform, a sergeant 'Anything?'

The answer was one of those minimalist but multifunction Italianate shrugs that subtly involves not only the shoulders, neck, and hands, but eyebrows, eyes, mouth, and chin as well: *Nothing important so far, but then we just got started and we're still*

166

looking, and with a little luck, who knows what we'll find — maybe nothing, maybe something.

Caravale gave him an almost equally complex, wrist-rolling wave of the hand in return: *Go ahead, keep on with what you were doing, I'll be around for a while. I'll check with you later.*

The colonel had described the physical situation to Gideon on the drive, but spatial relations in the abstract had never been Gideon's forte, and he hadn't really grasped it until this moment. Now he saw that a few yards ahead of them there was a turnoff from the road, over a drainage ditch that paralleled the road, and onto a small graveled parking or turnaround area. Through the bottom of the turnoff ran a culvert to allow the water to continue on its way down the ditch. The turnoff itself consisted simply of a few tons of gravel that had been dumped into the ditch over the ten- or twelve-foot length of culvert. The gravel had then been leveled to a three-foot height, effectively covering the pipe, bridging the four-foot-wide, three-foot-deep ditch, and providing a surface on which vehicles could cross. A second length of drainage pipe lay in the parking area, alongside the culvert.

The bones had been discovered late the

previous afternoon, by workmen from Aurora Costruzioni, Vincenzo de Grazia's company, which had acquired the land twenty years ago and was responsible for the nearby developments. One of the workers, using a spade to dig a channel for a second culvert pipe, had jammed it against something under the surface, had jerked the spade out, and had partly plucked out a human pelvis — or so the police physician who had been called to the site had determined. Gideon, remembering Caravale's earlier story about the bone-identification skills of local physicians, was reserving judgment but hoping it was a different physician. At the moment, the remains in question were out of sight, at the far edge of the turnoff, where the gravel slanted down and away.

'I see you have your men working everyplace but in the gravel itself. Have they already gone over that?'

'No,' Caravale said. 'Not where the remains are. I thought it would be best to leave that untouched for you.'

It was the answer he'd wanted. 'Good.'

'I looked you up on the Web,' Caravale said abruptly. 'I entered your name in Google.'

'And?'

'And I found one hundred forty-four references. Your friend was right, you are well known. And highly regarded.'

Gideon smiled. 'Well . . . '

'Look, I know I was pretty rude the other day,' Caravale said, speaking fast, 'and I feel bad about it. It was only that I had a lot on my mind, and besides, I didn't think you were really . . . Well, the thing is, I really appreciate your agreeing to help us out here.' He hesitated a second, then offered his hand.

Handsomely done, thought Gideon. 'There's absolutely nothing to apologize for,' he said, taking Caravale's hand. 'I guess I was a little brusque myself. And believe me, Colonel, you have no idea how glad I am to be here.'

'Well, good. Where are you from, Professor?'

'The Seattle area, Colonel.'

'Good, what do you say we dispense with the Colonel-Professor routine? I don't know about Seattle, but in New Haven we're pretty informal. My name's Tullio.'

★   ★   ★

The remains were at the upstream end of the culvert, in a depression that had been gouged out of the gravel slope angling down from the leveled surface of the turnoff to the floor of the ditch. All that was visible was the pelvic girdle — the hip joint — and half of the right femur, the thigh bone. The body was apparently lying on its back, with the legs bent and twisted sharply to the left, so that the right hip and femur were closest to the surface. The rest of the body — assuming there was a 'rest' — was lying on its left side, still covered by more than a foot of gravel.

With an 'it's all yours' wave, Caravale went to check on his crew, for which Gideon, who preferred to work without an audience, was grateful. He believed himself to be disciplined and objective when it came to drawing conclusions, but he knew that his manner of working — the process by which he found his way to his conclusions — was often intuitive and based on hard-to-quantify judgments, which made it cumbersome and sometimes impossible to explain to a lay observer what it was he was doing and why.

That was one reason he was disposed toward working in private. The other was that he liked to talk to himself when he examined a skeleton, and the things he muttered tended to be pretty pedestrian: 'Hmm, what's this?' Or 'Now what do you suppose could have caused that?' Or 'Say now, look at this.' So with people around he kept his mouth shut, which cramped his style.

'Well, now, let's see what we have here,' he said, settling down to his first cursory survey.

He didn't touch the bones, but simply squatted on his haunches to look at them.

The right innominate bone — that is, the right half of the pelvis — had apparently been the piece that had gotten caught by the spade, so that the rest of the pelvis had been tugged out of position, pulling the adjacent bones with them. Thus, the upper ends of both femurs, the sacrum, the coccyx, and the lowest two lumbar vertebrae were also partly exposed. Except for some scraps of dried ligament at the articular surfaces, there was no soft tissue to be seen. This, as far as Gideon was concerned, was a welcome sign. It meant that there was unlikely to be soft tissue — flesh, fat, decomposing organs — to contend with anywhere else on the body. The sacroiliac and sacrolumbar ligaments were just about the hardiest tissues in the body, other than the bones themselves. If they were dried up and essentially gone, he probably wasn't going to have to be scraping nasty stuff off the bones anywhere else.

That, he told himself, would save time, always a consideration to a professional. But he knew full well that time wasn't the main issue for him. As forensic anthropologists went, Gideon was among the more squeamish. After all these years, 'wet' remains could still make his stomach churn. He hated

171

handling them; the looks, the stench, the greasy feel of them. The older, the drier, and the less smelly a skeleton, the happier he was. In his opinion, hundred-thousand-year-old burials were perfect, but that wasn't a luxury that often came his way in forensic cases.

He leaned a little closer to the bones. The right iliac blade — the thinnest part — of the innominate had been snapped clear through at its narrowest point, through the base of the sciatic notch, just above the acetabulum, the socket into which the head of the femur inserts, but that had obviously happened only a short time ago, long, long after the body had been interred. Most of the skeleton was an ashy gray (bones eventually took on the color of their environment), with ugly black and rust-colored stains and splotches on it. If the fracture had occurred at or before the time of death, its edges would have looked like the rest of the skeleton. Instead, they were a fresh yellow-white, the normal color of bones that haven't been subjected to the bursting and decomposition of organs and blood vessels, or exposed to the weathering of time. So: no forensic significance.

A ragged, stained ribbon of fabric about an inch wide lay across the sacrum, apparently circling around under it. This, he was fairly certain, was the waistband of a pair of underpants. Cotton underwear on a decomposing corpse was quickly soaked through with body fluids and decayed rapidly, soon disappearing completely in most cases. But waistbands, usually being made of synthetic elastomers, didn't. There were also some shreds of faded blue cotton fabric — trousers or shorts, probably — mixed in with the bones and, in places, stuck to them.

After a couple of minutes of just looking, he reached out and ran his finger gently over the rim of the fifth lumbar — the lowest and largest vertebra in the spinal column, the one just above the sacrum — and then straightened up, wincing at the increasingly familiar creaks and pops in his knees. His own articular surfaces were beginning to show their age.

'Well,' he murmured, 'it's not a rabbit, that's for sure.'

★ ★ ★

It also wasn't Achille de Grazia.

The bones were not only essentially bare, they were heavily flaked, pitted, and abraded, and that wouldn't have happened in eight months, let alone eight days. Eight years, maybe, but fifteen or twenty was more like it.

On the other hand, he did have to allow for

their being buried in gravel, not soil. That meant that there would be more extreme ups and downs in temperature as the weather above ground changed, and that the moisture level would fluctuate more. When it rained, they would be soaked faster than if they'd been in soil; when the rain stopped, they would dry faster. All of that would hasten the processes of decay and weathering, as would the easy access that bugs would have. And then the gravel itself was composed of angular pieces, not rounded pebbles. Since there would necessarily have been some shifting and compression when vehicles rolled over them, the bones would have suffered more abrasion than they would have in ordinary soil.

He picked up a few of the individual stones. Granite. Granite, if he remembered right, had an acidic pH, and an acidic environment was one more thing that made bones weather faster. So maybe eight years was pretty close after all. 'Between five and fifteen years,' he announced to himself, mentally preparing the on-the-safe-side report he'd turn in to Caravale afterward.

He went back to the car and returned with his hat, a crumpled, tan canvas tennis hat with a brim all the way around (it was the back of the neck that got broiled in work like this), and with his tools. He'd brought no equipment with him to Italy, and it had been too late last night, and too early this morning, to buy anything, so he had borrowed a teaspoon, a tablespoon, and a ladle from the hotel kitchen, a ruler from the desk clerk, and a toothbrush from himself.

It was hardly the recommended assemblage for forensic exhumation, but since Caravale had told him the remains were in gravel, he hoped there wouldn't be any stubborn roots to be pruned, or hard, compacted soil to dig through, or fragile bones to free from a soil environment that could bond with them almost like concrete. As for containers, cameras, tape, etc., he knew the crime-scene van would be stocked with plenty of those; shovels too, if it turned out that he needed them.

He didn't. The gravel, as expected, was loosely packed, and he was able to scoop it away mostly with his bare hands, putting each handful into ten-gallon buckets, also provided by the van, for later screening by the technicians. He started at the exposed hip joint and slowly began to work his way outward, moving both up and down the body. As he worked, he concentrated on exposing the bones without damaging or moving them, rather than on examining them. That would be the interesting part, of course, and he preferred to save it for later, after he'd cleaned them up, in a morgue or laboratory that had good lighting and room to work standing up, instead of on his knees. Besides, he'd already made all the preliminary conclusions he was likely to come up with on-site. The remains, in addition to being human and having been buried about ten years ago, plus or minus five years, were those of an adult male, and an older one at that; at least in his fifties, probably more.

The sexing had been simple and sure. The pelvic girdle, the one part of the skeleton from which you could make a nearly one hundred percent certain sexual determination, was masculine in every indicator, from the narrow sciatic notch to the oval obturator foramen. That the remains were those of an adult was equally clear from his first quick look at the pelvic girdle and femur. The epiphyses, the separate sites of bone growth that appear at the ends of the long bones and along the edges of the innominate in infancy, and then ossify and attach to the body of the bone as the skeleton matures, were all fully attached. And that process didn't finish up until the twenties.

As for the specific age, his estimate of fifty-plus had come from running his fingers over the fifth lumbar vertebra. The vertebral 'lipping' that goes along with degenerative arthritis — unfortunately, a normal accompaniment of aging — was well advanced, and the surface of the bone showed mild but visible signs of osteoporosis and thinning, also age-related phenomena. There were diseases that could mimic these changes, so it was always possible he was off-base, but once he got to the lab, there would be other indicators to check; the pubic symphyses in particular. With luck, he'd be able to narrow down the age quite a bit more.

Work proceeded rapidly and relatively comfortably — Caravale had thoughtfully provided a knee pad from the van — although there were frequent pauses to allow for photographs and sketches by the crimescene team, and for one of the techs to help out as the few remnants of clothing turned up: the nylon cuffs and tab (the strip down the front with the buttons) of a jacket, a few of the buttons themselves, the soles and a little bit of the uppers of a pair of canvas deck shoes, a leather belt, and the zipper from the trousers, with a little of the fabric attached. These the rubber-gloved tech removed with tweezers and tongs, and carried them off to the van. Caravale popped in and out for updates, but was more interested in the work of his men than in the bones.

The whole process took two and a half hours, at the end of which Gideon got up, stretched, and walked up and down the road a little, working his cramped neck and shoulder muscles. He chatted with Caravale awhile. Then he came back for another look at what he had, before doing the bagging and labeling for the trip to the lab.

The remains were wholly uncovered now, and for once he seemed to be looking at a complete skeleton, right down to the hyoid, the terminal phalanges of the fingers and toes, and the irregular, pebble-like wrist and ankle bones — probably even the six tiny ossicles of the inner ear; all two hundred six bones of the human body (more or less: it depended on age — the older you got, the fewer you had, because certain adjacent bones tended to fuse together with time; on the individual — some people had thirteen thoracic vertebrae instead of twelve, some people had twenty-five or twenty-six ribs instead of twenty-four; and on how you defined 'bone').

Either there weren't any bone-stealing carnivores around, or the gravel had been a barrier to them. As he'd thought, the body had been buried on its back, with the legs flexed and turned to the left. The skull was also half-turned to the left, the mandible agape in a typical skeleton grin and a little awry. The right arm lay across the chest — that is, across the collapsed ribs — and the left arm was extended, palm up, alongside the body.

Although the remains appeared to have been unmoved since the burial, the skeleton had suffered some damage. In addition to the broken innominate, the vault of the skull was caved in on the right side, with several big pieces of parietal bone now lying inside the skull along with a lot of gravel and a shrunken, dried-up lump that was what remained of the brain. And the face — the maxillary bone — had suffered too. The right side of the maxilla was crushed from palate to orbit, and the strange, flimsy, curling bones inside the nasal cavity — the conchae, the vomer, the ethmoid — were pulverized beyond the possibility of reconstruction.

It struck him, not for the first time, how peculiarly fragile the human face was, considering the critical environmental monitoring devices it had to protect — sight, smell, and taste. The maxilla was one of the thinnest bones in the body, and hollowed out besides, by the big maxillary sinuses. If you held it up in front of a lamp, it was like eggshell; you could see the light right through it. Generally speaking, Gideon marveled at the astounding engineering of the human skeleton. But the face — that, as he sometimes told his students, he would have designed differently. Maybe left a little more hard, bony snout, just to be on the safe side, had he been in charge of human evolution.

The facial damage was unfortunate — who knew what evidence it might obscure? — but not significant in itself. It was clearly the result of repetitive, long-lasting compression, not of sudden blunt-force trauma; truck or heavy equipment pressure over time, in other words. The burial had put the skull a little higher than the rest of the body, and just where the right-side tires of a truck would roll over it on the way from the road to the parking area, and the left-side tires on the way back. Eight or ten years of that were more than it could stand.

The right ulna and radius (the two bones of the forearm) had also been broken, but these had been snapped, not crushed. Unlike the breakage of the pelvis, the broken edges were as gravel-colored as the rest of the skeleton. That suggested that they had already been broken when the body was buried. And not very long before, either, because there were no signs of healing. Of course, that didn't prove much because there wouldn't be any signs of healing for sixteen or seventeen days after a bone had broken. From simply looking at the surface of a fracture, you'd ordinarily have no way of telling if the break had occurred two weeks before death, or two seconds before.

But in this case, Gideon thought, there was a way. And his conclusion was that two seconds was about right.

'It looks as if you're done,' Caravale said.

Gideon jumped. As always, he'd been deep, deep in his work, and Caravale's coming up to stand behind him had startled him. 'Just about.' He turned his head and squinted into the sun. 'I could use a few dozen bags to get all this stuff into, and a marking pen to label them. Once they're in the morgue, they'll have to be cleaned up before I get down to a serious examination.'

'And how long will that take, the cleanup?'

'The rest of the day,' Gideon said with a weary sigh.

'It's unpleasant? Something you don't like doing?'

'Boring, not unpleasant. It's just drudgery.'

'Can I have someone help you with it?'

'You can have somebody do it,' Gideon said, jumping at the chance. 'It'd take me about five minutes to show him how.'

Caravale nodded. 'All right, I'll give you Fasoli.'

Gideon gave him a grateful smile. 'Wonderful.' He got gingerly to his feet, pleased not to hear any crik-craks from his knees. 'You'll also want to have somebody sift through the gravel underneath here, after the bones have been removed. I'd take it right down to the floor of the ditch. You can never tell what you'll find.'

'I know. Such as bullets, for example. When they stay lodged in the body, they can fall out into the ground as the tissues decompose, sink into it over time.' He was showing Gideon that he knew something about this sort of thing too.

'That's true enough, but in this case I don't think you're going to find any bullets.'

'And why would that be?'

'I don't think he was shot.'

Caravale scowled. He looked from Gideon to the bones and back again. 'Excuse me, but isn't it a little early to make such an assumption? Just because there are no bullet wounds on the skeleton, it doesn't follow that there wasn't any shooting. The slug, it might have gone through his throat, or between his ribs, or, or — '

'Sure, only the murder weapon wasn't a gun.'

'Not a gun.'

'No.'

Well, *probably* not, but Gideon was giving in to the secret vice and sport of forensic anthropology: the playful boggling of the minds of policemen great and small. Professionally speaking, he was going a bit beyond what he was certain of, which was admittedly reprehensible, but then he had just spent over two hours kneeling on sharp stones (the knee pad helped, but not that much after the first hour), hunched over a pile of musty bones and inhaling gravel dust under an increasingly warm sun, while Caravale had spent most of the time standing around, and sometimes sitting in a folding chair, in the pleasant shade of the nearby woods, giving orders and watching other people work. That being the case, Gideon felt he had earned the simple reward of enjoying the expression on his face. Or the expressions, to be more precise, as they went from perplexity to doubt, to outright skepticism.

'What are you telling me then? That you found the weapon?' His eyes darted over the area, looking for something that Gideon might have discovered and laid out on the gravel.

'Nope.'

'But you think you know what it was.' He

183

was beginning to show some impatience.

'No, not exactly. Sort of.'

Caravale sighed. 'Not exactly. Sort of. Are there signs on the bones then, or not? Wounds?' His eyes raked the skeleton again. 'The crushed skull?'

'No, I already told you, that happened over time. No, I haven't found any marks on the bones yet; that is, nothing to identify the weapon. Maybe later.'

'Then would you mind telling me how the hell you — ' An impatient blast of air hissed through Caravale's wide nostrils. 'Look, I don't have time — '

Gideon relented. He didn't really want to make Caravale angry. Besides, enough was enough, and he was starting to feel a little guilty. But only a little.

'Take a look at this, will you?' he said, leaning over to touch the broken right ulna and radius with the handle of a spoon. The breaks were next to each other, about a third of the way down from the elbow. 'This is what I was looking at just now. These fractures — they aren't new. They happened right around the time of death. Very close to the time of death, I'd say.'

'Because there's no difference in color, right.'

'Well, not only that — '

'But how do you know they weren't broken right after his death, during the burial, say — an accident with a shovel? They don't look hard to break.'

'No, they would have been easy enough to break, but the fact — '

'And whenever they were broken — before, after, during, whatever — I'm having a hard time understanding what they have to do with whether he was or was not shot.'

'Give me a chance now,' Gideon said, laughing. 'I'm trying to explain.'

'It's about time,' Caravale grumbled, but he was smiling.

With the colonel now an engaged audience, Gideon pointed out that the fractured ends of the broken forearm bones didn't lie adjacent to each other, as might have been expected. Instead, the lower halves of the ulna and radius had ridden up a couple of inches over their upper halves. That, he explained, was a just-about-sure sign that the fracture had occurred while the person was still alive. With the living muscles of the arm convulsing in shock, and the stability provided by the bones themselves suddenly gone, the two segments of each bone had been yanked together and pulled up over each other.

'I see,' Caravale said, nodding. 'That's very interesting.'

'And if you look carefully at the way the splintering occurred at the break points, you can tell the direction of the blow as well.' He offered a borrowed magnifying glass to Caravale, who gave it a try, but within a few seconds he handed back the lens, shaking his head.

'I'll take your word about the splinters, but let me guess the direction of the blow.' He held his left hand up, as if shading his eyes with his forearm, and with the fingers of his other hand, tapped his arm a few inches below the elbow.

'Here.'

Gideon nodded. Caravale had tapped himself on the ulnar aspect — the pinky side — of the forearm. It was the classic location of the fracture that resulted when a person threw up his arm to protect himself from an attack — the so-called 'nightstick fracture.'

'And what that tells me . . . ' Gideon began.

'What that tells you,' said Caravale slowly, 'is that it's extremely unlikely that he was shot. Because if the killer had a gun, he'd just go ahead and shoot him, right? Why would he have to attack him with some other object? Is that your reasoning?'

'That's my reasoning.'

Caravale, who had grown increasingly

absorbed, nodded thoughtfully several times. 'Well, I think you're on to something.'

Gideon felt as if he'd just passed a test. But then, so had Caravale.

It worked both ways. The man was a quick study. He'd caught on at once, had taken the basic idea, and had run with it.

'So here's what we think we know about him,' Caravale said a few minutes later. They were twenty yards from the burial, sitting in directors' chairs from the van, in the shade of some softly rustling poplars. Nearby, the crime-scene crew was also taking a break, sprawled on the ground, smoking and animatedly arguing the finer points of a soccer match the evening before.

'We have a burial that's been there for perhaps ten years — '

'Very approximately. Plus or minus five.'

'An adult male, fifty or more — '

'Make it sixty or more,' Gideon interrupted. He had upped his estimate as he'd gotten a better idea of the extensive porosity and thinning that was to be found in the bones. The scapulas in particular showed the atrophy and demineralization he'd expect in a man of seventy. 'Also, he was a fairly small guy, and lightly built.'

'Lightly built . . . do you mean thin? Not fat?'

'No, there's no way to tell fat or thin from the bones. What I meant was lightly muscled, what we call 'gracile'. I don't know what the Italian word is.'

'The same,' said Caravale. '*Gràcile*.' Grah-chee-lay.

'Ah, *gràzie*, Vaccari,' he said to one of his men, who had brought cans of Cola Light for him and Gideon. Popping the top on one, he arranged himself more comfortably in the chair. 'All right, to review: sixty or more, male, lightly built, probably killed with a blunt instrument — '

'No, not necessarily blunt,' Gideon said. He was working his cramped neck muscles, tilting his head back and rolling it from side to side, watching the tree branches move against a bright blue sky. 'It could have been a sharp instrument too; a knife, even.'

'A knife? You mean a knife could have cut through the bones like that? Both bones?'

'No. But remember, this was a fragile old guy, and the radius and ulna are thin bones to begin with. Say he threw up his arm to try to fend off a knife attack. His forearm could have been broken just from the force of the other guy's arm.'

'Yes, all right.'

'But I'm hoping it wasn't a knife. There are too many ways to kill someone with a knife

188

without leaving a mark on the skeleton. I'm hoping he was killed with something cruder — an axe or a club.'

Caravale laughed softly. 'A strange thing to hope for.'

'I only meant — ' Gideon shook his head and drank from the can. It was too hard to explain. Anyway, Caravale knew what he meant: Not that he wished this man or anyone else to have been hacked to death with an axe or clubbed with a steel pipe, but only that — inasmuch as the deed was already done and he was dead anyway — it would be nice if the weapon was the kind that would leave some skeletal evidence, and maybe provide a clue or two.

All the same, Caravale had a point. It was a hell of a thing to be hoping for. But then, this kind of work had a way of altering your perspective on things.

'Is there anything else you can tell me at this point?' Caravale asked. 'To help identify him?'

'Well, I'm pretty sure he limped,' Gideon said.

'Limped.' Caravale cocked his head and looked at him. 'Is that so?'

'Yes, there's aseptic necrosis over most of the right femoral head, probably avascular in origin — '

Caravale held up both palms and shook his head. His English, fluent as it was, had its limits, and Gideon didn't have the ghost of an idea of how to say it in Italian. He put his Coke on the ground and stood up. 'Come on, I'll show you.'

11

At the exact moment that Gideon and Caravale rose from their chairs, some five miles to the south in Stresa, Leonora Fucini was setting out the swiveling postcard racks in front of her souvenir shop on Via Bolongaro. She was nervous, thinking about getting Davide from the tobacco shop next door to come over and do something about the unkempt youth who'd been looking at an umbrella display in her window when she had arrived twenty minutes ago, and who was still there. Staring at four plaid folding umbrellas on a shelf for twenty minutes. He was dirty — she'd caught a whiff of him when she'd first brushed by on her way in — and swaying slightly, forward and back. He was on drugs, no question about it, or maybe coming off a drunken spree the previous night. Either way, she didn't want him out there. He was frightening away customers, and he was frightening her. She'd give him two more minutes, and then she'd call Davide.

But as soon as she went back into the shop, he stumbled in after her, a loose-lipped grin on his face. His eyes were frighteningly empty. She stiffened and backed against the counter, her hands raised in front of her.

He was wearing a shirt that said HOOTIE AND THE BLOWFISH. 'Is this . . . ' he said thickly, swaying so much he had to prop himself on a counter. His speech was slurred, his eyes only half-open. 'Is this a police station?'

* * *

'What we're looking at is the femoral head,' Gideon told Caravale, indicating the globular top of the thigh bone, the 'ball' that fit into the cuplike 'socket' of the hip. He had lifted the right femur from its place in the gravel to show to Caravale. 'And if you compare it to the other one, you can see that it's got this unhealthy, shriveled, caved-in look. That's because it was dead bone, not living; it wasn't getting any blood supply. It would have been painful, and it would definitely have made him limp, maybe use a cane or even go around in a wheelchair. From the looks of it, it's been this way for decades, maybe since he was a kid.'

'Childhood disease?'

'Possibly, but I doubt it. Most of the diseases that would do this would be bilateral; that is — '

'Two sides,' Caravale said. 'Yes, yes, I know.'

'Sorry. Yes, two sides. But the left one is healthy. So I think it was an accident, a fall, probably, that broke the neck of the femur. That's this part.' He tapped the diagonal, two-inch-long length of bone that connected the head to the femoral shaft. 'It's not an uncommon injury, especially in childhood, and if it's a bad break, it can tear apart the blood vessels that run to the femoral head. And when that happens, this is what you get: aseptic necrosis of the femoral head.'

Caravale ran his finger down the neck of the femur. 'I can't tell where it was broken, exactly.'

'Neither can I. It's repaired itself and I haven't found any sign of the actual fracture yet. If it's a really old break and was properly set, there may not be any sign. Or it could have been a stress fracture, in which case there might not be anything to see anymore. We'll see later, when we get this scuzz cleaned off. But the neck's a lot thicker and rougher than it ought to be, and that's what injured bone tends to do when it heals itself. Look at the left one in comparison.'

Caravale did. '*Gra-chee-lay*,' he said after a moment.

'Exactly.'

Caravale now lost interest in the femur and knelt to peer into the empty mouth cavity of the skull, between the crushed maxilla and the mandible. He straightened up and brushed gravel dust from his knees, 'It's true, isn't it, that it's possible to identify a body — I'm talking about absolute certainty — from the dental work on its teeth?'

'Sure. So we'll have your people take some close-up photos of the dentition and I'll draw up a chart that can be sent around. This guy has had a number of teeth worked on, and any dentist should be able to recognize his own work.'

'Right. Good.' Caravale seemed barely to be listening. 'Excellent.'

'I'm not sure you do see, Tullio. The identification itself is easy . . . once you find the right dentist. The trick is finding the right dentist. Where do you even start looking?'

'Colonel?'

Caravale turned. It was the uniformed sergeant. 'Yes, Rocca?'

Rocca was bursting with excitement. 'They've found him, the de Grazia boy.'

'Alive?'

'Yes, alive! He just walked into a shop in Stresa. He's been drugged, he thought it was a police station. Apparently they let him out of a car nearby and he walked — '

'He's not hurt?'

'I don't think so. Just drugged. He — '

'Where is he now?'

'At the shop, Colonel. This happened only a minute ago. The call just came in.'

'All right.' Caravale was already walking rapidly toward his car. 'I want him taken to the hospital to be looked at. I'll be there in ten minutes myself. And I want his father called and informed. And — oh.' An afterthought. He looked back over his shoulder. 'Gideon, is it all right if you go back to Stresa in the van later? With the bones?'

'With the bones is fine. I have a little more to do anyway. And hey — I'm glad the de Grazia boy's all right,' he called, but Caravale was already in the car, leaning over the wheel and gunning the engine.

★   ★   ★

By 11 A.M. the bones had been bagged, labeled, and boxed, ready for their trip to the morgue, which was in the hospital in Stresa, which turned out to be located on Via de Martini, only two blocks from the Hotel Primavera. Gideon, going along with them in the van, saw them safely delivered, took a break to clean up at the hotel and have lunch among the living and breathing at one of the

195

hotel restaurants on the Corso Italia, shopped for the few forensic supplies that would be needed, and walked back to the hospital.

There he found Corporal Fasoli waiting for him. One of the youngest of the officers, he seemed genuinely interested in the bones and paid close attention as Gideon demonstrated, with some of the metacarpals, how it was to be done. Each bone was to be cleaned with nothing more than the fingers and the small paint brush or soft toothbrush that Gideon had provided, using water or acetone if necessary, to get the dried glop off. If any of the adhering tissue was stubborn, it was to be left for Gideon to deal with. The stains were not to be worried about. The most important thing, aside from taking care not to clean too vigorously, especially where there had been abrasion or breakage, was to be careful not to lose anything. If bones were washed in the sink, it was to be done over the screen-bottomed tray he'd brought. When the cleanup was finished, the bones were to be laid out on paper toweling on one of the autopsy tables to dry overnight, and in the morning Gideon would position them in anatomical order and get to work.

Fasoli, who had already rolled up his sleeves, nodded crisply, eager to begin. He understood perfectly. It was a privilege to

196

assist the famous *detective delle ossa*. Would the professor like him to try to place the bones in the proper anatomical positions himself? He could surely find an anatomy book here at the hospital, and it was a task he would like to try.

In the face of Fasoli's natural enthusiasm, Gideon felt no guilt whatever about leaving him to the cleanup, and at one-thirty in the afternoon he was sitting happily on the grass in the sunshine, eating mortadella and tomato-and-cheese *panini* with Phil and Julie (by his reckoning, having had no breakfast entitled him to two lunches) at Camping Costa Azzurra, a giant camping village on the lake near Fondotoce, between Stresa and Ghiffa. As scheduled, the Pedal and Paddle group had pulled in early to allow for a visit to the little stone Oratorio of Saint Giacomo, said to be from Roman times, and to take it easy for an afternoon before embarking on the two-day bicycling excursion to Lake Orta the next morning.

'Leave it to you,' Julie said in mock wonderment when he had finished telling them about the events of the last few hours. 'Come to Italy for a vacation and wind up digging a skeleton out of a shallow grave in the woods. Amazing.'

'Just another knack, I guess,' Gideon said.

'But that's really great news about Achille,' Phil said. 'I was starting to get worried when he didn't show up.'

'So was everybody else. Caravale looked as if someone just took a hundred-pound load off his shoulders when they told him.'

'Speak of the devil,' said Phil, pointing with his chin.

Gideon, following his gaze toward the parking area, was surprised to see Caravale himself climb out of his black Fiat and look around, shading his eyes with his hand, obviously searching for someone. As to who that might be, there wasn't any doubt. Gideon had given him the group's itinerary in case there was any reason to find him. 'I'll be damned,' he said and got up on one knee to wave.

'Tullio — over here!'

Phil and Julie looked at him. ' 'Tullio'?' Phil said. 'My, my.'

Caravale, not seeing them, headed off toward the campground office, creating a rolling wave of concerned looks from the campers who saw him. He had changed into his uniform, which didn't surprise Gideon. At the excavation site, he'd had the impression that Caravale felt anything but at home in jeans and polo shirt. And with reason: A spiffy, well-tailored uniform — especially one with shoulder boards — did a lot for a pudding-shouldered, dumpy type like Caravale.

They caught up with him on the steps of the log cabin office, but a noisily idling diesel-powered tour bus a few yards away drove them back to the lawn to talk.

'How's Achille doing?' Phil asked at once.

'About the way you'd expect. Shaken up, filthy, but that's about all, except for the drugging. They treated him fairly well, apparently.'

'Was he able to tell you anything?'

'Not a great deal. He was in a tent the entire time; they never let him out.'

'A tent?' Julie asked. 'You mean they kept him outside?'

'No, he's sure it was indoors. A tent inside a building of some kind. But he has no idea where.'

'What about descriptions?' Gideon asked. 'Did he get a look at them?'

Caravale shook his head. 'One of the men didn't have a mask on when they kidnapped him, but he was too terrified by all the shooting to have a clear memory of him. He was 'big', that's all he can remember. It doesn't help much.'

'Who wouldn't have been terrified?' Julie asked. 'Poor kid.'

'What about later?' Gideon asked. 'He never saw them?'

'Later, whenever they came in, they made him put a blindfold over his head first — some kind of elastic bandage. He thinks there were two of them, both men, but maybe three. I'm starting to wonder if he might not have been drugged — sedated, at any rate — for the whole time. He says he doesn't think so, but I'm not so sure.'

'So you don't have much to go on, do you?'

'Much?' Caravale laughed. 'You must be seeing something I missed. I didn't think I had anything to go on.'

'Well, the main thing is, he's out and he's all right,' Phil said, as usual pointing out the bright side. 'Is he home now?'

'Oh, sure, with his papa and his loving family. They're all making a fuss over him, he's very happy. All is well on Isola de Grazia.' He rocked back and forth on his feet, his thumbs hooked in the waistband of his Sam Browne belt.

Something's funny here, Gideon thought. Caravale was looking too pleased with himself. No doubt he was relieved that Achille had come out of it alive, but at the same time he was now a cop with a big, unclosed case on his hands and nowhere to go with it; not a lead in sight. In Gideon's experience, that usually made cops cranky.

'Is there something else on your mind, Tullio?' Gideon asked.

'Something else?' He pretended to think. 'Oh, yes, that's right, I almost forgot. Those remains you were kind enough to help out with this morning? We have a positive ID on them.'

Gideon was astounded. 'But . . . I left Fasoli with them not even two hours ago. They can't even be clean yet. How did you — '

'Why, I did what you told me. I got a dental identification.'

'But how, how did you — '

'We found his dentist and asked him.'

'I understand, but how could you possibly — I never made any charts, we didn't — '

He stopped in mid-sentence. Caravale was grinning at him, revealing a surprisingly perfect row of small, square, brown teeth. It was the first full smile that Gideon had seen on his face, and it made him look like a wicked Cupid. Obviously, he wasn't above taking pleasure in a little mind-boggling of his own.

Fair enough, a little tit for tat. 'OK, I give up,' he said. 'I'm completely mystified. How about letting me in on how you managed that?'

'It wasn't so hard. I decided not to wait for your charts. I simply had our digital photography person photograph the jawbone from a lot of different angles and e-mailed them to the dentist — his office is in Milan — and a little later he called back with a hundred-percent positive ID. Nothing to it. The whole thing took . . . oh, twenty minutes.'

'But — '

'But how did we manage to find the right dentist? That was no problem. You see, I was already ninety percent sure I knew who those bones came from.'

He looked from one to the other of them, saving the last, longest look for Phil. His expression composed itself, flipping from self-satisfied to grave. 'They are the remains of Domenico de Grazia.'

Phil's mouth opened, shut, and opened again. 'Domenico de — '

'Your uncle. The old *padrone*. The father of Vincenzo de Grazia. I'm sorry.'

12

They got powdery, lukewarm coffee from a vending machine on the porch of the office building — an expansive Caravale paid for them all — and took it to a shaded picnic table beside a tiny corral in which a pot-bellied, sad-eyed donkey stood in a corner and quietly snuffled its dinner from a nose bag. It was the limp that had been the final clue, Caravale explained. That, and the age of sixty or more, and the 'small, gracile' description, and the ten-year length of time it had lain in the gravel. Put together, it all pointed to Domenico.

Phil was shaking his head. 'I don't get it. This is nuts. Sure, Zio Domenico had a limp and all that, but he drowned in a boating accident on the lake. I came for the memorial service. Are you saying he *didn't* drown?'

'That's exactly what I'm saying,' Caravale said gently. 'I was with the force then, but I was only a lieutenant. I wasn't the investigating officer, but I remember the case. Your uncle liked sailing. We used to see his boat on the lake sometimes, but he was never out for very long. The day he disappeared he'd left early, and when he didn't come back by late afternoon, everybody began to worry. It wasn't a good day for sailing; the wind was rough, the water had a chop to it. So they started a search for him. The boat was found the next day, overturned in shallow water, across the lake, off Porto Valtravaglia. The conclusion seemed reasonable enough: an unfortunate accident. But Domenico, he was never found. So it was never completely settled.'

Phil's eyes were on the paper cup that he was turning round and round in his fingers. 'So if this is true, somebody actually killed him. I'm sorry, but this is really hard to believe.' He looked up, almost challengingly. 'Everybody loved the guy. Everybody.'

'That's what I would have said,' Caravale agreed.

'Not quite everybody, I guess,' Julie said.

Gideon was beginning to wonder what Caravale was doing there. This was an unexpected development, yes, but there was no reason for him to have jumped in his car and driven right out to tell them about it. It could have waited until morning. It could have waited longer than that.

'Uh, Tullio, is there something I can do for you?' he asked.

'Well, yes, maybe, now that you ask.

204

Naturally, I told Vincenzo about it,' Caravale said. 'He asked me to come out to the island again to talk with the family — another goddamned council, I'm afraid. The boat will take me up at three.'

'And?'

'And I was hoping you might come along with me.'

'Me? Why?'

'They'll ask questions about the remains. I don't know how to answer them.'

'But what can I tell them? Wait till I've had a serious look at them and know something — tomorrow, the next day.'

'I'd appreciate it if you'd come with me today.'

'Well . . . sure, if you like, but I don't know what I can tell them.'

'A lot more than I can,' Caravale said. 'Can you meet me at the police dock in Stresa at three, then? An hour from now?'

'I'll be there.'

'Damn,' Phil said, 'I'd really like to be there too. I still can't believe it. And I'd like to see Achille, see how he's doing.'

'Come, then,' said Caravale. 'I'm sure they'd be glad to have you.'

'Can't.' Phil shoved away his untouched coffee. 'I have to get the group up to the oratorio in an hour. It's on the schedule. And then there are things to see to — getting the bikes ready — '

'Oh, go ahead,' Julie said, 'you belong with your family at a time like this. I can see to things here. Heaven knows we've been over everything enough times.'

'Yeah, but — '

'Go ahead, let me earn my pay.'

He gave in with a reluctant but appreciative sigh. 'Thanks a million, Julie.'

'You're not getting any pay,' Gideon observed.

She laughed. 'Let me earn my keep then.'

Caravale looked at his watch and stood up. He seemed relieved. 'Good. I'll see you both at three, then.'

* * *

The drive to Stresa would take no more than ten minutes, which gave Phil and Gideon three-quarters of an hour before they had to leave. Phil immediately began to go over logistics with Julie. Lax and slipshod in his personal affairs at home — he could be counted on to be at least twenty minutes late for any appointment — he ran his tours with a near-fanatical attention to detail, and Julie lasted about five minutes before exploding.

'I *am* a park ranger, you know? I deal with bears, and cougars, and drunks, and hostile bikers. I think I can probably handle anything that comes up here. So get lost, I'll take care of things.'

Gideon smiled. She was cute when she was angry, and even cuter when she was making believe she was angry.

Phil jumped up immediately. 'Sorry, I get a little carried away.'

'I'll say,' Julie muttered.

'Just let me change,' he told Gideon, and ran off to the platform tent he was sharing with three of the other men.

Thirty minutes later he emerged. 'Sorry about that, thought I ought to shower. I was getting a little grungy.'

They stared at him for a full ten seconds before Julie spoke. 'Shower, and put on clean clothes, and shave off your beard, and — ' Her eyes narrowed. 'Did you give yourself a haircut?'

'I just trimmed it a little,' he said with one of his gawkier shrugs. 'You know, to show some respect.' He squirmed under their continuing scrutiny. His face was pink. 'So I cleaned up. What, is this a big deal? Gideon, come on, let's go already.'

★ ★ ★

The *consiglio*, for reasons Gideon couldn't fathom, was held in a stuffy, windowless little room in the otherwise spacious and elegant villa. He had seen paintings by seventeenth- and eighteenth-century masters on the walls of the corridor outside — he recognized Titian, Rubens, Velazquez, or at least their schools. But this grim little room seemed to have been chosen for ugliness and discomfort. Surrounded by tiers of gloomy family portraits, some competently painted, mostly not, and hemmed in by the living members of the de Grazia clan, he sat on an amazingly uncomfortable, hard-backed wooden chair, feeling very much the stranger at an intimate family gathering. Lighting came from a single antique hanging lamp that had been converted to electricity and now bore four unpleasantly glaring, candle-shaped bulbs. The seats, some of them chairs, some heavy chests, but all of them looking every bit as uncomfortable as his, had been arranged along all four walls, leaving a five-foot square of scarred, planked wooden flooring open in the center.

Including Gideon, there were eleven people in the room, necessarily shoulder to shoulder. On his immediate right was Phil, and on the far side of Phil a slender, soft-spoken woman whose name Gideon hadn't caught when

Vincenzo had made a round of pro forma introductions. Phil had briefed him earlier on who would probably be there, but if she'd been mentioned, Gideon didn't remember it.

Directly across from him sat old Cosimo de Grazia in his old-fashioned suit and starched white shirt, buttoned to the top but without a tie this time. Eyes closed, he sat lost in thought or in dreams, with his veined, mottled hands clasped on the silver lion's-paw-and-tea-bud knob of his cane, his goateed chin resting on his knuckles, and Bacco asleep and snoring between his feet. In the chair beside him was a rumpled, portly, bespectacled man of Cosimo's age who sat with an unlit, half-smoked cigar clenched between his teeth.

This, according to Vincenzo, was Dr Gianluigi Luzzatto, who had been Domenico de Grazia's physician and closest friend and was still Cosimo's doctor, though otherwise retired from practice. He had been making one of his twice-weekly visits to Cosimo, who had been refusing for two decades to see a younger, more up-to-date physician, and he had been invited to the consiglio by his patient out of respect for his longtime relationship with the de Grazias. It wasn't strictly by the book, but Vincenzo had always allowed Cosimo some extra latitude in matters of family protocol. Like Cosimo, Dr Luzzatto wore a dark, old-fashioned suit, including a tie and even a tobacco-ash-spattered vest. Unlike Cosimo, he somehow managed to make them look as if he'd been sleeping — and eating — in them for two days.

Phil had looked at him, pointed his finger, and blurted: 'You're Dr Luzzatto! I remember you!'

'I'm flattered.'

'When I was a little kid,' Phil said, 'I mean really little . . . you were carrying me through a . . . was it a hospital corridor? There were benches, white walls . . . '

Luzzatto nodded, pleased. 'You're right. It was in Milan. The Gaetano Pini Institute. You were not even five. A long time to remember an operation.'

'I don't remember any operation, I just remember being carried. In your arms. I was crying . . . you thought I was scared, but I was embarrassed. I was in my underwear, and there were all these women there . . . '

'It was insensitive of me,' Luzzatto said, smiling and placing a hand over his heart. 'I humbly apologize.'

Along the same wall as Luzzatto, seated together on a chest and looking like a male-female version of Tweedledum and

Tweedledee, were Phil's aunt, Bella Barbero, and her husband, Basilio. Then again, she might have been his cousin; Phil hadn't been sure. If Gideon remembered correctly, the affable, rambling Basilio was an officer in Vincenzo's construction firm.

The entrance to the room was on the wall to Gideon's right, a doorless opening on either side of which were the only two chairs with armrests, a matched set of high-backed, thronelike affairs with carved Gothic backrests. In one sat Vincenzo, in the other, Caravale, like coreigning monarchs waiting for their court to get itself settled.

The two remaining people, the lean, vinegary, malcontented-looking Dante Galasso and the striking but equally vinegary Francesca de Grazia Galasso, sat along the remaining wall, next to each other, but as far apart as space would allow. Dante, according to Phil, had been an ardent and articulate Marxist professor in Bologna years before, but somewhere along the line he had stopped calling himself a Communist and seamlessly turned himself into a 'postmodernist,' apparently considering it more in step with the times. His formidable wife Francesca — Vincenzo's sister — was both the CFO of Aurora Costruzioni and the de facto mistress of the de Grazia estate, someone, Phil had warned darkly, of

211

whom it was a good idea not to get on the wrong side.

Gideon had been hoping to get a look at Achille de Grazia, but the boy preferred to stay in his room. Phil had gone up to see him and reported that he seemed to be all right, but was markedly unassertive and subdued. 'I doubt if it'll last,' Phil had said, 'but we can always hope.'

'Well, then, it looks as if we're all here,' Basilio Barbero observed when the settling process had gone on too long for him. 'Ready to start, eh? When I hold a conference at work, I make it a rule to begin promptly on schedule. Otherwise, you see, those who come late are rewarded by having the meeting start the moment they arrive, while those who came early are punished by having to wait for the latecomers. Thus, one sets in motion — '

'Yes, yes, let's begin,' Vincenzo said. 'Colonel?'

Caravale opened in formal fashion. 'At 12:45 P.M. this afternoon, skeletal remains found buried on land owned by the Aurora Construction Company on Mount Zeda, not far from the construction site of the new golf and country club, were positively identified as those of Count Domenico de Grazia.'

Astonishment. Consternation. Except for Vincenzo, who'd been briefed earlier, they had thought the council had been called to talk about the kidnapping.

'Mount Zeda?' Bella Barbero said when the immediate hubbub had died down. 'What are you talking about? That's impossible. He went sailing that morning. We all know that. His boat was found across the lake, at Germignaga.' She made it sound as if she was accusing Caravale of manufacturing the facts.

'It was Valtravaglia,' Francesca Galasso corrected. 'Not Germignaga.'

'I don't see —'

'His boat, yes. His remains, no,' Caravale said.

'But what would Domenico have been doing at Mount Zeda?' a puzzled, troubled Cosimo asked. 'By that time he no longer had any interest in the construction business. It had all been turned over to Vincenzo. What would bring him to Mount Zeda?'

'Could it have been before the land was purchased?' Basilio asked. 'Maybe it was when he was considering buying it.'

'No, no, my boy. I tell you, by then he had removed himself from such affairs, am I not right, Vincenzo?'

'That's true, Uncle. Besides, the land had already been in our possession for several years.'

'You see?' Cosimo said. 'Believe me,

213

Colonel, I knew my brother. Like me, he was no longer at ease off the island. He disliked leaving it, other than to sail. Why would he have gone to Mount Zeda?'

'Ah, but can one really ever 'know' another person's life?' Dante Galasso asked — gratuitously, thought Gideon. 'Or does one simply choose his own reality from the web of stories, the 'narrative', that each of us constructs for the consumption of the Other?' He spread his hands and looked around the room, smiling, waiting for acclamation.

'Asshole,' Phil grumbled to Gideon, who thought Phil had a point. His Italian wasn't good enough to grasp every word, but he'd gotten the gist. He'd heard the same opaque sophistry, or close enough, from the post-modernist academicians at the university.

Seated next to her husband, Francesca rolled her eyes and let out a pained sigh. 'Lecture number three hundred thirty-four,' she said, seemingly addressing the assembled ancestors who looked sternly down from the walls. 'Reality as a Social Construct.'

Dante looked pityingly at her. 'Ha, ha.'

Caravale, talking around the Galassos, replied politely to Cosimo. 'We don't believe he went there of his own free will, Signor de Grazia. We believe he was brought there, or carried there after his death, and buried.'

'But — ' It was Basilio, bouncing with nervous energy, his pink face gleaming. 'But — but that must mean . . . doesn't that mean someone must have murdered him?'

Dante, apparently one of those compulsive talkers who either didn't notice that other people paid no attention when he spoke, or else didn't care, laughed. 'What a privilege it is to see such an incisive mind at work, eh, Doctor?' he said to Dr Luzzatto, sitting around the corner from him.

Luzzatto, chewing hard on his cigar, glanced at him without comment, then returned his attention to Caravale.

Out of the corner of his eye Gideon saw Bella Barbero's plump bosom rise in indignation as she gathered her resources to defend her husband. But a couple of nervous, placatory pats on the arm from Basilio quieted her down.

'Do I detect an edgy undertone or two around here?' Gideon whispered to Phil.

'Always,' Phil cheerfully agreed.

'We're proceeding on that assumption, Signor Barbero,' Caravale said. 'As of today, the case has been reopened as a homicide investigation.'

'Finally,' said Vincenzo pointedly. He, too, was clearly simmering about something, and had been from the moment they'd seen him waiting on the dock to meet the launch.

Caravale looked at him. 'Excuse me?'

'I have thought all along that my father was the victim of foul play.'

Caravale stared at him. He doesn't like being surprised like that, thought Gideon. And he especially doesn't like it in public. 'And why is that, exactly?' he asked.

'My father was a prudent man. He knew he was not an expert sailor. When he sailed, it was with a companion, often myself. Why would he go alone this one day, without telling anyone? Why would he leave so early, before anyone was up? That was not his usual practice. Why would he choose a day when the water was rough?' He shook his head. 'It made little sense then, it makes little sense now.'

Muttering as much to himself as to anyone else, Dr Luzzatto spoke around his fat cigar. 'Not so, not so. When he had something to think about, some decision to ponder, he would go alone. It made his mind clear.'

'Once in a while, yes — '

'And on that day,' Luzzatto went ponderously on, scowling, his eyes focused inward, 'I can tell you for a fact that he did indeed have something important to ponder.'

'Be that as it may, Doctor, as the colonel so rightly points out, his body was not found.'

216

Angrily, Vincenzo turned to Caravale. 'Do you suppose it might have helped if the *carabinieri* had looked into the possibility of homicide then and there — instead of waiting for ten long years after the fact?'

'What might have helped,' a tight-lipped Caravale shot back, 'was your saying something at the time.'

Vincenzo leaned aggressively into him. 'I did considerably more than say something. I gave your predecessor a list of my father's enemies, men who would benefit from his death. He chose to pay no attention.'

Another surprise for Caravale. 'You talked to Colonel Pontieri about it?'

'Of course I did. Look in the case records.'

Caravale looked as if he couldn't decide whether to believe this or not. 'Let's move on,' he said after a moment.

'If you please, signore?' Cosimo de Grazia was gently waving his raised hand. With the starched white cuff of his shirt having slipped down, his wrist was like a dissection drawing in an anatomy text. Beneath the papery skin Gideon could make out not only the usual bony landmarks, but structures invisible in most people: the pisiform, the tubercle of the scaphoid, the tendon of the *Extensor pollicis brevis*, even the fluttery throbbing of the radial artery. Gideon could have taken his pulse visibly from across the room.

'I would like to ask the colonel when it will be possible to have the body of my brother returned to us,' Cosimo said. 'I think he has suffered enough indignities. I would like to see him at rest with his family, here in the de Grazia vault.'

'I understand completely, signore, but Professor Oliver has yet to make a full examination. I'm sure you can see the necessity.'

'I'll be starting in the morning,' Gideon said, his first contribution of the afternoon. 'It shouldn't take — '

'I fail to see the point of further examination,' Francesca said with considerable heat. 'What more is there to be learned? I must agree with my uncle. My father was a de Grazia, a count of the House of Savoy. He should be treated with respect. It is an affront to his memory to have his bones pawed over by strangers only to satisfy some morbid — '

'It's the law, signora,' Caravale told her. 'In a case like this, there has to be an autopsy.'

'An autopsy of bones?' A harsh laugh. 'How does one perform an autopsy of bones?'

Caravale, happy to get off center stage, gestured to Gideon. 'Professor?'

Gideon took advantage of the opportunity to get out of the torture device he was sitting

218

in and stood up, a position from which he was also most comfortable lecturing, if lecturing was going to be called for.

'Permit me to assure you, Signora de Grazia,' he said in language every bit as flowery as Cosimo's, 'that your father's remains are being treated with the utmost respect and esteem. At this moment they are being most carefully cleaned' — with his old Oral-B toothbrush, he chose not to point out — 'and tomorrow morning I will begin the examination.'

With Phil and Caravale to help him over the words he couldn't handle in Italian, he explained what he would be looking for and, in simple terms, how he would go about the job. Ordinarily, the primary purpose of a forensic anthropological examination was to assist in the identification of skeletal remains by determining race and sex, estimating age and stature, and distinguishing 'nonmetric factors of individualization,' as the anthropologists called them: signs of past or existing trauma, pathologies, and stress-related changes in the bones that might reveal the occupations or habits of a lifetime.

Gideon would indeed be doing these things, but inasmuch as Domenico had already been identified from his dentition, his analysis would merely provide confirmation that would go into the record — an important precaution if and when there was a courtroom proceeding. His most important task, however, would be to search for anything on the skeleton that might reveal the cause of death.

The dusty, scientific talk of bones and measurements seemed to take the wind out of them. There were no questions while he spoke, and for a minute after he sat down, no one had anything to say.

'And how long will all this take?' Vincenzo asked wearily.

'It shouldn't be long. Usually, not more than a day or so,' said Gideon.

'And then we may have my father's remains back?'

Caravale answered him. 'That depends. If Professor Oliver does find evidence of the cause of death or other important information, we would probably have to hold them as evidence. We'll have to see. But in the end they'll be returned to you.'

'I understand,' Vincenzo said. 'Gentlemen, thank you both for coming.' He glanced around the room. 'Is there anything more?'

'Only to thank God that Achille has been returned unharmed,' Cosimo whispered.

'If it's God we've been relying on in that

matter,' Dante Galasso said with a crooked smirk, 'I can only say — '

'Nobody here cares what you can only say,' Bella Barbero said sharply, 'so why don't you just keep it to yourself, for once in your life?'

'Now you just wait one minute,' Francesca said, leveling a crimson-nailed finger at her. Criticizing her husband herself was one thing; listening to her non-de Grazia stepsister do it was entirely different. 'Dante is entitled to say whatever he feels like here, and if anybody in this room is not in a position — '

'Well, well, well,' chirped Basilio Barbero, jumping up and rubbing his hands together, 'will you look at the time? Clemente will have finished setting out the aperitifs in the library by now, and I, for one, am certainly ready for mine. There's nothing like a Cynar before dinner to get the gastric juices flowing. It's not only pleasant, it's amazingly helpful to the digestion, something that many people fail . . . '

★ ★ ★

While Caravale and Phil had a few final words with Vincenzo, Gideon waited outside, near the head of the stone steps that led down to the dock, looking south along the western shore of the lake toward Stresa, visible only as a clump of shimmering yellows between the blue of the lake and the green of the mountains. After a few minutes, however, feeling the stony, mirrored gaze of the guard, Cesare, on the back of his neck, he went around the side of the house to the breakfast garden, where he sat at the table he'd shared with Julie a few days before. No marmoset this time, but either the same white male peacock or its twin brother was once again in full display, strutting and quivering at the far edge of the clearing with his tail feathers spread, quills audibly rattling. A few yards away the object of his affection, a dull, green peahen who couldn't have been less inter-ested, wandered aimlessly about, pecking mechanically at the ground or staring in jerky, birdlike fashion in every direction but at her suitor, who kept after her with a dogged, expectant, never-say-die determina-tion. Tough life, Gideon thought. Of course, if you had a pea brain, it probably didn't seem so bad.

'There you are!' Phil called, coming around from the front of the building. 'We need to stick around awhile. Caravale wants to talk to Achille again.'

Beside him was the woman who'd sat next to him inside. As far as Gideon could remember, she'd said nothing during the

222

consiglio, but had merely watched and listened.

'Lea,' Phil said in English as Gideon got out of his chair, 'I'd like you to meet my very good friend Gideon Oliver. Gideon, this is my cousin Lea Pescallo.'

'Lea Barbero,' she gently corrected him, at which Phil looked immensely pleased.

'*Piacere di conoscerla*,' Gideon said, sensing that she wasn't too comfortable with English.

She smiled, and he was aware of how attractive she must once have been. In her forties now, and looking her age, with weary eyes and mouth, and slightly bowed shoulders, there was still a pale, nineteenth-century kind of beauty that clung to her. She looked like the type of woman on whom swooning would look good. 'I am too 'appy to know you, sir,' she said. 'What you sayed about the bones. Very interesting.'

'Thank you. I hope it'll be of some help in determining what happened.'

As he spoke, he realized with a shock why she seemed familiar. He'd seen her before, only a few days ago. Lea Barbero, in her crisp, pink-striped Oxford shirt, her fashionable, mid-calf-length khaki slacks and new-looking, open-toed leather clogs — Lea Barbero with her under-stated makeup and softly layered

223

blond hair — was the drab, hunched woman in sneakers and old sweater that he and Julie had taken for a maid the other day; the woman that had turned and fled the moment she'd seen them.

He turned to look at Phil — he of the new haircut, fresh shave, and clean shirt — and realized that there was a look on his face that was totally unfamiliar, a cocky, jaunty, hey-look-at-me expression that was wholly unlike him. Even his posture seemed different: he was practically strutting.

He looked, in short, an awful lot like a love-dazed peacock.

Son of a gun.

13

It was called the Napoleon Room because Napoleon was supposed to have slept there for two nights during the Italian campaign of 1797, and it was one of the more impressive rooms in the villa. The heavy canopy bed, easily big enough for four, was in a curtained alcove off the larger sitting room. The sitting room floor was inlaid marble, the walls and the high ceiling decorated with intricate stucco work. There were several de Grazia coats of arms, and cupids and angels peeped from around every corner. There were gilded mirrors and ornately framed landscapes on the walls, and from the ceiling hung an elaborate chandelier of Venetian glass. Over the white marble mantel there was a life-size, full-length portrait of Napoleon standing next to his horse. There were upholstered divans and chairs, console tables, commodes and cabinets, and directly under the chandelier an elegant, round, marble-topped table with four armchairs. There was room to spare for everything, and everything, even the elaborate prisms of the chandelier, looked as if it had been dusted within the last hour. Caravale had lived in four-room apartments with less space than this.

It was Achille de Grazia's bedroom, and had been since he'd been six years old.

Three people were seated at the table: Vincenzo de Grazia, Achille, and Caravale. In front of Achille was a transcript of his statements earlier in the day. 'Should I sign it, or should my father?' he asked.

'You,' Caravale said. 'And initial each page. Read it first, though. Make sure it's right.'

'Yes, sir.'

Physically, Achille looked better than he had when Caravale had seen him at the hospital. They'd been unable to do anything about a ferocious flare-up of acne, but he'd been thoroughly spruced up and now wore a soft-collared blue shirt, dress jeans, and a pair of buttery tasseled loafers, much like his father's, that had probably cost the equivalent of half a month's salary for Caravale. Otherwise, he seemed about the same — downcast, listless, docile, numbed . . . as if there were nobody inside.

From everything Caravale had been told about him, this was a striking departure from his usual bullying self-centeredness, and it seemed to worry Vincenzo, who sat close to the boy, as if to prop him up if he should need support. Vincenzo even had his arm around Achille's shoulders. Well, not quite around his shoulders, but over the back of his chair. Even so, it seemed to Caravale a noteworthy show of concern, considering whom it was coming from.

Achille pretended to read the transcript, but Caravale could see his eyes darting away from the print, as if on their own initiative. He signed it as requested.

'I would like to see it too,' Vincenzo said.

'Of course,' Caravale said. Above his head a stray eddy of air set the chandelier to tinkling.

Keeping one arm over the back of Achille's chair, Vincenzo hungrily read the statements — muddled memories of the kidnapping itself, and a description of his days in the tent — while Achille leaned gratefully into him, like a puppy responding to his master's closeness.

With a grunt, Vincenzo finished the transcript and slid it across the table to Caravale. 'All right. I trust you're finished with him and would have no objection if he goes away to school in Switzerland.'

'You mean right now?'

'In a few days.'

'Do you want to go away to Switzerland?' Caravale asked Achille.

'Of course he does. It was his idea. This terrible experience — '

'I'd prefer Achille to answer for himself. Do

you want to go to school in Switzerland, son?'

Achille nodded. He looked like a four-year-old that had had a bad scare. 'Yes, sir, please,' he mumbled. 'I . . . I don't want to stay here anymore.' A little firmness, a touch of the old Achille, crept back into his voice: 'I'm not going back to La Sacca.'

'He was supposed to start in Switzerland next fall anyway,' Vincenzo said. 'Saint Gotthard's School in Bern. It's a boys' school, mostly for the sons of businessmen and government officials. Highly rated, with excellent security. Given what's happened, they've agreed to take him early. They'll send somebody from Bern to accompany him.'

'All right, I have no objections, as long as you understand that we'll probably have to contact him later, and we might have to ask him to come back.'

'All right, then. Achille, thank the colonel.'

'Thank you, sir,' Achille said. He had yet to meet Caravale's eyes, even once.

Caravale wasted no time getting out of his chair. He hadn't liked that damned chandelier hanging over his head.

★ ★ ★

Vincenzo and Caravale walked in silence down the central corridor, between hanging

228

rows of old tapestries, but once out on the portico, Caravale stopped.

'I was wondering, Signor de Grazia, where the money to pay the ransom came from.'

Vincenzo seemed puzzled by the question. 'From my bank. As I told you.'

'Banca Popolare di Milano.'

'Yes.' And again, with a lilt of annoyance: 'As I told you.'

'That's so, but you didn't tell me where the money *came from*.'

Vincenzo shook his head impatiently. 'I don't — '

'The Banca Popolare di Milano wired the money for you to the Bank of Rezekne, yes. We've established that. But they didn't lend you the money. And you'd only had a few hundred thousand euros in your accounts there. I'd like to know where you got the rest.'

Now Vincenzo was surprised. 'Why? What difference does it make? Why have you been looking at my accounts?'

'Are you refusing to tell me?'

'I'm not refusing anything. I'm asking you why it should be of importance.'

'It's a routine question, signore.' Which was true, although now he was beginning to wonder if he'd hit on something. 'Surely you can see that.'

Vincenzo turned so that he faced Caravale

squarely. 'I don't see it at all. I will tell you frankly, Colonel. I don't appreciate your sticking your fingers into my financial affairs. My advice to you is to stick to the matter at hand.'

Saying nothing, Caravale stared steadily back, although he had to tip his head back to do it, and after a few moments it was Vincenzo who broke from the locked gaze. 'All right, then, I borrowed against my stock holdings, if it's so important. As I said I would. My broker took care of it.'

'All five million euros?'

'Yes,' Vincenzo said shortly. 'Now, if that's what you wanted to know, I'd like to get back to work. And you, I believe, have a ten-year-old homicide to solve.' Caravale considered pressing him a little more — Which stocks did he borrow against? What exactly was the lending arrangement? Who was his broker? — but he could sense the workings of the gears in Vincenzo's mind, a step ahead of him, already framing ambiguous replies to whatever he might ask, so he let it pass. Besides, if the man, in desperation, had done something not-quite-legal to get the money to ransom his son, Caravale wasn't about to go after him on account of it.

All the same, his cop's soul told him that there was something here that didn't add up, and he made a mental note to have his people look a bit more closely into the financial end of things as they pursued their investigations.

'All right, signore,' he said pleasantly. 'As you say.'

★ ★ ★

Back in Stresa after dropping Phil off at Camping Costa Azzurra, Gideon was in a rotten mood. He picked at a hole-in-the-wall restaurant meal of *pollo ally cacciatora*, watching with ethnocentric and unanthropological disapproval as a five-year-old was encouraged to sip his father's red wine (but had his hand slapped when he reached for his coffee). The dinner was good, but he had little appetite and left half of it on the plate. His hands hurt. He had unthinkingly done his digging that morning without the benefit of gloves, and although it hadn't bothered him at the time, it now felt as if the gravel had inflicted a hundred tiny paper cuts. Stupid.

On his roundabout way back to the hotel, he stopped at a *gelateria* on the Corso for his usual dessert. For the first time, however, he found himself annoyed rather than charmed by the baffling Italian custom of adding two inexplicable steps to the purchase. Going up to the *gelato* counter, he was required to tell the woman behind it what he wanted, in return for which she gave him, not his two-scoop cone of chocolate and pistachio, but a piece of paper on which she'd scrawled some arcane symbols. This he had to take back to the cashier near the door, to whom he gave his 1.30€; and from whom he received a receipt. The receipt was then taken to the counter (again), and the *gelato* finally given to him. The process had never bugged him before, but it did tonight. And the standard, useless, plastic *gelato* spoon that came with it — not only absurdly minuscule, but spade-shaped rather than spoon-shaped (why, to make eating the stuff more of a challenge?) — was one more irritant.

He knew what it was that was really bothering him, of course. While his solitary, footloose dining arrangements had been enjoyable at first, after five evenings they were getting depressing. So were his solitary sleeping arrangements. He missed Julie; missed her company, missed her presence through the night. Next time, if there was a next time, he'd be less finicky about his demands for material comfort. He thought briefly of checking out of the Hotel Primavera in the morning and joining the group after all, but there was only one more night to go after this one, and he'd be spending it in a tent with two or three other men anyway, so what was the point?

Unable to focus on the *International Herald Tribune* or a book, and too lazy to go out for another walk, he kicked off his shoes and turned on the television set. The Primavera brought in only one English-speaking channel: Eurosport, a British import that was showing cycling at the moment, but was promising, with barely controlled enthusiasm, to move on to an exciting weight-lifting competition from Sofia at the top of the hour. There was a German station with talking heads and a French one that had a noisy, laughy game show. The rest were in Italian: another couple of game shows, including a homegrown version of *Who Wants to Be a Millionaire?*, a Judge Judy-type program, two dubbed American sitcoms with the usual weirdly assorted families and creepy children, and *Law and Order (La Legge e le Forze dell'Ordine)* with Jerry Orbach chasing down perps in Italian (*'Alt! Polizia!'*).

He watched the last twenty minutes of *La Legge e le Forze dell'Ordine*, and at nine o'clock he switched off the TV and went to bed.

14

At 3:22 that morning a remarkable telephone call was received at Stresa's Polizia Municipale headquarters on Piazza Marconi. According to the caller, Sister Susanna, the nighttime receptionist at the hospital, there were strange sounds coming from the morgue in the basement. 'As if,' she whispered, 'something is trying to get out.'

'No, no, Sister,' said Ettore Omodeo, the police dispatcher, with a reassuring laugh. 'After all, how could anyone get out of a morgue? But it's chilly out tonight, it might be someone trying to get in, to keep warm. You stay where you are, Sister. I'll have someone there right away.'

Omodeo contacted the lone patrol car on duty and gave them the message. Then he shook his head.

What kind of a person would want to break into a morgue?

★ ★ ★

Gideon had always been an early riser, often earlier than he wished, and going to sleep at 9 didn't help any. By 5:00 A.M. he was awake and restless, itching to get moving. And he needed coffee. He did some stretching and enough push-ups and sit-ups to get some blood into his muscles, showered, shaved, slipped on a windbreaker against the predawn chill, and trotted downstairs, feeling a bit more positive about the world in general. He nodded to the teenaged nighttime desk clerk, who greeted him with a mournful shrug.

'No breakfas' yet, signore. Seven o'clock.'

'I know. See you then.'

He walked past shuttered shops and restaurants to the quiet Corso Italia and crossed it to the Lungolago, the lakeside promenade. Near the ferry terminal there was an espresso and snack stand that he knew from past experience would be open for the benefit of early-arriving ferry workers.

By now the barista knew him by sight. '*Buongiorno. Cappuccino. Doppio. Senza cioccolato.*'

'*Si, grazie,*' said Gideon, smiling. It was practically like being in Seattle.

Relatively contented now, he walked along the promenade, slowly sipping coffee from a giant Styrofoam cup. The only other people he saw were a couple of elderly men walking their dogs and looking lonesome and pensive in the way of early-morning dog walkers

235

everywhere. The ornamental fountains had still to be turned on, and with no traffic whizzing down the Corso yet, he could actually hear the gentle lapping of the lake against the stone bulwark on which the promenade had been built.

It was very peaceful, very pretty. The air smelled of camellias and lemon oil, cut by the pungent, not unpleasant scent of creosote from the ferry terminal pilings. The globe lamps along the promenade were still lit, but the sky had begun to lighten, so the perfectly pruned trees, the brick walking paths, and the dark lake itself were all highlighted with streaks of rose and gold. After a while he stopped to lean on the balustrade and look out over the water, waiting for the sun to top the mountains on the other side, shoot out its brief explosion of brilliant yellow rays, and touch the graceful towers and parapets of the Borromean Islands with the day's first light. He'd watched it before, and with a still-warm double cappuccino in his hand, it was about as good a way to start the day as any he could imagine; given, that is, that he had to start it without Julie.

It was the smell that brought on the first trickle of apprehension. Old sweat, stale clothing. Someone was standing too close to him. This was Italy, of course, where the perception of personal space wasn't as expansive as it was in the States, but it made him wary all the same. And now he could even smell the person's breakfast on his breath — a ham and cheese *panino*, espresso laced with grappa . . . Even for Italy, this was getting a little —

As he began to turn, there was an intake of breath startlingly close behind him, and then his cup went flying and the hot coffee was in his face, the crushed Styrofoam jammed up against his mouth by a bare, muscular forearm pressed against his throat. At first he thought someone was trying to shove him over the balustrade into the water a dozen feet below, but when a knee was forced into his lower spine to bend him over backward, he realized he was being strangled. Somebody had a choke hold on him from behind, clamping his neck between upper arm and forearm and tightening the resulting vise by pulling on his wrist with the other hand.

For a second, gripped by the primal terror that came with having his air cut off, he struggled, clawing at the hold and pummeling futilely behind him with both hands. At six foot one, Gideon was a fairly big man, and strong — he'd been a boxer in his college days and still stayed more or less in shape — but his attacker had forearms as thick as thighs. It was like being squeezed by a boa constrictor. Still, he managed to twist his head a couple of inches to one side so that the front of his neck was now in the small hollow that made up the crook of the man's arm. The direct pressure was off his windpipe and it was possible to suck in a gasping breath.

With the return of air came sanity. Blind impulse gave way to something like rational thought. And with rational thought came the realization that he had only made matters worse, and not just a little worse. By turning his head, he'd inadvertently changed the man's grip from a 'bar arm' hold, with the forearm pressed directly — and painfully — against the trachea, to a judo hold, the so-called 'sleeper hold.' With the crook of the arm now at the front of his throat, his windpipe was free, but the forearm and upper arm, now at either side of his neck, were compressing the carotid arteries. He could breathe again, but the blood supply to his brain was being cut off.

This was bad. The need for air, as overpowering as it was on an instinctive level, was the lesser of his worries. Cutting off a person's air by compressing the trachea was excruciating, yes, but it could take two or three minutes to shut down the brain. But pressure on the soft tissues of the superior carotid triangles, squeezing shut the arteries — and it didn't take that much pressure to squeeze them shut — immediately starved the brain of oxygen and created a toxic excess of carbon dioxide. Hypoxia and hypercapnia. And that deadly combination would take only ten seconds to cause unconsciousness, fifteen at the outside. Death would follow. He had very little time. Already he was seeing whirling stars at the backs of his eyes, the first sign of oxygen deprivation to the brain. The first sign of blacking out.

He made himself stop his ineffectual flailing, which was using up what little oxygen he had left. His fingers, already weakening, were never going to budge that tree trunk of an arm, and the feeble blows he was aiming behind him were useless. Instead, he strained to reach his attacker's face, trying for the eyes or the nose or the lips; anything he could tear at or grind his fingers into. He touched what he thought were nose and upper lip, but the man shook him off and jerked his head back out of the way.

The hold tightened, as if by resisting he'd gotten his attacker good and mad. Gideon could feel the muscles of the biceps and brachioradialis harden and bulge. He could feel the wiry hairs of the forearm against the bottom of his jaw. He was hearing popping sounds in his head now, like static. There were pinprick sensations crawling spiderlike over his face and scalp, a scattering of minute explosions, and all at once he was overpoweringly sleepy, so that all he really wanted was to be allowed to lie down and go to sleep. He realized his arms were hanging limply at his sides now. When a bright yellow flash seemed to sear his eyes, he didn't know if it was in his brain or if it was the sun clearing the mountains. He wasn't sure if his eyes were open or closed.

But one small part of his cerebral cortex was still working; enough to tell him he had perhaps two seconds of consciousness left. If he was going to live, he had to act now. Now. With a tremendous, gasping effort of will, he arched his body and threw his head backward with all his remaining strength. He heard an 'Uff!' as his head struck the other man's face. The hold loosened slightly, and with the returning flow of blood to his brain came a partial return of strength, of clarity of mind. His head had smashed into the bastard's nose and it had hurt him. What worked once could work twice. He braced his right foot against the balustrade for added leverage and shoved off as hard as he could, flinging himself backward and sharply snapping his head back at the same time.

This time there was a howl of pain, accompanied by the crunch of breaking bone and a strangled '*Merda!*'

At the same time, there was a cry somewhere off to the right. '*Ehi! Che fai la? Cbe succede?*'

The man cursed again, released his hold, and staggered off. Gideon, deprived of support, found his knees didn't have the strength to hold him up. His legs were like seaweed, squelchy and boneless. He collapsed to the promenade, twisting as he fell and ending up with his back against the balustrade, trembling and barely able to move as the postadrenaline crash hit him. He lay there with his eyes closed, watching the last of the starry pinpoints blink out and listening to the wary approach of his rescuer ('*Signore, si sente bene?*'), who seemed to be eons off, in some echoing, parallel universe.

There was a piece of something stuck to his lips, and he thought at first that one of his teeth had been broken, but it was only a fragment of the Styrofoam cup that had been smashed against his mouth. He flicked it off. Then, realizing that the hair at the back of his head was sticky, he touched it and opened his eyes to check his fingers. Blood, but not his. He'd broken the guy's nose, all right. Good.

And from the crackling sound of that crunch, it wasn't just the *ossa nasalia* — the two bones that formed the bridge of the nose — that had snapped, but some of the delicate bony structures inside as well: the ethmoid, the vomer. He sure as hell hoped so. That sonofabitch was going to remember him for the rest of his life, every time he heard himself breathe. With any luck Gideon had deviated his nasal septum for him as well, so he'd remember him every time he looked in the mirror too. Fine.

Never again, Gideon thought as he slipped into something like an exhausted, relieved doze, would his students hear him utter a word of complaint about the fragility of the human face.

15

When the *polizia* arrived a few minutes later, they found him still on the ground and a little muddled, but sitting up against the parapet, surrounded by four or five solicitous people, one of whom was trying to get him to swallow some brandy from a paper cup.

'*Inglese?*' the police wanted to know once they'd heard him say a couple of words in Italian.

'*Americano,*' he said.

The two cops exchanged an I-thought-as-much glance. Still, they were courteous and concerned, and they dumbed down their Italian to his level. They wanted to run him over to emergency, but by then, with his mind clearing, Gideon was able to convince them that he was all right, that the blood on his collar wasn't his. And he knew that ten or twelve seconds of having his carotids compressed wasn't going to do his brain any permanent harm. Twenty seconds, you were a vegetable. Twelve seconds, no problem. Strange but true. So no hospital, thanks all the same.

They used a cotton swab to collect some blood from his hair, presumably for evidence, and then while one of the cops talked to the witnesses, the other one sat him down to take his statement in the front seat of their cruiser — a white Fiat minihatchback with a snazzy green stripe running horizontally around it, the kind of car Gideon might have mistakenly hailed for a taxi if he'd seen it drive by.

With a portable tape recorder running, Gideon told him what he could, which wasn't much. He'd never seen the man. He'd come up behind him, dug a knee into his back, wrapped one hefty arm around his neck, and squeezed. About all he could say was that he was big and he was strong. But with a little artful probing on the policeman's part, he was able to come up with a little more: The man had been wearing a short-sleeved shirt, he was Caucasian, with wiry black hair (at least on his forearms), and he'd had a ham and cheese roll or something like it for breakfast, along with a *caffè corretto*. Oh, and he was pretty definitely Italian: his reaction to getting his nose broken had been a heartfelt '*Merda!*' That was about it.

'He communicated nothing to you? He didn't try to take your money?'

'He said '*Merda*', but I doubt if that counts as communication. And he wasn't interested in money. He was interested in killing me.'

'And you don't know why?'

'Well, I'm not sure. I'm working on a case with Colonel Caravale — '

The cop sat up. 'Colonel Caravale? The *carabinieri* commander?'

'Yes, I'm an anthropologist — '

'A moment, please, signore.' The cop got on his car radio to relay this information. Then, while Gideon drank some bottled water that the second cop offered him, the first one waited to be called back. Five minutes later the call came rattling out of the speaker. Gideon couldn't understand it, but the cop started up the engine and his partner got in back and slammed the door.

'He wants to see you. Caravale.' He looked impressed.

'How about letting me clean up first? I'm just up the street at the Primavera.'

The cop had his doubts, but when Gideon wiped a hand through his hair and held up bloody fingers, he changed his mind. 'OK, five minutes. We'll drive you.'

In the lobby, the nighttime clerk, on his final hour of duty, looked up from his copy of *Playboy Italy* to see Gideon step out of the police car and come in, bloodied and disheveled, and still a little unsteady.

He blinked slowly a couple of times. 'Sorry, signore, no breakfas' yet for one more 'alf-hour,' he said.

★ ★ ★

Carabinieri headquarters were at the corner of Viale Duchessa di Genova and Via Fratelli Omarini, one block from the railroad station and two from the water, in what passed for Stresa's low-rent district. Surrounded by a grim, spike-topped wall of rough-hewn stone, the featureless concrete building was painted white, but that had been done long ago. Now it was splotched and streaky with a black mold that seemed to spread as you looked at it. On one side the three-story building overlooked an eighteenth-century church; on the other a ruined villa with a jungly, once-ambitious estate garden that looked as if it hadn't been pruned in a century.

But hidden within the forbidding walls that surrounded the unlovely building was a beautiful little ornamental garden of flowers and shrubs, devotedly tended, and it was onto this garden of fresh reds and pinks that Caravale's ground-floor office looked. The office itself was as neat and orderly as a monk's cell, but considerably more plush. Thick, plum-colored carpet, a big old wooden desk near the window with a few framed family photographs on it, two matched, leather-upholstered desk chairs, and in a corner on the opposite side of the room a large chestnut butler's table with four more soft leather armchairs. It was at the table that Gideon and Caravale sat, with two cups of killer espresso, as thick as Turkish coffee, that had been brought in from a vending machine in the hallway. Unlike just about every other cop's office he'd ever seen, there were no taped-up maps or charts or reminders on the walls. The only object on the beige grass-cloth wallpaper was a corroded pair of giant pincers centered in pride of place above the butler's table.

Caravale saw him looking at them. 'Those? They're for use on uncooperative prisoners. And,' he added darkly, 'on consultants who get above themselves.'

'I'll keep that in mind.'

Caravale smiled at him. 'They belonged to my grandfather,' he said, turning to look fondly at them. '*Nonno* Fortunato. They're ice tongs. All his life my grandfather, my sainted grandfather, drove an ice wagon. A runt of a man, soaking wet he didn't weigh fifty kilos, but with those tongs he'd lift a block of ice half his own weight, throw it over his shoulder, and walk up three flights with it. And then come down and get the next block. A truly good man, worth all those de Grazias put together, and yet all his life what did he have? Nothing. Just work, and poverty, and worry. But from those heavy, freezing blocks of ice that finally broke him, he sent my father to college. And my father sent me.'

Gideon was as surprised by these confidences as by the depth of feeling that came with them. 'He sounds like a wonderful man.'

'He was, indeed,' Caravale said appreciatively. 'It was because of him that I enrolled in the police academy. I had to fight my father every step of the way.'

'Your father didn't want you to go into police work?'

'My father,' Caravale said wryly, 'was of the opinion that we *carabinieri* are no more than an apparatus of the established order — willing tools of the oppressor class.'

'Ah,' Gideon said, not knowing what else to say.

'I beg your pardon. I'm talking too much. It was the tongs.' He hunched his shoulders. He was in civilian clothes again, and without the shoulder boards, there wasn't much to hunch. 'Ah, it's all long ago. They don't make men like that anymore. Now what about you, Gideon, are you all right? Not hurt or anything?'

'No, I'm fine. Thanks for the coffee. It's just what I need.'

Caravale nodded. 'I just listened to your statement.'

'It wasn't much help, I'm afraid.'

'Oh, I wouldn't say that.' He permitted himself another small smile. 'All forces in the region are now on the lookout for a large man with ham and cheese on his breath.'

'And who speaks Italian, don't forget that part.'

'Yes, of course.' Caravale, pretending to write in the notebook on the table, murmured: 'Large man. Ham. Cheese. Speaks Italian. Wonderful, he's as good as caught. It's only a question of time now.'

Gideon laughed. 'Next time I'll be more observant.'

'Good, I'll appreciate it.' He vacuumed up his espresso, swished it once around his mouth, and swallowed. 'So tell me, what do you suppose this was about?'

'I've been thinking about that,' Gideon said. 'My first thought was that it had to be about those bones, that somebody didn't want me to examine them. But the more I thought about it, the less sense I could make out of it.'

'Why?'

'Because I could understand it if the idea was to keep us from finding out that Domenico de Grazia didn't drown in the lake after all, but that somebody killed him and then hid his body in a culvert on Mount

Zeda. But we already knew it was Domenico, so what would the point be — unless this somebody who tried to strangle me didn't know you'd gone ahead and made the identification?'

'Possible, but doubtful. It would mean he would have had to be aware that the remains had been found, but not that they'd been identified. Who could that be? The de Grazia people — they're the only ones we told, and they all know it's Domenico. Who else would know anything about it?'

'Well, then, I don't know what the point was.' He thought for a few seconds. 'I haven't found anything that indicates the cause of death yet. Maybe somebody doesn't want us to know how he died, and thinks I might come up with it?'

'But why wouldn't they want us to know? Knife, club, axe . . . what difference does it make? Why would someone commit murder to prevent its being known?'

'I already said I don't know,' said Gideon with some annoyance. Caravale was holding something back. 'Twice. Let's hear your theory.'

Caravale tipped his chair back and folded his hands in front of his belt. 'I don't know either. But I think you might have it right.' He paused. 'Oh. I meant to tell you. They tried to steal your bones last night.'

'Uh . . . come again?'

'At three o'clock in the morning. Someone tried to break into the morgue. When the Polizia Municipale showed up, he ran off. But he'd been trying to force the door of the room where Domenico's bones were being kept. And there was nothing else in there but some linens.'

'So first they tried to get the bones,' Gideon said slowly. 'And when that didn't work, they came after me.'

'It looks that way.'

'Then that's why the attempt on me was so . . . so crude, so risky — I mean, coming up behind a guy in a public park and choking him? Not exactly brilliantly planned. But they were running out of time, they'd already failed to get the bones, and I was going to examine them in a couple of hours. They were desperate. So they hung around the hotel waiting for me to come out, and . . . well, there it is.' Thoughtfully, he finished the last of his cooling, grainy coffee and took a sip from the glass of water that had been brought with it.

'Yes, there it is.' Caravale slapped the table with the palm of his hand and got briskly out of his chair. 'If you're up to it, let's get to them, then.'

Gideon, whose thoughts had been straying, looked up at him.

'To what?'

'The bones. Let's see what it is they don't want you to find out.'

*   *   *

Domenico de Grazia's remains were no longer at the hospital. After the attempted break-in, Caravale had ordered them brought to *carabinieri* headquarters, where they had been placed in the evidence room, a cryptlike vault deep within the building, far from any windows; a blockhouse within a blockhouse, with one wall consisting of a steel-barred grille, like the door to a cell. Two of the other concrete-block walls were faced, floor to ceiling, with wooden pigeon holes in which there were tagged items in bags or boxes. Against the remaining wall was a chipped, stained, Formica-topped table. In the corner, standing on end, was a tagged crossbow, along with other objects — a mangled tire rim, a music stand, a kitchen stepladder — too large for the pigeon holes. It was, Caravale told him, probably the most secure room in the city of Stresa.

The bones were in two cardboard cartons and a large paper bag that had been laid on the table. Whoever had put them in had apparently used size as his sole criterion for sorting. The big ones — the cranium, pelvic bones, and arm and leg bones — were in a printer-paper box; the medium-sized bones — the mandible, ribs, vertebrae, scapulas, clavicles, and sternum — were in a canned mushroom carton; and the small ones — the wickedly irregular, tiny, exasperating-to-sort bones of the hands and feet, all one hundred six or so of them (more than half the body's bones were in the hands and feet) — were in the bag, along with a few loose teeth. If the good Corporal Fasoli had really gone to the trouble of arranging them anatomically, it had all gone to waste.

But at least they were clean. 'He did a good job, your Corporal Fasoli,' Gideon said, beginning to get them out onto the table. The bones showed the usual unappetizing stains of blood, mold, earth, and body fluids — it would have taken bleach to get them out, and there really wasn't any good reason for doing that (Gideon's aesthetic sensitivities weren't good enough reasons) but the clotted dirt and the dried remnants of ligaments, tendons, and who-knows-what were pretty much gone.

He squinted up at the ceiling lights, four long neon tubes behind pebbled, translucent sheets of plastic.

'Something wrong?' Caravale asked.

'The light's awfully flat. I need something that will cast sharper shadows, bring out texture. A desk lamp would do if it's bright enough. Maybe there's a goose-necked one somewhere that I could use? Oh, and a good magnifying glass?'

'Goose-necked?' It was an unfamiliar term to him, but when Gideon demonstrated with his hands, he nodded and moved toward the open door. 'Give me two minutes.'

'OK, yeah,' Gideon said, already absorbed in gingerly removing the mortal remains of Domenico de Grazia from their containers. Ordinarily, the next task would have been to lay the bones out anatomically, every single one of them, including those tricky hand and foot bones, but this wasn't an ordinary case, and he was eager to get to the crucial question: Was there anything here that could shed light on old Domenico's death? What Gideon did, therefore, was to separate the bones he wanted to look at first, the ones most likely to hold clues to the cause of death: the skull, for obvious reasons; the ribs, for injuries that might indicate damage to internal organs; and the metacarpals and phalanges of the hands, for nicks or small fractures that might have come from clutching at a blade in self-defense or warding off a blow.

The skull was first. The shriveled husk of brain still lay within. For forensic purposes, it was useless. He lifted it out with two fingers and placed it in a clean sack, to eventually go back to the family with the bones.

A cursory examination of the cranium showed nothing. Unquestionably, the broken parietal and maxilla were recent damage. But sometimes new injuries could cover the signs of old ones, so he went over the broken areas with care. Still nothing. As for the loose teeth in the bag — an upper incisor and first molar — the sharp-edged, unbroken sockets from which they'd come showed that they'd fallen out long after death, a normal occurrence as the soft tissue holding them in place shrank and disappeared. There were four other teeth missing as well, but they had come out decades before death; their sockets barely existed now, the bone having been slowly reabsorbed over the years. There seemed to be nothing else, no signs of —

'Gideon?'

He jumped. Caravale was standing behind him with a goose-necked desk lamp in one hand and a rectangular magnifying lens with a built-in light in the other. 'Will these do?'

'They'll do fine, thanks.'

'It's all right if I watch?'

255

'Sure, stay.' Why not, it wouldn't kill him not to talk to himself for a while.

Gideon plugged in the lamp and set it up on the table, adjusting its neck so it cast a sidewise light that would emphasize textural irregularities — depressions, cracks, nicks, anything. Then, using the magnifying glass, but without flicking on its bulb (a direct light would only flatten everything out again), he began going over the skull one more time.

Meanwhile Caravale, whom Gideon hadn't seen smoke before, opened a packet of Toscano cigars, pulled out one black, twisted stick, snipped it in two with a tiny pair of blunt-edged scissors he produced from somewhere, and put one of the evil-looking halves back in the packet.

'For later,' he said. 'One a day, half in the morning, half in the afternoon.' He lit up — it smelled as bad as it looked — leaned against the grille, and watched; asking nothing, saying nothing.

Gideon worked steadily and silently, pulling over a stool when he got tired of bending over. There was nothing useful on the cranium, nothing on the mandible. The metacarpals and phalanges of the hands showed an old, healed fracture of the right fifth metacarpal and plenty of arthritis, but nothing else. After twenty intent, focused minutes he straightened up, stretched, and massaged the back of his neck. Caravale, who had left without his noticing, came back with a couple of cold bottles of Brio. Gideon accepted the quinine-flavored soft drink gratefully, taking a couple of long gulps and then turning to the ribs, examining them one at a time.

Ten minutes passed before he found anything. 'Well, well,' he said, separating one rib from the rest and laying it aside.

Caravale came closer, leaned on the table. 'What?'

Gideon motioned for him to wait another minute, which Caravale obediently did. Another ten minutes passed. 'Ah, so,' Gideon said with satisfaction. A second rib was separated from the others.

He turned to Caravale, holding up a rib in each hand like a couple of batons. 'Success. Got a cause of death for you.'

16

'This is the seventh rib, right side,' Gideon said. 'And this is the vertebral end of it, the end in back, where it connects to the spinal column.'

'I never knew you could tell one rib from another. They all look the same to me.'

'If you have them all, it's easy; you compare the relative lengths and the shapes of the arcs. But there are plenty of other differences too. See, here there are variations in the articular facets and tubercles of the first, second, tenth — '

With a raised palm, Caravale warded him off. 'Please. I'll take your word for it.'

'Well, you asked me.'

'And I deeply regret it, I assure you. Continue, please.'

Coming out of Caravale's porky, beetle-browed face as it did, it made Gideon laugh. 'OK, I won't try to educate you. Now take a look at the top side of the rib — this is the top side — near the back end. This is the back end. Do you see the — '

'This little sliver, coming out of the bone?'

'That's right. That's a knife cut.'

Caravale adjusted the lamp and bent interestedly over the rib. 'It's like a shaving, like what you get when you're whittling a piece of wood.'

'That's just what it is. When bone is green — when it's alive — it's soft, and if a knife slices into it at a shallow angle, a sliver of bone is likely to curl away from it. Like this. Once bone dries, it doesn't happen. Try to cut it with a knife after it's dry and the piece would just chip off.'

'Ah.' Caravale absently pulled out and lit the half-cigar he'd put away for the afternoon. 'And this one small cut, this cut you can hardly see without the lens — this proves he was stabbed to death?' He was thinking ahead, to the presentation of evidence in a court of law, and he had his doubts.

'There's more, Tullio.' He pulled the other rib into the circle of brightest light and pointed with a ballpoint pen. 'This nick? That's also a knife cut.'

'Is it?' He scrutinized it with the magnifying glass. 'But it's completely different. There's no sliver. This is more like a, like a — '

'It's more like a gouge. Which is what it is. It's not a sharp slice, it's a relatively blunt, V-shaped notch. If you use the glass again, you can see where the fibers at the edges have been mashed down into it.'

Caravale shrugged. He was willing to take Gideon's word for that too. Smoking, he studied the gouge, 'It's like what you'd expect from an axe, or from an extremely dull knife . . . '

'Yes.'

'But the other wound is from a sharp blade.'

'Yes.'

'So . . . two different weapons?' He looked confused, as well he might.

'No, no, no, I'm sorry, I didn't mean to mislead you. See, this one — wait, it'd be easier to show you. Is there a kitchen in this place?'

'A — ? Yes, just down the hall there.'

'OK, don't go away.'

In the kitchen he startled the cook by barging in, saying he needed to borrow something, and snatching an eight-inch chef's knife from the knife block. The frightened cook was looking mutely around for help when Corporal Fasoli, who was having a cup of coffee and a pastry, called through the opening from the dining room: 'It's all right, he's with the colonel. He's harmless.'

The cook recovered himself as Gideon was on his way out. 'Just make sure you bring it back,' he called after him, brandishing a spatula to show he meant it.

When he returned to the evidence room, Gideon laid the seventh rib on the table, right side up, so the curling slice-mark was on top. With care, he slipped the knife blade gently into the slice, under the shaving of bone. At an angle of about thirty degrees, the fit was perfect. The knife remained propped there without the need for additional support.

'Now, this other bone, that's the sixth rib, the one right above, and the V-shaped gouge, as you see, is in the bottom of it, the underside. If I place it in position above the seventh and lower it . . .'

'The gouge was made by the back, the spine, of the knife!' Caravale exclaimed on seeing the snug fit. 'A single weapon, a single thrust!'

'Exactly. It's V-shaped, not square, you see, even though the spine of the knife is square, because it went in at an angle. See, a single sharp weapon can make a lot of different-shaped wounds depending on the way it goes in, or how far it penetrates, or whether it was twisted in a manner that — ' He realized he was on the verge of lecturing again and caught himself. 'Anyway, with the blade going in like that' — he gestured at the knife and the two ribs, locked together in a circle of light like some grisly museum exhibit — 'the point couldn't have missed penetrating the left atrium of the heart. Death inside of a minute, probably sooner. What? Is something bothering you?'

Caravale had been frowning, fingering his side, near the bottom of his rib cage, like a man whose ulcer was worrying him. 'I don't mean to question your expertise, but . . . well, a few years ago I fractured a rib in an automobile accident. Down here.'

'Yes?'

'The doctor said . . . Well, I'm fairly certain he said . . . that it was my seventh rib.'

'That looks about right,' Gideon agreed. 'The seventh or eighth.'

'But the heart, isn't it up here?' He put his other hand, with the cigar, on his sternum. At Gideon's nod, he went on. 'Well, then, how could a knife thrust here, at the seventh rib, go into the heart? That is, unless it was practically straight up — which our knife there isn't. It would go into, into . . . '

'The left lobe of the liver, correct. Several inches below the heart.'

'So . . . ?' Caravale shook his head, lost.

Gideon laughed. 'What you're forgetting is that the ribs don't go straight around, they angle upward from front to back. Yes, that's the seventh rib down there in front, but by the time it curves around and connects to the vertebral column in back, it's way up here.' He reached around and with one finger tapped Caravale on the upper back, between the left scapula and the spine. 'And that's where the knife went in.'

'Ahh,' said Caravale with his brown-toothed grin. 'I see. Straight into the heart.'

'Well, it would have had to get through a few muscle layers first, and the left lung, but yes. Straight into the heart.'

'Stabbed in the back.'

Gideon nodded. 'Yup.'

They stood looking down at the bones. 'So he put his arm up to ward off the blow — that's how he got it broken — succeeded for a moment . . . ' Caravale took a final drag on his cigar stub and ground it out in a metal ashtray. ' . . . but must have fallen and gotten himself knifed in the back.'

'That's pretty much it, but from the angle of the thrust, it doesn't look to me as if he was on the ground when the blade went in. I think he probably just twisted around, maybe trying to get away, and got stabbed before he could make it. He was an old man, and he was lame.'

Gideon finished his Brio and tossed the bottle into a wastepaper basket under the table. It still surprised him how easy it was to talk about these hideous events as if they hadn't really happened to a living human being, as if they hadn't involved agony and terror and unspeakable, bloody horror.

'All right, so what do we know now that we didn't know before?' he asked, musing, getting his mind back on the clean, comfortable present.

'Several things,' said Caravale. 'We know the cause of death. We know for certain that he was murdered. Until now it was strictly circumstantial — he was buried, therefore, he must have been murdered. But now we *know*.'

'Yes, sure. But why did somebody try to steal the bones? Why was I attacked? What was that all about? Okay, so we know he was murdered with a kitchen knife or something like it. So what? Why kill me to keep that from coming out?'

Caravale pensively scratched his cheek. 'It could be to make sure we didn't identify the murder weapon and somehow connect it to the killer.'

'So throw away the knife. They've had ten years to do it. Wouldn't that be a whole lot simpler?'

'And safer.' Nodding, Caravale plucked a dark fleck of tobacco from his lip. 'There must be something else.'

'Maybe, but I sure can't imagine what. I'll go over every single bone, though. Give me an hour.'

With Caravale gone, Gideon worked bone by bone by bone, sliding each one into the light, turning it over in his fingers to see and to feel every angle and facet, scanning it with the magnifying glass, putting it aside into the 'discard' pile, and moving smoothly on to the next one. He could work far more quickly than usual because there was no reason to measure them, apply height or race formulas, or do anything else to help in the identification process. All he had to do, basically, was look for anything unusual; in particular, trauma and pathologies.

There was nothing that amounted to anything. Some dental caries, a lot of expectable age-related arthritis, and various long-standing deformities of the lumbar vertebrae and of the knee, ankle, and foot joints, all of which were clearly related to the old man's hip problem, but that was all. Nothing new, nothing that explained anything.

Still, it ended up taking quite a bit more than an hour, and when he found Caravale in his office to tell him the results, Caravale simply looked up with a grumpy expression and said: 'Jesus, it's about time. I've been sitting here listening to my stomach rumble for the last twenty minutes. Let's go and have some lunch.'

★ ★ ★

Caravale preferred not to eat in Stresa, where so many people knew him. Instead, they drove a few miles up the lakeshore road, past graceful villas and Art Nouveau hotels, to the quieter town of Baveno, where they pulled into the parking lot of a rustic, homey restaurant called Il Gabbiano, the seagull. The owner knew Caravale and his preferences, and without being asked he showed them to a wooden table more or less hidden in a niche beside an arched entryway separating the two small rooms that made up the place. The place smelled of oregano and baking bread. It was like sitting in somebody's country kitchen.

As Gideon had surmised, Caravale took his eating seriously.

After a brief but thorough scan of the menu, he rattled off an order for artichoke pie appetizer, risotto Milanese, veal pizzaiola, parsleyed potatoes, and sauteed fennel, with cheese, grapes, and coffee to follow. Mineral water to drink. This was a stupendous initial order (for a native) in a country in which doggie bags do not exist because one's stomach is supposed to plan ahead, and people generally choose one course at a time, not an entire meal that they might not be able to finish. The restaurant owner was not surprised, however. Without writing it down, he grunted, then turned to Gideon and said, translating as he went: 'The *tròta*, trout, is very fine, fresh this morning in the *lago*, the lake. Very good *fritto*, fried.'

Gideon went along with that, ordering a bowl of minestrone and some bread and mineral water to accompany it. Coffee afterward, but no dessert.

'That's all you want?' Caravale seemed disappointed. 'Your meal is courtesy of the Carabinieri di Piemonte e Valle d'Aosta. That doesn't happen every day. You should make the most of it.'

'I didn't realize that, but really, that's all I want. And thank you.'

'A small expression of our gratitude.' He rubbed his hands together and looked over his shoulder. 'So, let's go and see what awaits on the antipasto table.'

With a platter of olives, sauteed peppers, salami, stuffed zucchini, and marinated shrimp and mussels between them, Gideon picked at a slice or two of salami, then raised something that had been at the back of his mind for a while.

'Tullio, I had a nasty thought. What you said before, about who could have attacked me, who could even have known that you'd found the bones . . . '

'Ahh,' said Caravale with an evil, knowing grin. So he'd had the same nasty thought.

'Assuming you or your men haven't been broadcasting it around,' Gideon went on, 'the only people who'd know would be — '

'The de Grazias, that's right. We're back to them. And that doctor, Luzzatto. Or maybe other people they might have told. But that's easy to check. For the time being, it looks as if we're talking about the nine fine people that were in that room with us yesterday.'

'Eight people. I think you can pretty safely exclude Phil Boyajian.'

Caravale said nothing, but only tipped his head to one side and waggled his hand, palm down. Maybe yes, maybe no.

Fair enough, Gideon thought. From the police point of view, at this stage of the game no one was to be excluded, certainly not on the testimony of an old friend.

Gideon did a little more pondering. 'If it is one of those people — '

'One or more of those people.'

' — then that pretty much has to mean that the same person — '

'Or people.'

' — was behind Domenico's murder ten years ago, or at least involved in it in some way. Right? Why else try to hide anything about the bones?'

Caravale's answer was a head-tilted, open-handed shoulder shrug that as much as said that the conclusion was self-evident; the facts spoke for themselves.

'His own family,' Gideon said.

'Or Luzzatto. One of the nine people in that room,' he said again.

Gideon shook his head. 'The guy that choked me — he wasn't in that room, I can tell you that much. Believe me, I would have remembered those arms.'

'A hired hand.'

They paused while the owner-waiter set down Gideon's soup and Caravale's wedge of artichoke pie.

'Hired hands kidnapping Achille last week, a hired hand trying to stop me from examining the bones of his murdered grandfather today,' Gideon said. 'Isn't that a lot of hired hands? You can't have that many criminals for hire wandering around Stresa. Doesn't it make you wonder at least a little if the two things might be related?'

'Wandering around Stresa, no. But not so many kilometers away, wandering around

Milan, yes. Look, Gideon, the kidnapping, the murder, they happened ten years apart.'

'To the same family.'

'Yes, the same family. So? What are you suggesting, that one of the de Grazias not only murdered Domenico, but kidnapped Achille too? We had a liquor store robbed the day before yesterday in Stresa. Do you think that might have been the de Grazia gang as well?'

'No, of course that's not what I'm suggesting — well, I don't know, maybe I am. All I'm saying is that the two things might possibly be connected one way or another. I had an old professor who used to talk about what he called the Law of Interconnected Monkey Business. I don't know how that would translate into Italian, but what he was saying was that when too many seemingly unrelated incidents occur to the same set of people in the same — '

'I understand what he was saying, but what do you say we just deal with the facts that we have instead of coming up with complicated theories? We have a decade-old murder of an old man. We have a week-old kidnapping of a boy. Two separate cases, ten years apart. Believe me, we have enough resources to deal with them both on their own merits. And as things stand, I don't see a good reason for assuming they're part of anything bigger.'

Gideon held up his hands in defeat. Caravale had just delivered a pretty good précis of Gideon's standard classroom presentation on Occam's razor, the Law of Parsimony: 'Entities are not to be multiplied beyond necessity. The simplest theory that fits the facts is the best one upon which to proceed.'

And Gideon believed in that. Absolutely.

On the other hand, there was Alfred North Whitehead's take on the subject: 'Seek simplicity and distrust it.' That was the nice thing about theories. If you looked hard enough, you could always find one to fit what you were thinking.

17

'Gideon?' Caravale said on the drive back to Stresa. 'Do you remember yesterday, at the *'consiglio''* — he put a sourmouthed set of quotation marks around the word — 'that Luzzatto said something about Domenico de Grazia's having something to ponder on the day he died?'

'Yes.'

'Can you remember exactly what he said?'

'Everybody was speaking Italian, Tullio. I didn't pick up every word. But didn't he say he knew — knew for a fact — that Domenico had some kind of decision on his mind?'

'But not what? No specifics?'

'If he did, I didn't hear it.'

'Nor did I. Then that will be an interesting question to ask him, don't you think?'

'What important decision Domenico had on his mind just before somebody killed him? Yeah, I'd say it would be.'

'I would too,' said Caravale.

As Caravale slid the car into a parking space at the Hotel Primavera, the question of Gideon's safety was raised and quickly disposed of. The colonel needed to go out to the island that afternoon to interview the family and get statements. While there, he would make sure that everyone was informed that Gideon's examination of the remains was done and his report to Caravale had already been made. He'd do the same with the local press, which was naturally showing interest. That would, or should, remove any new danger to him. Unless, of course, Gideon wished protection, in which case it would be provided.

'Thanks, no.' Gideon had been through the well-meaning intrusiveness and inconvenience of police protection before. He got out of the car, closed the door, and leaned in the open window. 'I'll be fine, Tullio. I appreciate the offer, but I'd be happier not seeing a cop every time I turn around.'

Caravale looked up at him and mournfully nodded. 'So would I.'

★   ★   ★

It took a while for Gideon's parasympathetic nervous system's post-stress reaction to fully kick in, but when it did, it was a lulu. Saying 'ciao' to Caravale, he'd felt all right, but by the time he'd climbed the three flights to his room, his leg muscles were twitching and the strength was running out of him like water.

Fumbling weakly at the door with his key, he could practically feel the adrenaline overdose draining out of his system. He made straight for the bed and flopped on his face. Before he could take his shoes off, he was asleep.

When the telephone rang two hours later, he was still on his face, his feet over the edge of the bed. He lifted his head and cocked one eye open to see the time and to gauge how he felt. Better than he'd expected: no shakiness, no palpitations. Homeostasis pretty much restored. But the short, deep sleep had made him dopey. It took four chirps of the phone before he was sitting up and groping for it.

Caravale was on the line.

'Listen, are you up to coming over to my office? If not, I can come there.'

'No, I'm fine. I could use the fresh air. What's up?'

'I have a picture I want to show you.'

★ ★ ★

There were six color photos, not one, arranged along the edge of the desk for his inspection. Four of them were dual, full-face-profile mug shots, the other two candid photographs. The men in them all looked superficially similar.

'Do you recognize any of them?' Caravale

asked, tilting back in his chair and crossing one stocky thigh over the other.

Gideon glanced along the row. 'Is one of these the one who tried to strangle me?'

'Ah? What makes you think so?'

Gideon shrugged. 'Because they look strong, and they look dumb. And why else would you be showing me photographs? Anyway, no, I don't recognize any of them. Which one did you think it was?'

'This one.' Caravale leaned forward and put his finger on the set of mug shots that was second from the left.

Gideon scrutinized them more carefully, thinking that perhaps he had caught a glimpse of the man's face without realizing it, and that it might come back to him. The man had oily, receding black hair, eyebrows like caterpillars, a jowly lantern jaw, and a glowering aura of bull-headed obstinacy.

'Sorry, not familiar at all. Doesn't look like anybody I know,' Gideon said, which wasn't entirely true. What the guy looked like was a muscle-bound version of Tullio Caravale. 'Sorry.'

'Too bad. It would have been better if you could verify it. But he's the one, all right. We have someone else who picked him out.'

'You found a witness? I thought it was too dark, I thought they were too far away.'

'Not a witness to the attack, no . . . not exactly. But we have someone who can verify his breakfast.'

'Verify his . . . Tullio, you're losing me again.'

Caravale smiled. 'Ham and cheese, remember? Coffee with grappa. You're the one who told us.'

'Yes, sure, but . . . ' He shook his head. 'Help me out here. I'm still a little slow.'

At five forty-five in the morning, Caravale explained, the only café in Stresa that was open was old Crossetti's stand next to the ferry building, which started serving at five o'clock for the benefit of the ferry workers.

'Where I got my coffee,' Gideon said.

'Right. And that's where Big Paolo here' — he tapped the photo again — 'got his ham-and-cheese *panino* and his *caffé corretto* half an hour before that. We described the order to old Crossetti, and old Crossetti promptly described the buyer to us. There'd been only two orders like that so far — five fifteen is a little early for *panini* — and the other person was an old lady with a goiter — Crossetti has a keen eye for his customers. And when we showed him the photographs I just showed you, he picked out Big Paolo without hesitation.'

'Big Paolo. You even know his name.'

'Paolo Tossignano. Also known as Dumb Paolo, but not to his face. Another thug-for-rent from Milan. As I thought,' he reminded Gideon.

'Tullio, you don't waste any time, do you?' Gideon shook his head in genuine admiration. 'Two hours after he came out of the ground, you had Domenico identified. And now you figure out who this guy is almost as fast — without any eyewitnesses. No wonder you got to be a colonel.'

Caravale's pouty, pock-marked face gleamed with pleasure. 'You haven't heard the most interesting part. We didn't just happen to have Paolo's picture handy, you know. Would you like to know why we had it?'

'That would be nice,' Gideon said.

'Because,' Caravale said, enjoying himself, 'he'd just been identified as taking part in another recent crime. You see, there was one reliable witness to Achille's kidnapping — a grocer, Muccio. He got a good look at the one kidnapper without a mask, and a few days ago he was able to identify him as — '

'Dumb Paolo.'

'Correct, the very same.'

'But that would mean . . . that would mean . . . ' Maybe he was groggy. He was having a hard time sorting out the implications. 'What would it mean?'

'It would mean,' Caravale said, 'that there just might be something to this theory of interconnected whatever-it-is after all.'

'Monkey business,' Gideon said.

'Whatever. But the one thing we can say for sure is that Big, Dumb Paolo Tossignano not only tried to twist your head off, but was also one of Achille's kidnappers.'

'So,' said Gideon, thinking out loud to clarify his thoughts, 'that leaves us with the de Grazias again. We know that they were the only ones who knew where the bones were and that I was working on them, so it had to be one of them that sicced him on me. And unless he got himself hired to do the kidnapping by somebody completely different, somebody unconnected to the first person — which would put a hell of a strain on the interconnected monkey business theory — it must have been the same person — a de Grazia — who hired him for both things. Is that the idea?'

'That is the idea.'

Gideon shook his head. 'Whew. So one of them is hooked up in both Domenico's murder and Achille's kidnapping?'

'It looks that way.'

'But it seems so . . . I don't know, I guess I can imagine one of them murdering the old man for his money or something, but the idea that one of his own family had Achille kidnapped? That's too . . . too . . . '

'It might be too — too,' Caravale said a little impatiently, 'but I can tell you on good authority that it happens. Now would you like to hear something really interesting?'

'You mean it gets more interesting? I don't know if I can stand it.'

'Remember Luzzatto?'

'The doctor — the one who was going on about what Domenico had on his mind before he was killed. Have you talked to him?'

'He's dead.'

'Good God, that can't be. He was just — '

'I know, I know. He was alive yesterday, how can he be dead today? Well, so were you, almost. That's the way it works. First you're alive, then you're dead. He went off the road on his Vespa, going up to where he lives in Gignese.'

'Luzzatto drove a motorcycle? The guy must have been eighty.'

'In America that might be strange. Here, a lot of old people do it. A Vespa is not exactly a Harley, you know.'

'And you think it was — you don't think it was an accident?'

'The timing's a little suspicious, wouldn't you say? What was that theory again? I'm starting to really like it.'

'I don't know, Tullio. An eighty-year-old man riding a motorcycle on a mountain road, you have to expect — '

'An eighty-year-old man who's been driving a Vespa since before either of us was born, and he's never been killed before. He certainly picked an inconvenient time for it. Inconvenient for us, quite convenient, I'd say, for someone else who had something he didn't want to come out.'

'Coincidence?' Gideon offered weakly.

Caravale snorted. 'God doesn't like coincidences like that.'

That was pretty much what Gideon thought too. 'Tullio, if he was really murdered, and it was because of what he said at the *consiglio* yesterday, that has to mean the person who killed him was also somebody who was there. One of the de Grazias — again. Or am I not seeing this clearly?'

'You're seeing it the same way I am.' He suddenly banged his desk with the side of a hammy fist. 'I should have interviewed him right away. I never should have put it off.'

Gideon shook his head. 'I don't see how you can fault yourself for that. There was no way of knowing what was going to happen to him. We were talking about a crime from ten years back. Who could guess somebody else was going to be killed?'

'All the same . . . ' He leaned back in his chair and stretched. 'Listen, my friend, it's almost dinnertime. What would you say to a glass of wine and some antipasti, and we can talk this through a little more? I have a few more ideas I want to try out on you.'

'No, sir!' Gideon said firmly. 'This is your case, not mine. I've done my job, I'm out of it. My head hurts. I'm going back to bed.'

Caravale shrugged good-naturedly. 'As you like. I'll give you a lift.'

★   ★   ★

The following day, Monday, was the final day of the Pedal and Paddle Adventure. At 7:30 A.M. the bus for which the ever-efficient Phil had arranged arrived at Lake Orta to pick up the members, most of whom were showing serious signs of having been cooped up too long with the same small group of people, and to take them to Milan's Malpensa Airport. Gideon, who had intended to go along to help out, overslept — something unusual for him — and went down to the breakfast room with mixed feelings of relief (Paula Ardlee-Arbogast no longer clouded his horizon) and guilt (had he purposely, if subconsciously, overslept to avoid her?). Liberal helpings of ham, brioche,

281

and soft Bel Paese cheese from the buffet table took the edge off his guilt, however, and the usual enormous serving of caffè latte, with the coffee and the hot milk brought to the table in separate steaming pitchers, left him feeling quite fine. The fact that he would soon have Julie back to himself undoubtedly had a lot to do with it too.

After a walk around the town — the lakefront promenade didn't appeal to him this morning — and a stop to pick up some fruit at the GS *supermercato* on Via Roma, he settled down to spend the day at his notebook computer, happily catching up on e-mail and munching green grapes.

Phil and Julie, both looking frazzled, showed up at 3 P.M. Phil went up to his room to nap ('Call me when it's time for dinner'), and Julie announced that she was in extreme need of three things: a truly scorching shower with water that would stay hot for more than three minutes at a time; a chance to buy some new non-camping-style clothing, preferably involving a skirt, and shoes that didn't take laces; and a decent meal in an actual restaurant that served things on nondisposable plates. In that order.

Gideon returned contentedly to his computer, having only briefly considered offering his assistance, if needed, in the shower. She had been pretty explicit in her priorities, and right now it was more than enough just to have her around again.

At five thirty, with Julie looking splendidly dewy and fresh in a crisp, new, just-above-the-knee sleeveless dress and new sling-back, open-toed, leather-weave sandals, they met Phil in the lobby of the Primavera.

'Where to?' Phil said. 'There's a great pizza place right around the corner — What?' He had caught Julie's grimace.

She looked from Phil to Gideon and put on her wistful face, the one with the pouty lips and the puppy eyes. 'Could we eat someplace — no offense, Phil, I enjoyed all those stews and pizzas but do you suppose we could eat someplace really nice? You know, with actual courses?'

'Oh, jeez,' muttered Phil.

'Having thoroughly researched the matter,' Gideon said, 'I know just the place. You'll love it.' He turned to Phil. 'But you'll need to get some long pants, buddy.'

Phil glowered at him. 'You're kidding me.'

'There's a nice men's shop up the block at Via Roma,' Julie told him.

'And you probably ought to wear a shirt with a collar,' Gideon said. 'I can lend you a shirt with a collar.'

Phil looked wildly around the lobby, as if for help, found none, and gave in, letting his shoulders sag in utter dejection. 'What I don't do for my friends.'

18

During his morning walk Gideon really had researched the town's restaurants, and it was to the Grand Hotel des Iles Borromées that he brought them. The graceful, wedding-cakey Belle Epoque pile had been open for business since 1863, with a well-publicized celebrity guest list that had included the usual European royalty, plus Mussolini, the Rothschilds, Clark Gable, and ambulance driver Ernest Hemingway, who had recuperated there from his wounds in the First World War, and had later used it in *A Farewell to Arms* as the peaceful retreat where Frederick Henry lies low, planning his escape to Switzerland. Nowadays the celebrity clientele was mostly rock bands with names that Gideon couldn't keep straight and frequently couldn't believe. They had before-dinner drinks on softly padded Empire-style chairs in a gleaming lobby with gilded wall and ceiling sculptures, huge chandeliers, and terrazzo floors ornamented with Oriental carpets. Naked marble infants — *putti* — stood on one chubby foot atop pedestals, holding multibranched bronze candelabra. The drinks were carried from a teal blue bar by a tuxedoed waiter who wore rubber-soled shoes and spoke in whispers.

'It's wonderful,' Julie sighed as her Cinzano was set down on a low marble table. 'Just what I had in mind.' She rubbed her bare arms. 'I feel so *clean*.'

As expected, Phil didn't agree. 'I think I remember this place. My grandfather used to take us here for lunch sometimes, in the days when he still went off the island sometimes. I always felt like I didn't belong.' He held up the glass of Beck's beer he'd ordered and shook his head. 'Seven bucks for a beer, and you don't even get the bottle. Sorry, folks, but this place is not going to make it in the *On the Cheap* guide.'

'I'm sure they'll be desolated,' Julie said. 'Didn't some superstar chef kill himself a few years ago when his restaurant didn't get into *On the Cheap?*'

'No, that was Michelin,' Phil said seriously. When it came to *On the Cheap*, his sense of humor was rarely in evidence.

They paused to watch half a dozen slim, attractive, trendily dressed people in their twenties and thirties come out of an elevator and sit down at the far end of the lobby, chattering and laughing like movie extras who'd been told to look rich and happy. 'Look at them. So confident, so . . . entitled.

They act like they think they deserve to stay in places like this, like they have it coming to them — '

'Strange talk coming from a bona fide representative of the gentry,' Gideon said. 'You sound like your buddy, Dante Galasso.'

'Representative of the gentry, where do you get that from? Bite your tongue, man.'

'You are, though, Phil. You're a member in good standing of the de Grazia clan. I've seen you at their *consiglio* with my own eyes. You might as well face it.'

'Might as well own up to it,' Julie said. 'No point in denying it. What's true is true.'

'I,' said Phil, squaring his shoulders, 'am an Ungaretti and damn well proud of it. As far as I'm concerned, you can take that whole bunch of patronizing, condescending, self-satisfied . . . well, except for my grandfather . . . you can take them and . . . hell . . . ' He subsided, muttering, into his Beck's.

'If you feel that way about it,' Julie said, 'why are you staying on with them at the island for our last few days? Why not keep your room at the Primavera?'

'Yeah, well.' He wiped foam from his upper lip with the back of his forefinger. 'My grandfather, you know . . . if I didn't spend a couple of nights there, Cosimo'd really be hurt.'

'Uh-huh, I see,' Gideon said, letting a moment go by while he took a flinty, freezing sip of his martini and set down the stemmed glass. He'd ordered it straight up instead of on the rocks for once because it seemed like the right drink for the Grand Hotel. 'Oh, by the way . . . will your cousin Lea still be there? Just wondering.'

'Well, what the hell — '

'Inquiring minds wish to know,' said Julie.

'Jesus,' Phil said, looking around the room with a sigh. 'What do you say we pick on someone else for a while now, or is that too much to ask?'

'Phil,' Julie said, 'seriously — are you sure it's such a good idea to be there? I mean, one of them could be a murderer, a kidnapper . . . '

She looked at Gideon, who had told them earlier about the extraordinary string of events in the forty-eight hours or so since he'd last seen them: the abortive theft of the bones, the attack on him, the identification of Big Paolo (both as a kidnapper of Achille and as Gideon's assailant), and the death of Dr Luzzatto.

'One of them almost certainly is a murderer and a kidnapper,' Gideon said. 'Big Paolo ties Achille's kidnapping and Domenico's death together, and the de Grazias are the only ones who knew about finding Domenico's bones. And they're sure as hell the only ones who heard Luzzatto say he knew what was bothering Domenico. Counting Achille's driver, that's three murders we're talking about. That's some family you have there.'

'Shee,' said Phil.

'Oh, and you're a suspect too. Caravale's going to be talking to you. I thought you'd want to know.'

'I'm a suspect?'

'Because you were there with them when the news came about Domenico. And you heard what Luzzatto said too. I tried to tell Caravale that you probably weren't guilty, but of course I couldn't say for sure.'

Phil grumbled something and swilled the last two inches of his beer. 'Boy, I'm sure glad I came out with you guys. This is turning into a swell evening.'

The waiter glided over, whispered that their table was ready, and pointed the way down an arched corridor lined on either side with gilded mirrors that alternated with nineteenth-century paintings.

'Who has any appetite anymore?' Phil grumbled.

But once they'd taken their seats in the quiet, softly lit dining room, he found his appetite again, and all three of them ordered the fixed-price, multicourse menu of the day, choosing to see what the chef came up with.

'For sixty-five bucks this better be good,' Phil said.

It was. They worked steadily through the antipasto, the seafood crêpes, and the port-laced consommé, and started on the main course of poached Lake Maggiore whitefish stuffed with prawns and olives before the talk veered away from the food.

'I'm telling you, I just can't believe it,' Phil said, putting down his fork. 'One of those people murdered my uncle Domenico? It's been going round and round in my mind. I mean, yeah, they had some grudges, like any family — you saw the way they are, Gideon — but kill him? I don't think so.'

'I wouldn't quite say like any family,' Gideon said. 'What do you mean, 'grudges'?'

'Well, like . . . you were talking about Dante before.' He paused. 'Dante's married to Francesca,' he explained to Julie. 'Francesca is — '

'Vincenzo's sister,' Julie said. 'I know. Gideon explained your family tree to me.'

'As far as I can figure it out,' Gideon said.

'OK, well, the thing is, Domenico couldn't stomach Dante. You have to understand, at the time Dante Galasso was this wild-eyed radical professor. You name it, he was for it: armed revolt, aristocrats to the wall, the elimination of private property and differential incomes, the whole schmear. It was really hard on Domenico, because Francesca'd always been his favorite, even more than Vincenzo. Everybody knew it. You know, firstborn and all that.'

He paused to extract a stray bit of crayfish shell from his teeth.

'Francesca was nuts about Dante — I know, it's hard to believe now, but she was — but Domenico put his foot down and told her he wouldn't have the guy as a son-in-law. He'd disown her if she married him. So she did and he did. But then she got on his good side again, even though he wouldn't let Dante in the house. Wouldn't even allow her to say his name when she came over. Seriously. She was welcome, but Dante had to stay home in this dinky apartment they had in Modena.' Another longer, more meditative pause as he chewed.

'And?' prompted Julie.

'And then Domenico dies, and, like, two months later they move in. Free room and board for the rest of their lives, and Francesca has a whole household staff to boss around. But Jesus, be serious, that's no motive for murder . . . '

The three of them looked at each other.

' . . . is it?' Phil finished weakly. And then: 'Yeah, I guess maybe, in a cop's mind, it would be.'

'No, in a cop's mind, it would be two motives,' Gideon said. 'One for Dante, one for Francesca. You need to tell Caravale about this, Phil.'

'But won't he just think I'm trying to cast doubt on others to disguise my own dastardly motives?'

'Seriously. You need to tell him. And you said 'grudges'. Is there something else?'

Phil shook his head. 'Aw, this is ridiculous. I mean — '

Julie put her hand on his arm. 'Phil, it's not ridiculous. We're not playing some kind of gossip game. One of those people *is* a murderer. If there's something else you know — '

'Well, there's Basilio — I can't believe I'm saying this — but I guess if you're going out of your way to dig up stuff, you could say Basilio had a reason to kill him too.'

Basilio Barbero, it seemed, had gotten himself into a mess not long after a payroll supervision position had been found for him at Aurora Costruzioni. Whether it involved embezzlement or incompetence had never been firmly established (although Phil,

292

knowing Basilio, leaned toward the latter), but it was common knowledge that the angry Domenico was thinking of firing him, expelling him from the nest at Isola de Grazia, and possibly even prosecuting him.

And then — as with Dante's case — Domenico had conveniently died, and the situation had blown over. Vincenzo, the new man in charge, had kept him on, and even made him the chairman of the morale committee.

'I guess you'd have to call that a motive, wouldn't you?' Phil said disconsolately.

'Two motives again,' Julie said. 'Don't forget his wife. Bella.'

'Actually, Bella makes more sense. I can't see Basilio killing anybody.'

'Either way, you have to tell Caravale about it,' Gideon said. 'Anything else?'

'You want more motives yet?' Phil, never a big eater, pushed away his half-finished plate and thought about it. 'That's it, I'm afraid. Nobody else would have any reason to do away with Domenico. Not that I know about, anyway.'

'Sure, you do,' Gideon said. 'Vincenzo.'

'Vincenzo? What are you talking about? All right, the guy's an asshole — sorry, Julie — but why would he kill his own — oh. The inheritance, you mean.'

'Yes, the inheritance. When Domenico died, Vincenzo became *padrone* — of the Isola de Grazia, of the company, of everything. And I assume the money went to him too. Right?'

Phil shrugged. 'As far as I know, sure.'

'A lot of people have been killed for a lot less, Phil. Even by their own sons. Or maybe it was because he didn't want to wait any longer to get control of the company.'

He offered around the bottle of wine they'd ordered, a straw-colored, fruity Lugana from Lake Garda. Phil, who wasn't much of a drinker either, covered his glass with his hand. Julie held hers up.

'Damn, Gideon,' Phil said, shaking his head, 'I never knew you had such a nasty mind.'

'It's the first axiom of the forensic scientist,' Julie said. 'When in doubt, think dirty.' She sipped some of the newly poured wine. 'I even have a motive for your grandfather, if you're interested.'

'For *Nonno* Cosimo? That sweet old man? You gotta be kidding me.'

'Now, I'm not saying I believe this. I'm just trying to imagine what Caravale's probably thinking.'

'Which is?'

'Which is that, on some level, Cosimo must

have hated him — well, resented him anyway — because it was Domenico who got everything, who became the *padrone*. He was even a count. And all because he was born a few years earlier. Cosimo, as the kid brother, got nothing at all. Or don't I understand the way that works?'

'No, that's the way it works, all right, but if what you're saying is true, which I don't buy for a minute, why didn't he kill him years ago, before Vincenzo was born, so he would've inherited? What good does it do to wait till they're both in their seventies?'

Julie dabbed at her lips with her napkin. 'Mm, yes, that could be a sticking point.'

'Not necessarily,' Gideon said. 'It could have been from emotions that finally got out of hand from playing second fiddle his whole life. From what you told me, Cosimo lived his entire life, first in his brother's house, and then in his nephew's house. Never even had his own home. That could build a lot of resentment. Who knows what might have kicked it off?'

Phil leaned back in his chair and regarded them both. 'Do you people really believe what you're saying, or are you just playing with my mind?'

'We're just playing with your mind,' said Gideon. 'But you can bet Caravale will have it on his list of possibilities. He'd be crazy not to.'

'OK, as long as we're covering all the bases, what about Lea?' Phil asked, bristling. 'Anybody got any reasons for her to bump off Domenico?'

'Not me,' said Julie.

'Not me,' said Gideon.

'Huh. OK, then. All right, then.'

They had finished the vegetable course of stewed fennel, begun on their salads, and ordered their espressos before Phil picked up the conversation again.

'And something else. You said whoever killed Domenico was probably behind Achille's kidnapping too. Well, how the hell do you figure that? What would be the motive there?'

'How about five million euros?' Gideon said.

'What do any of them need money for? How could they spend it without everybody else noticing? Even if they moved off the island, it'd be obvious.'

'I don't have any answers for that, Phil.'

'Well, all right then,' Phil said. 'Huh.' He continued picking at his salad, his head down. 'Listen, Gideon, I've been meaning to ask you something. About Lea. I'm kind of . . . well, interested in her.'

'Really?' said Gideon.

'Really?' said Julie.

'But I'm worried about . . . well, she's my cousin. I mean . . . you know, should I . . . well, what are the genetic implications? I'm not too good at that stuff.'

Gideon drank the last of his wine and set the glass down. 'Let's work it out. Let me make sure I have it straight. Lea is the daughter of Bella and Basilio, correct?'

'Correct.'

'And Bella is Vincenzo's . . . what?'

'Half-sister, I think.'

'No, describe the relationship. Exactly how is she related?'

'Bella? She's the daughter of Domenico's wife from her first marriage. Vincenzo's half-sister, right?'

'So they have the same mother? That's their relationship?'

'Uh — no, actually. It was Domenico's second marriage too. They were both widowed. Vincenzo was his first wife's kid. Stefania, I think her name was. I don't really remember her. Bella's mother's name was Clara. Nice lady.'

'OK, then Bella is Vincenzo's stepsister, not his half-sister.'

'There's a difference?'

'A big difference. As far as you're concerned, a huge difference. You want to know how close your relationship is to Lea, and whether there'd be any danger if the two of you had children together, right?'

Phil blushed, literally to the roots of his hair. 'Well, I wouldn't put it that way . . . I'm just exploring . . . I mean, we're not even close to thinking about . . . we don't even . . . well, yes.'

'And the answer,' said Gideon, 'is that there's no genetic problem at all. She's not related to Vincenzo, and you're not related to her.'

Phil was amazed. 'You're right, of course! I guess I never thought it through.' He frowned. 'But she's always been my cousin. Everybody thinks of us as cousins.'

'Among the Arunta, maybe, but not here. Look, you can call her whatever you want to call her, but you don't have any blood in common. None.' Gideon reached for his pen. 'It's not that hard. Here, I'll draw it out for you.'

'No, that's OK.' He grinned stupidly at them. 'Not related. Son of a gun.'

'Not yet,' Julie said with a smile.

19

At the Primavera, there was a message waiting from Caravale. 'Please call.' The message listed his cell phone number. Gideon made the call from their room while Julie settled down with a *Time* magazine she'd bought earlier that day. 'I'll be damned,' he said softly as he hung up five minutes later.

'What's up?' Julie asked distantly, not quite looking up from the magazine on her lap. 'Anything new?'

'Not on the cases, no. But . . . well, they've found Phil's father.'

It took a couple of beats, but that got her attention. 'They found Phil's father?' she exclaimed, flipping the magazine shut. Then she knit her brows. 'Wait a minute, what does that mean, they found Phil's father?'

'Caravale has a couple of people poking around up in Gignese; that's a few miles from here, the village that Dr Luzzatto lived in — '

'The one that got killed in the motorcycle accident.'

'Right. And they were going through his records and talking to people, looking for any kind of lead, and the name 'Franco Ungaretti' came up as a recent patient of Luzzatto's, and since they'd been out at the Isola de Grazia doing interviews, they knew who Phil was, and they asked this Franco if he was related to those Ungarettis, and he is.' Gideon came and sat on an ottoman beside her, his elbows on his thighs. 'He's Phil's father.' He tapped a notepad on his knee. 'I have his address and phone number.'

'That's fascinating. What's he like, do you know? Does he want to see his son?'

'I have no idea if he wants to see Phil, but the guy who talked to him wasn't too impressed. He's a familiar figure with the local police up there — scuffles, public drunkenness, bar fights, that kind of thing. In and out of jail, but never for anything terribly serious. The reason he'd been to Luzzatto was to get a cut cheek patched up. Somebody'd taken a chunk out of it with a broken wine bottle.'

'Ick,' she said.

'He lives with a woman — Caravale thinks she's his common-law wife — who everybody says fried her brains with drugs years ago. Still hires out to do housework when she can find somebody who doesn't know her reputation, which isn't too often.'

'Whew, not exactly Ozzie and Harriet. What does his father do? Does he have a job?'

'He's a part-time night watchman at the Umbrella Museum up there.'

'At the what?'

'Il Museo dell'Ombrello e del Parasole. Caravale says it's Gignese's number-one tourist attraction. Well, its only tourist attraction.'

She couldn't help laughing. 'An umbrella museum. Only in Italy. OK, go ahead, I'm all ears.'

'There isn't any more. That's it.'

'About his father, I mean.'

'That's all.'

She shook her head, perplexed. 'That's all extremely interesting, but why is Caravale calling you about it?'

'He didn't know what to do with the information. I mean, he talked to Phil the other day, and he knows the way he feels about his father — '

'Not too warmly. Let's see,' she said, ticking off the items on her fingers, 'there was "creep", "lousy", "no good" . . . '

'Exactly. So he wasn't sure whether he even ought to mention it to him, and he figured that since I was an old friend, he'd leave it up to me.'

'And will you? Mention it to him?'

'What do you think? Should I? I don't want to upset the guy for no reason, but — '

'I think he has a right to know. He can decide for himself if he wants to see him. It's his father, Gideon. You can't keep something like that to yourself.'

He nodded. 'I guess that's what I think too,' he said, but without much certainty. 'I'll call him now.'

★ ★ ★

Phil was adamant about wanting nothing to do with Franco Ungaretti. 'That sonofabitch? He abandoned us,' he yelled bitterly into the phone. 'He never came to see us again, he never wrote, he never told us where he was. And she really loved him, you know? But he just took off, 'See ya around sometime'. I don't have a single happy memory of him, not one. He didn't give a damn about me, why would I give a damn about him? Screw him.'

They had been happy to let it go at that, but the next morning he showed up in the Primavera's breakfast room as they were finishing their coffee and plopped down on a chair at their table.

'OK, you win,' he said, 'I'll go and talk to him. But only on one condition.'

'What do you mean, we win?' Julie asked. 'I don't recall that we were pressing you.'

'No, but if I act as if I've gotten pushed into it, then that lets me not admit to myself that I'm kind of curious to see him. See? It's my technique for dealing with cognitive dissonance. Does that make any sense?'

'With you, it does,' Gideon said. 'So what's the condition?'

The waiter, seeing Phil, brought another caffé latte setup: pitchers of milk and coffee, and a giant cup.

Phil poured the milk and coffee in at the same time, Italian style. 'The condition is,' he said to Gideon, 'you gotta come with me.'

'Me?' a surprised Gideon exclaimed. 'No, thanks, leave me out of this. What do I have to do with it?'

'Nothing, I just . . . ' His skinny shoulders peaked up toward his ears. 'I don't know, I just feel like I need some moral support. This is kind of a weird thing for me, you know?'

'Phil, I'd like to help out, but sitting in on something as . . . as personal as that . . . I'd feel . . . well . . . '

'Oh, do it,' Julie told him. 'I'd do it in a flash if I knew enough Italian to be any help.'

'Thank you, Julie,' Phil said warmly. 'You don't know how good it makes me feel to know that I have one real friend anyway, someone to stick by me when I need support. But never mind, I guess I can get along without seeing my poor, old, long-estranged old father, who I haven't set eyes on in — '

'OK, OK,' Gideon said. 'I'll go with you. But I'm not getting involved. I'm just there for — '

'Moral support, right. I really appreciate this, Gideon.'

'You owe me, pal. I hate this stuff. Well, you better call him and set something up then. We only have a couple of days before we leave.'

'I already did, last night. I used the number you gave me. Guess what, it's a bar. He doesn't have a telephone, but one of the waiters knows him and gives him messages.'

'You didn't actually talk to him?' Julie asked.

'Nope, left a message. Told him I'd be there, in the bar, at ten o'clock this morning. He could come, or he could not come, it's up to him. If he shows up, fine. If he's not interested enough to see me' — he shrugged — 'then at least I know he hasn't changed, he's the same useless crud he always was.' He glanced at his watch. 'It's about a twenty-five-minute drive from here, so either way we should be there and back before noon. I don't intend to make this very long.'

Gideon folded his arms and leaned back in his chair, tipping it onto its rear legs. 'So without even talking to us, you just assumed

I'd give in. You just assumed that, whatever plans we might have, we'd change them to suit you. You just assumed Julie would be glad to entertain herself for two hours so I could squander my valuable time propping you up so you'd have the nerve to face your poor, old, long-estranged old father.'

Phil grinned amiably at them. 'Yup.'

★　★　★

Gignese was one of a scattering of out-of-the-way villages along a twisty, switch-back road up the slopes of Mount Mottarone. At an elevation of over a thousand feet, it commanded a spectacular view over Stresa, the Borromean Islands, and the vast blue expanse of Lake Maggiore, but Gignese itself was a distinctly modest, working-class hamlet with a paper-thin tourist veneer (two small family hotels) optimistically based on the drawing power of the Umbrella Museum. Indeed, the museum, a surprisingly large, good-looking structure of brick and concrete standing by itself at the entrance to the town, was the one modern building they saw. The rest of the village consisted of a one-block commercial center — a gas station, a church, the two hotels, a couple of bars, a grocery store — surrounded by a few concentric rings of aging houses and apartment buildings in various shades of yellow-brown, mostly running from mustard to ochre.

All in all, a depressing place after Stresa's perfect, postcard prettiness, and Phil looked as if he was having second thoughts about getting out of the car when they pulled up across the street from the Bar Ricci.

'Up to you,' Gideon said. He had left the engine running. 'If you want to forget about it, no problem. Don't do anything on my account.' He was still squeamish about the idea of horning in on what was sure to be an emotion-fraught encounter between father and son.

'I know, I know.' Phil was raking the place with his eyes. The Bar Ricci was the kind of no-frills establishment found in every village in Italy, no matter how small; a bar-café, actually, with a newspaper rack and a single metal table and chairs outside on a tiny terrace. Inside they could see eight or nine men — no women — sitting in groups of two or three, reading newspapers or chatting over coffee or brandy. The door was open and it wasn't yet 10 A.M., but already the room was blue with cigarette smoke.

'Is he in there?' Gideon asked.

'Who knows? All I remember are some pictures of him in a scrapbook, mostly from

306

before, when he was a skier.'

Gideon looked at him. 'He was a skier?'

'Are you kidding? He was the best downhiller in Italy, or at least the wildest. The Avalanche, they called him. It's a long story. I'll tell you about it sometime.' He jerked his head. 'Jeez, Gideon, I wish you hadn't told me they found him.'

'Well, hell, Phil — '

'I know. You did the right thing, it's only that — ' He started. 'Oh, Jesus, there he is, that's him. Sonofabitch, that's my father!'

He was staring at a lean, sinewy man in his sixties, with lank, thinning, iron-gray hair, sitting at the lone outside table. Beside him was a hunched-over woman of about the same age, wrapped in a shawl despite the mild weather, and wearing a shabby, ink-black wig that wasn't quite straight. They were facing slightly away from each other, not speaking. The man's eyes were constantly on the move. The woman seemed to be talking to herself. There was nothing on the table in front of them.

'Are you sure?' Gideon asked. 'You haven't seen him since you were a little kid.'

'It's him,' Phil repeated. 'I remember. See the way he holds his head on the side, like he's right on the verge of getting an idea? That's from when he broke his neck or something. It ended his career. See the way his fists are kind of curled all the time, almost clenched? See the way he's, like, always looking around and around, waiting for someone to insult him or challenge him to a duel, or something? See how — '

'Phil, I thought you didn't remember him. I thought all you had were some old pictures in a scrapbook.'

'Yeah, well, I guess I was wrong, because a lot of things are coming back. Man,' he said wonderingly, 'I've got neurons that haven't fired in forty years popping away like mad. All kinds of memories and associations. He looks so *small* to me — I mean, I remember him as this big strong guy, but I guess that's because I was so little myself. I remember . . . who's he sitting with? You think that's his wife? His so-called wife?'

'I suppose so.'

'Yeah. Jesus, look at her. She looks like her brains are cooked, all right.' He clasped his hands on his head and pressed down, as if he were trying to keep the top from coming off. 'Oh, God, what am I doing here?'

'Phil, if you don't want to — '

'No, no, I want to. You know me, I like to whine. But he wasn't supposed to bring anybody, so what's that all about?'

'You weren't supposed to bring anybody either.'

'Yeah, that's true. OK, what the hell.' He took a breath, reached for the door handle, and looked at Gideon. 'Ready?'

'Let's go,' Gideon said as they got out. 'And Phil . . . good luck, pal.'

'Good luck what?'

Gideon looked at him over the roof of the car, not sure what he'd meant. 'Whatever you want.'

20

Franco Ungaretti had no trouble identifying Phil either. 'Fili, yes?' he said in Italian as they neared the table. 'When did you get so old?' He seemed determinedly sullen, as if making sure that they knew he'd come against his better judgment. He continued to scrutinize Phil as they sat down. 'Look at that gray in his hair, do you see that?' he said to the woman. 'My son looks older than me, isn't that something?'

The woman, absorbed in counting something off on her fingers, quirked up the corners of her mouth in a mechanical smile.

'You don't look so terrific yourself, Franco,' Phil said, which was true enough. The older man looked like a broken-down old featherweight who'd been in the ring a few times too often. His nose had been broken more than once, one ear had been partially cauliflowered, and there was healed scar tissue above his eyes. An uglier scar on his cheek, spongy and shiny and pink, looked as if it had been left by a claw hammer, but was probably the one from the broken bottle. He had poorly fitting upper and lower plates that clacked as he spoke, and made the tendons of his neck jump as he tried to keep them from shifting.

'I don't . . . is it true there are no snails in Ireland?' said the woman, momentarily surfacing, before going back to her fingers without waiting for an answer. The joints, Gideon saw, were puffy with arthritis and had to be painful.

Franco stabbed a finger at Phil. 'You,' he said sharply, 'can call me 'Father'.'

'Oh, really? I figure I can call you whatever I want,' Phil shot back, and the two of them glowered at each other.

'Well, this has certainly started off well,' Gideon murmured in English to Phil; and aloud in Italian: 'Why don't I get us some coffee? Anyone?'

'I can buy my own coffee,' Franco said, seeming to notice Gideon for the first time. 'Who are you supposed to be, anyway? What do you want here?'

Gideon, sitting across from him, leaned back and away from an almost-visible gust of brandy and stale tobacco fumes.

'He's a friend of mine, Gideon Oliver. I asked him to come. I wanted to give him the chance to meet my esteemed and beloved father,' Phil said with heavy-handed sarcasm. 'So who's your lady friend?'

311

'This is Mrs Ungaretti.' Franco clamped his teeth together, *clack*, and fixed Phil with a you-got-a-problem-with-that? stare.

'I don't like being touched,' the woman murmured to no one in particular. 'I never have. I don't know why that should be, unless it's a family trait.' No one paid any attention to her.

Phil started to answer his father, but decided to let it pass. He didn't have to say it: As far as he was concerned, there was only one Mrs Ungaretti, and it wasn't this addled lady.

'As long as you're a friend of the family,' Franco said to Gideon, 'I'll have a brandy, a cognac. Make it a double.'

'Yes, I will too,' the woman said vaguely. 'Make it a double.'

'She'll have an espresso,' Franco said.

'Espresso, yes, that's what I meant,' she said docilely. 'With a twist of lemon, if such a thing is possible.'

'Phil?' Gideon asked.

But Phil didn't hear him. Father and son were engaged in locking glares like a couple of bellicose ten-year-olds trying to stare each other down.

Gideon was grateful for the chance to escape, even temporarily. Not a man who was at ease with emotional fireworks in any case, he was surprised and disturbed by the way Phil was acting. In all these years, he realized, he had never once seen Phil angry — irritated, grouchy, fractious, yes; plenty of times. But really angry? Meanly sarcastic? Never. This was the first time he'd ever seen this gentle, go-with-the-flow man act rudely to anyone, and that was most unsettling of all. It seemed to go against nature.

He took all the time he could getting the drinks — brandy for Franco, espresso with lemon peel for Mrs Ungaretti, cappuccino for himself — then carried them back out on a tray as slowly as he could get away with doing it. He was pretty sure things were going to get worse before they got better (if they got better, which was looking doubtful), and he was in no hurry to get back.

Indeed, when he returned, they were practically at each other's throats. Phil's face was white, with the muscles in his cheek pulsing, and Franco was half out of his chair, bending over the table, his fingers clutching the edge, shouting hoarsely at him. 'Don't you get so high and mighty with me! I'm not your damned father anyway, and for that, you can take my word for it, I thank God every morning of my life!'

'You're right, you're not my father,' Phil yelled back into his face, 'and I'm not your son. My father was Mark Boyajian. You, you're nothing!' He was trembling across his shoulders and down his arms.

'I'm nothing? *I'm* nothing? Don't make me laugh! *You're* nothing! You're not even your mother's son!' He, too, was deeply agitated. He snatched up the double brandy and tossed it down in two quick gulps with what started as a stage laugh and quickly became a ragged cough. Inside the café, people were nudging each other and faces were turning to take in the show.

'Phil,' Gideon said in English, 'maybe we should just — '

Phil shook him off. 'No, don't you want to hear what he has to say? I mean, how often do you get the chance to hear this kind of bullshit? What's that supposed to mean, I'm not my mother's son?'

'What does it mean?' Franco said wildly. 'You want to know what it means?' He lost his focus, let go of the table, and dropped heavily back into his chair, eyes closed. 'What does it mean,' he sighed.

'I'm waiting,' Phil said.

'Come on, Phil,' Gideon said, putting a hand on his arm, 'the guy's obviously smashed, he's just coming up with things to get you upset. Don't you think we ought to — '

'You really don't know, do you?' Franco muttered. 'They really never told you? In all this time?'

'Know what?' asked Phil.

'Ah,' said Franco. 'Ha, ha.'

'Ah,' said the woman. She reached under the wig, scratched enthusiastically at her scalp with a finger, and readjusted the black mat on her head.

A shiver traveled down Gideon's back. Something bad was coming; you could feel it hovering in the air, waiting for its chance. He was sorry now that he'd told Phil about his father.

'It's Vincenzo, the great Vincenzo, who is your mother's son,' Franco cried. 'Not you. What do you think of that? Isn't that funny? To be not your own mother's son?' He tried a laugh, but his muscles were too rigid to bring it off. He sounded, in fact, a little crazy. His fists, loosely curled on the table until now, were clenched, so that the extensor tendons on the back of each hand stood out like drinking straws.

Phil gawked at him. His mouth opened and closed twice before he could get even a few garbled words out. 'Vinc . . . what . . . ? How can . . . ? I don't . . . I don't . . . ' He threw a perplexed, apprehensive look at Gideon, who was as clueless as he was.

Franco got to his feet again, more unsteadily this time, propping himself on the table with his fists and bathing them in a wash of alcohol and tobacco fumes. 'Now I'm going to tell you a very interesting story,' he said, raking them with his eyes.

At which point Gideon, to his surprise and embarrassment, burst into a brief but noisy snort of close-mouthed laughter, managing to more or less snuff it out after a couple of honks. They stared at him, even the woman. 'I'm sorry,' he said. 'I didn't mean — '

But there was no way he could explain, especially in Italian, that when Franco had leaned over them and peered so intensely at them, an image of the Mad Hatter's Tea Party, the famous old Tenniel illustration, had jumped into his mind with amazing clarity. In his memory, the parallel was almost exact. There was Franco, the Mad Hatter himself, running the show according to rules that nobody understood, with the docile, dopey Dormouse — the woman with her shabby wig, in this case — slipping in and out of awareness beside him. Phil was the March Hare, who, if he wasn't nuts before, seemed well on his way now. That left Gideon as Alice, the observer from outside who didn't quite belong and couldn't quite comprehend what was going on or where it was headed. A

316

perfect fit all around.

Franco's story fit too: a bizarre, jumbled tale of switched babies, bamboozled rich uncles, and confused identities straight out of a Victorian potboiler. Gideon's Italian was just barely up to the job of following him, and even then, only because an increasingly incredulous Phil interrupted after almost every sentence with a befuddled '*Che?*' or '*Como?*' or a helpless, hands-spread '*Non capito.*'

This was the upshot, as near to it as Gideon could make out:

In 1960 or thereabouts, Domenico de Grazia, whose wife was barren, had arranged with Franco and his wife Emma —

'My mother,' Phil had put in hopefully.

'Wait and see,' Franco said.

— had arranged with Franco and his wife Emma that Emma, through a process of artificial insemination, should secretly bear Domenico's child, the object being to provide him with a genetically suitable heir. The process was successfully accomplished and Franco and Emma were secluded here in Gignese for several months, awaiting the baby's birth. Emma wasn't good at being pregnant — sick every morning — and complaining from morning till night, so much so that Franco couldn't take it anymore and went home to Caprera after a while, until the baby was born, leaving Caterina, the live-in housekeeper, to deal with Emma's moods. But finally it was over, and it was the old doctor — Lazzero? Luzzatto? — who delivered it, a baby boy that met Domenico's requirements: a son and heir.

'Vincenzo?' Phil exclaimed dazedly. 'You're talking about Vincenzo?'

'Of course, Vincenzo, what do you think?'

'So Vincenzo and I are brothers — half-brothers? We have the same mother? Wait a minute, we're the same age, how could — are you telling me we're *twins*?'

'Stop interrupting,' Franco said. 'Do you want to know or not?'

'Sorry,' Phil said meekly.

'All right, then.' Franco looked at Gideon and gestured at his empty glass.

This time Gideon wasn't as anxious to leave and managed to signal the barman from where he sat. Franco watched hungrily as his second double brandy was carried out to him and set down, then quickly drank half of it and licked the residue from his lips.

'I can't help wondering what happened to all those towels,' the woman mumbled. 'Where could they have gone to? After so many years. It was so strange.'

318

Franco glanced at her, wiped his mouth with his fingers, and continued.

After the birth, Emma moped about until Franco, with Domenico's assistance, persuaded her to adopt a child of her own, which Domenico 'purchased' for her from a young neighbor girl she'd become friends with, an unmarried teenager, who was unable to care for her newly delivered baby.

Franco looked at Phil, his eyebrows lifted, waiting for him to speak.

Phil cleared his throat. 'And that . . . that baby, that's me? The one that was bought?'

'Yes, yes, that's right,' Franco said meanly, 'the one that was bought, that's you. Five hundred dollars, American, was the price.'

Gideon had his doubts about Franco's reliability and his intentions, but Phil seemed not to. 'So you're really not my father.'

'You're finally catching on?'

'And my — and Emma Ungaretti isn't really my mother.'

Franco nodded.

Phil swallowed. 'Who else knows about this?'

'I'm pretty sure Vincenzo knows. The snotty sister, Francesca, she knows. Oh, and the servant, what was her name — Genoveffa, if she's still alive. She was right here the whole time, snooping around and spying on us.'

'And . . . ' Phil hesitated. 'And Cosimo? Does he know?'

Franco puffed his lips dismissively. 'Of course not. He wouldn't believe it anyway.' He finished the brandy, lost his balance, and flopped back into his chair.

Phil looked as if he didn't know what had hit him. 'So I don't even know who my mother is.' He murmured it in English, with an arid laugh.

'Listen, Phil,' Gideon said, 'you better get some verification on this. This guy . . . '

'Why did you tell me all this, after all these years?' Phil asked, switching back to Italian. 'Why did you bother coming to meet me at all? You're right — I'm nothing to you, you're nothing to me.'

'Why did I come?' He snickered and used his chin to point at the woman. 'Because this one wanted me to, and I'm a nice guy, that's why.'

Phil turned to her. 'Why did you — ' But she was off in cloud-cuckoo-land again, trailing a fingernail around the rim of her cup and tipping her head toward it as if she could make out a tune.

'Why should she care?' he asked Franco.

'Why should she . . . ?' Franco guffawed, a real laugh this time.

'Haven't you been listening to what I've

been telling you? This is your mother, idiot!'
He shook her roughly by the shoulder. 'Gia,
look! It's Filiberto! It's your darling baby
boy!'

She looked foggily up from her cup. Her
eyes filled with tears. 'My boy,' she said.
Then, as an afterthought, she opened her
arms to him.

Phil couldn't have shied back any more
violently if she'd come at him with a knife.
'You're my . . . Who's my father, then?'

She let her arms fall to her sides. 'Your
father?' She looked at Franco as if for
help, but he merely shrugged. He'd lost
interest. He raised his arms and waved at the
men watching from inside the café — a
performer who'd given them a good show.
Some of them waved back with jeers and
mimed applause. As café entertainments in
Gignese went, this one had obviously been a
hit.

'Your father,' she said again, thinking hard.
'I remember him. A very nice boy, so sweet.
Pietro, I think his name was. Yes.' She knitted
her eyebrows, put a nail-chewed finger to
chapped lips, and pondered some more. 'No,
that's not right, Pietro was the one with the
two sisters, remember? Pasquale? No, Pasquale had the warts, ugh. Guglielmo? Mm,
no . . . '

'Can you believe that?' Phil said as Gideon started up the car. 'Can . . . you . . . believe that? I am really ticked off.'

'I'm not surprised,' Gideon said, edging out into the light traffic on Via Margherita. 'That was quite a story. If it's true.'

'You don't think it is? Why would he make up something like that?'

'I'm not saying he made it up. But he didn't strike me as the most reliable informant in the world either. I'd check it out with Vincenzo if I were you.'

'No way. I wouldn't give him the satisfaction.'

'Francesca, then.'

'Francesca,' Phil mused. 'I think I'm beginning to see why she always treated me like dirt — I mean, even more than she treats other people like dirt. I always thought it was because I was the runt of the litter, and even as a kid I was gimpy.'

'Phil, you're not — '

'And besides that, I was just a lousy Ungaretti, not a de Grazia. Now I see it was way worse than that. In her eyes, I'm barely human. No, forget it, I'm not talking to Francesca about it either.'

'Well, then, with the servant — Genoveffa, was it? You can't just take Franco's word for it.' But the truth was that as the time passed, Gideon found himself more and more taking Franco's word for it. Why would he have concocted such a wild story? Was he even capable of inventing it? And what about the woman? That addled, tearstained 'My boy.' Surely that hadn't been an act.

'Genoveffa,' Phil said. 'Yeah, maybe Genoveffa.'

He didn't say it with any conviction, but Gideon didn't press, and for a few minutes Phil stared stonily ahead with his arms folded. Then, as they picked up the winding road down the mountain, he raised his fists and let out a tooth-rattling growl. 'GHAAARGHH! I am really ticked off!'

'Phil, I believe you. Truly.'

'Here's this guy,' Phil railed, 'this so-called father I despised my whole life. I mean I've loathed him for, like, almost forty years now. There were a lot of times I would have strangled him if I could have gotten my hands on him. And now, after all this time, I find out he's not my father after all. I wasted all that hating! It is really annoying.'

'That's what you're mad about?'

'Sure,' Phil said, turning his baseball cap around so the bill was backward. And suddenly he looked reassuringly like the old, familiar Phil again. 'What'd you think I was mad about?'

'Well, I thought maybe the fact that you weren't related to any of the people you thought you were related to.'

'You mean Vincenzo and the rest of them? Nah, that's a relief. That feels great. That never felt right. I should have known.'

'Or — if what he said is true — that you're actually, well — '

'A bastard, right. No longer in name only. And I have a mother who barely knows who I am, let alone who my father was, and who talks like Ozzy Osbourne.' He considered. 'No, that's OK too. That's interesting, actually. Anyway, I know who my real mother was, and she's the same as she always was. As for my father . . . ' He started laughing. ''Pietro? No. Mario? No. Guglielmo? No. Arturo Toscanini? No. Enrico Caruso? No.' I think it gives me an air of mystery, don't you? Makes me even more dashing than I already am.'

'Definitely, no doubt about that.'

'And hey, now Lea's definitely not my cousin, right? How about that?'

'She never was your cousin, Phil.'

'Right, whatever.' He settled back with a sigh.

'So what are you going to do?' Gideon asked after a few minutes passed.

Phil glanced at him. 'What is there to do?'

'Well . . . you can't very well just keep stringing things along the way they were before, can you?'

'Sure I can, why not?'

'I mean, visiting them, acting like one of the family — '

'Sure, why not?'

'Well, why would you want to? I don't think you were ever too crazy about them. Anyway, it'd be a fraud, a sham.'

'So? It always was a sham, what's different now?'

Gideon shrugged. 'I'm just surprised. I assumed — '

'Look, let me give it to you in a nutshell. Vincenzo, Dante, that whole bunch — I couldn't care less if I never saw them again for the rest of my life. But Cosimo — my grandfather, even if he isn't really — it would break his heart. He believes in this good-blood crap, and if he found out that I was just . . . well, it wouldn't be good. After he goes, it'll probably be a different story. But until then, I remain his grandson.'

'Ah,' said Gideon. Now he understood.

As they turned from the highway into Stresa's bustle, Phil started laughing again. 'Mussolini? Mm, no. Rudolph Valentino? Mm, no . . . '

21

'Colonel, you got a minute?'

Caravale, on his way back from the soft drink machine with a Brio, stopped at the door to his office. 'What do you have, Lombardo?'

Lombardo and Rigoli were his financial specialists, and at his instruction they had spent the last few days probing into Vincenzo's situation. This morning they had gone up to Ghiffa to interview the people at Aurora Costruzioni.

'Well, you were right,' Lombardo told him. 'De Grazia didn't pay that ransom by borrowing on his stocks. He didn't have any left to borrow against. Not enough for this, anyway.'

Caravale frowned. 'What do you mean?'

Lombardo, knowing full well that finance was not Caravale's strong point, kept it as simple as he could. 'See, he'd already pledged just about all his holdings, at a fifty percent margin, as collateral to buy more stocks, mostly Internet stuff . . . a chain of Internet bars he was interested in. Well, not only did that not pan out, but the collateralized stock lost almost twenty-five percent of its value, so at a fifty percent margin, that meant his equity was down to a little more than thirty percent . . . are you still with me here?'

'Not only am I not with you, I already have a headache. If you could get to the punch line, I'd appreciate it.'

'The punch line is, not only does he not have stocks to borrow against, but his collateral is damn near the point where his broker is going to be making a margin call any day now.'

'You mean call in the loan? How much is he in for?'

'Three hundred thousand.'

Caravale leaned his back against the wall, thinking. 'Wait, let me get this straight. You're telling me that Vincenzo is three hundred thousand euros in debt, and the axe is about to come down on him if he doesn't come up with it?'

'It's at *least* three hundred thousand,' Lombardo told him. 'Could be more we don't know about. You think he was desperate enough to kidnap his own kid to get the money?'

'Five million euros,' Caravale said. 'That's a lot more than he needed.'

'As far as we *know*. Anyway, if he thought he could get away with it for three hundred thousand, why not make it five million? It's always nice to have a little spare cash on hand.'

Caravale, who had been thinking much the same thing, nodded. 'I *knew* there was something funny going on,' he said half-aloud. He started into his office and beckoned Lombardo to follow him. 'So how *did* he pay the ransom? Come on in, tell me what you found out.'

'I can do better than that,' Lombardo said. 'We brought a couple of the Aurora officers down for formal statements. Aldo's in there with the CFO right now. I think you might want to sit in too.'

'The CFO? Vincenzo's sister, right? Francesca.'

'That's the one.'

Caravale took a swig of the Brio and put the bottle on a table just inside his office. 'Let's go. I don't want to sit in, though. We'll watch through the one-way.'

Once in the darkened observation booth next to the interrogation room, Inspector Lombardo rapped sharply on the wall to let the interrogator, Inspector Aldo Rigoli, know that they were there.

'Now then, Signora Galasso,' Rigoli said in his courteous, hesitant manner, 'these microphones will record our conversation and a typed transcript will be prepared from it.'

Rigoli and Lombardo were two of Caravale's better interviewers, but two very different types. Rigoli was an unassuming, bespectacled man who looked and spoke like an assistant bank teller. Unlike the hulking Lombardo, he didn't frighten people. When it seemed more desirable to put the fear of God into the interviewee, it was Lombardo who took over.

'Afterward, the transcript will be sent to you so that you may — '

'Yes, yes,' Francesca interrupted. 'May we get on with it, please? I'd like to get done as quickly as possible. I assume it's the damned loan you want to hear about again?'

The only makeup she wore was a touch of eyeliner and a vivid slash of dark red, almost black, lipstick on what otherwise would have been a wide but thin-lipped mouth. Her long, squared-off fingernails were painted the same predatory shade. She was in a work outfit: a scarf wrapped tightly around her head like a turban, a high-collared, open-throated white shirt with bloused sleeves, a single strand of black pearls, spike-heeled, open-toed shoes, and trim slacks narrowed at the ankles. The slacks were made of a glossy gray fabric — sharkskin, Caravale thought, but maybe that was because sharkskin seemed right for Francesca Galasso.

It occurred to him that they might have done better to use Lombardo for this.

'If you please, signora,' Rigoli said.

'Very well. It's exactly as I told you before.'

Matter-of-factly, but with a distinct air of condescension, as if it might be difficult for police minds to grasp, she explained. As the company's chief financial officer, she had signed off the previous week on a five-million-euro loan to Eurotecnica Servizi, a Milan subsidiary of Aurora Costruzioni that specialized in preparing historical buildings for restoration. In actuality, however, Eurotecnica Servizi performed only three or four jobs a year, had no permanent staff (other than Vincenzo himself), and existed chiefly as a dummy corporation, a repository in which to bury occasional loans to Vincenzo when one or another of his varied investments needed an infusion of cash.

'In your opinion — ' Rigoli began.

'You want to know if, in my opinion, such an arrangement is legal.' She folded her graceful hands on the table in front of her. 'In a technical sense, possibly not. But when the cash flow problems were repaired, the money would be promptly repaid, so where exactly was the harm? In effect my brother was borrowing from himself, and

330

paying himself back. Who suffered? And the economy, the companies he invested in, obviously, they benefited.'

'And the loans, they were always paid back? There are none outstanding?'

'Yes, absolutely, do you think I would have been a party to it otherwise? You can examine the books for yourself if you wish.'

'We've done that,' Lombardo told Caravale. 'What she says is true. Seven loans to Eurotecnica in the past ten years, all of them paid back in full, with interest, well inside the loan period.'

'And now,' Francesca went on, speaking louder, working her way into a righteous indignation, 'we turn to the same mechanism to rescue my dear nephew from these repulsive bastards. Of course we do, what choice did we have? Time was short, the money had to be raised within a few days. Are you now going to accuse us of doing wrong? Should we have let them kill him? You've seen the boy — how grateful he is to be home, how relieved the entire family is that he is safe. The money will be returned the day the insurance is paid. What would you have had us do? Do you think we did wrong?'

'Personally? No,' said Rigoli.

'Personally, neither do I,' Caravale said, 'if

that's all there is to it.' And a moment afterward, to Lombardo: 'Don't tell anybody I said that.'

'And I would like to make it quite clear for the record,' Francesca said, speaking directly to the microphones rather than to Rigoli, 'that I did this voluntarily, eagerly. I was in no way coerced by my brother. It was I who suggested it. As chief financial officer, it was my responsibility, my duty, to decide, and I decided. I accept full responsibility. I would do it again.'

'I see,' Rigoli said.

'Are we done? I would like to be taken back now.'

'Yes, signora, you may go. However, please keep yourself available for further contact in the event — '

'Thank you.' She was up and striding to the door on her three-inch heels.

At the door she stopped and nodded an ostentatious good-bye to the one-way glass, just to let them know they hadn't put anything over on her.

As she shut the door, Rigoli turned to look straight at them too, dipped his chin, and tugged his lower eyelid down with his forefinger: *Whew, how about that one?*

'Interesting,' Caravale said, turning from the window. 'Now I want — '

'Wait, stick around another minute, Colonel. I think you'll want to hear this too.'

A moment later, a nervous, somewhat tousled Basilio was led in, looking confusedly around him, as if he'd been prematurely roused from hibernation.

'Now then, Signor Barbero,' Rigoli said in his reassuring voice, pointing to the chair that Francesca had just vacated, 'what I'd like you to do is to tell me again what you were telling me just before we came here.'

'About the chauffeur, you mean?'

Caravale looked at Lombardo. 'The chauffeur? What about the chauffeur? What's he talking about?'

Lombardo smiled and put a finger to his lips. 'Patience.'

'That's right, the chauffeur.'

'Should the microphones be closer?' Basilio asked. 'I should probably speak directly into them, because, you see, I've found that my voice is difficult to record clearly. It has something to do with a defect of the soft palate — '

'No, just continue to speak normally to me, as you are. The microphones will do their job.'

'Very well. Enrico. A sad case. What exactly do you want me to say?'

'What you told me before. The facts, that's

333

all. About how he never should have been there . . . all that.'

Caravale frowned. 'What's he talking about? Never should have been there . . . ?'

'Just listen, will you?' Lombardo said. 'For God's sake.'

Caravale muttered something, fumbled in a pocket, and stuck half of an unlit cigar in his mouth.

Basilio, having already told his story several times that day, was unusually concise. Aurora Costruzioni employed two chauffeur-body-guards. On the day of the kidnapping, Enrico Dellochio, the one who had been killed trying to protect Achille, had actually been scheduled to have the day off. His alternate, Casimiro Praga, regularly worked mornings and generally was the one who drove Achille to school. But on this particular day Praga had telephoned half an hour before he was due to arrive, complaining of a severe stomach-ache. The office had called in Dellochio instead, and it was he, to his very great misfortune, who had been driving at the time of the kidnapping.

At the same moment that Rigoli's heavy-lidded eyes flickered in the direction of the one-way glass, Caravale impulsively clenched his fist, inadvertently snapping the half-cigar in two. The pieces fell to the floor.

'An inside job!' he said excitedly. 'Of course! It's all coming together now. Praga is in on it. He's supposed to go along with it. At the last minute he loses his nerve, he backs out. He's replaced by Dellochio, who has no idea what's going to happen. That's why there was all that shooting.'

He smacked his forehead and turned angrily on Lombardo. 'Why didn't we know about this before?'

Lombardo, who had been nodding his agreement as Caravale spoke, was affronted. 'How could we know? Even today, it only came out by accident.'

'Where is this Praga?' Caravale said. 'Do we have him?'

Lombardo pointed through the glass, where Rigoli was just asking the same question.

'And Casimiro Praga, what happened to him?'

'That was the last we saw of him. He never returned, never came back for references, never picked up his pay, never anything.' Basilio shrugged. 'Would you like my opinion? I think he decided to look for a safer occupation back home in Padua. When you think about it, after all, it's only sheer luck that he's alive. By all rights, he should be dead. I saw an extremely interesting television program about the inexorability of Fate — '

'Are we hunting for Praga?' Caravale asked as they stepped away from the window. He patted his pockets irritably. 'Didn't I have a cigar?'

'We have a call in to Padua,' Lombardo said, 'and our own people are working on it too. So what do you think about all this, Colonel? Pretty interesting, eh?'

'Lombardo,' Caravale said, 'did you ever hear of the Theory of Interconnected Monkey Business?'

22

With a few free days tacked on to the end of the Pedal and Paddle Adventure for R and R (Phil had predicted they would need them), the Olivers' plan had been to spend them in Milan and Verona, seeing the sights, while Phil spent most of his time on the island with his ersatz relatives. But on Wednesday, Gideon and Julie were slow getting out of bed — they were making up for lost time, after all — not rising until almost eleven, which made a lengthy day trip impractical. So instead they stayed in Stresa, strolling the paths and gardens of the Lungolago, doing a little shopping — a wallet for Gideon, a handbag for Julie, postcards to send home before leaving (if they actually got around to it for once) — skipping meals and grazing among the cafés instead whenever the mood hit; in short, not doing much of anything beyond relaxing in each other's company. An exceptionally lovely day.

On Thursday morning (up late again, but not quite as late as Tuesday), Julie decided that what she really wanted to do was ride in a boat without having to paddle, so they took the longest ferry ride available, an hour-and-a-half cruise north across the border to Locarno, had an outdoor fondue lunch in Switzerland, and came back, stopping for an hour in Ghiffa, a fellow passenger having assured them that the famous hat museum located there — Italy seemed to be well supplied with oddball museums — was well worth seeing, which it turned out to be. Drinks with Phil at a café-bar on the Lungolago while they watched the sun go down, then dinner on their own at the Grand Hotel des Iles Borromées again, but this time on the back terrace, beside the extravagant garden. They sat long enough over their coffees to see the last of the daylight fade away and to feel the moisture around them as the dew gathered on the camellias. Another highly successful day, they both agreed, although perhaps they were more up to snuff on eighteenth-century hat-making tools than was strictly necessary.

The next day was their last full day in Italy and, as usual, they were making plans for what was left of it over another late breakfast, tossing around and discarding various ideas.

'You want to know what I'd really like to do?' Julie asked over a bowl of anonymous, Wheaties-like cereal she'd gotten from a plastic jar on the buffet table.

'Yes, I do. You'd like to take the day off from being tourists, not have any schedule at all, start getting ready for tomorrow. Check on our airline tickets, do some packing, make sure we have some clean clothes, take care of the postcards, rest up for the trip home, that kind of thing, so we don't wind up all stressed out.'

The spoon stopped halfway to her mouth. 'How in the world did you know that?'

'Because whenever you quit on the breakfast croissants and the cold cuts and go back to eating cereal, I know that means you're ready to go home. Your mental gears have shifted.' He himself was working on his second brioche, split and filled with sliced ham and cheese.

She continued to look at him for a few moments, then shook her head. 'We've been married too long,' she said, returning to her cereal.

'Actually, not having a schedule suits me too. I'd like to go have another look at Domenico's bones.'

'Domenico's bones? Why?'

'I'm starting to wonder if I might have made a mistake with them.'

'A mistake? You mean they're not Domenico's? Caravale's going to love that.'

'Oh, no, they're Domenico's, all right. No question there.'

'What then? The cause of death?'

'No, I don't have any doubts about that either. He was stabbed to death. But I think I might have misinterpreted something.'

She waited for him to go on, but he didn't. 'And you're not going to tell me what it is, right?'

'Well, let me look at them first.'

'Is it something important?'

'Could be, if it's true. Which it almost certainly isn't. But it might be.'

She watched him finish his sandwich and dab pensively at his lips without saying anything more. 'Thank you so much,' she said, 'for that lucid and comprehensive explanation.'

'More later,' he told her, smiling. 'Heck, I'm probably all wet anyway.' He finished the last of his coffee and kissed the back of her hand with a smack. 'See you in a couple of hours.'

＊　＊　＊

Ah, no, he was informed by a sympathetic corporal at *carabinieri* headquarters, unfortunately it would not be possible for him to look at the bones because they'd been sent to the Rome laboratory for further forensic analysis. But a thorough set of photographs had been taken. Would the *dottore* care to see those? Copies could be made for him if he wished.

That might be even better, Gideon said, and a few minutes later he was sitting in an interrogation room with five dozen large, sharp, well-lit color photographs of Domenico de Grazia's remains. He spent half an hour over them, talking to himself all the way, at the end of which time he carried them back to the clerk who'd given them to him.

'I'll take this one, and this one, and this one,' he said. 'This one too.'

They were quickly reproduced and brought back. The *carabinieri* had good equipment; the copies were as crisp as the originals. He slipped them into the manila envelope provided.

'Thanks very much. Oh, and is the colonel here?'

'Ah, but he's not in the office this morning, Signor Oliver,' she said regretfully. 'He can possibly be reached, however, if it's a matter of importance. Would you care to speak with him?'

'No, that's all right,' he said and was almost out the door with his photographs when he turned around and came back. 'Well, yes, on second thought, I guess I would.'

He found Julie back at the Primavera. She had started her to-do list and had pulled the armchair and the ottoman up to the wide-open French windows to work on it, but her eyes were closed and her hands lay comfortably folded over the note pad. The list had gotten as far as a double-underlined 'To Do' at the top of the page, but no further. Soothing sounds of quiet conversations in Italian and German drifted up from the open-air cafés in the street below, and the breezes off the lake were stirring a few unruly strands of black hair at her temples. All told, she looked about as stressed out as a house cat dozing on a sunny rug in front of the living room window.

He smoothed the hair back, then bent to breathe in its clean, familiar fragrance and to kiss her gently on the temple, her hair springy and supple against his mouth. 'What's this?' he murmured in her ear. 'I thought you had all kinds of things to do.'

'I'm planning,' she replied without opening her eyes. 'That's the key to my efficiency. I thought you knew that.'

He tapped the note pad. 'Is that so? You don't seem to have gotten — '

'Shuddup and gimme a real kiss.' She lifted

her arms, opened her eyes wide, and puckered up extravagantly.

'I bet this is what it's like to kiss a guppy,' he said, laughing, but of course he complied.

'That's more like it.' She stretched and yawned. 'So did you find what you were looking for?'

'I'm not sure.' He slid her feet over so that he could sit on the ottoman beside her.

'Still playing your cards close to the vest, eh? Oh, by the way, Vincenzo de Grazia called. The *padrone* himself.'

'Here? What did he want?'

'Achille's going off to school in Switzerland, and there's a party for him at the villa tonight. We're invited. Very informal, so you don't have to worry about fancy clothes.'

'Why are we invited?'

'Because of your kind assistance to the family in the matter of his father's remains, is what he said. Because Phil probably asked him to invite us, is what I think. Want to go?'

He hunched his shoulders. 'I don't know, it's our last night . . . do you?'

'Actually, yes,' she said, surprising him. 'I haven't been inside the house, you know. I'd love to see it. And after all I've heard, I'd hate to miss the chance to see the de Grazias in action.'

'Well, they're worth seeing, all right, but

what happened to resting up for tomorrow?'

'Oh, come on, be a sport. How bad can it be?'

'OK, let's do it,' he said, doing his best to get into the spirit. 'Might actually be fun. What time?'

'They'll send a boat to the pier for us at five thirty.' She looked at her watch. 'Which gives me just three hours before I have to start getting dressed. Yikes.' She swung her feet to the floor and stood up.

'Have to get going. Lots to do.'

'Need any help from me?'

'No,' she said, as he knew she would. 'No offense, but things go better if you just stay out of the way.'

'That's fine,' he said, unoffended. 'I have a phone call to make, and then I was thinking of going up to Gignese again.'

'Gignese? Do you have a burning desire to see the Umbrella Museum? Or don't tell me you want to talk to what's-his-name, Franco, again?'

'Not in this lifetime, thanks. But Caravale's going to be up there with some of his people, going through Dr Luzzatto's records, and I'd like to stop by and look at some things myself. I already called him. He said OK, he'll let them know to expect me if he's not there himself.'

He stood up too, and they embraced contentedly, looking out across the lake at the red-roofed villages climbing the far hillsides.

'And are you planning to tell me anytime soon why you want to go to Gignese and look at some things in Dr Luzzatto's office?' she asked after they slowly rocked back and forth for a while. 'Or why it was so important to look at Domenico's bones, for that matter?'

'Julie,' he said, 'I've got this idea . . . well, it's too crazy to even talk about at this point'

She nuzzled up beside him again. 'Come on, what? You can trust me.'

'No, this is really crazy. Let me do some more checking first; think it through a little more before I talk about it.'

'Oh, dear, our relationship is on the rocks for sure. You never hesitated to tell me your crazy ideas before.'

'I know, but this is probably the craziest one I ever had.'

She dug a knuckle into his ribs and laughed. 'Now that,' she said, 'would really take some doing.'

★ ★ ★

'Professor O'Malley?'

'Yes?' The voice on the other end of the line was guarded.

'This is Gideon Oliver, sir.'

'Oliver, for God's sake, you make me feel a million years old when you do that. I hereby give you permission for the two hundred and sixty-seventh time to call me just plain 'O'Malley', or even 'Bill', if you can bring yourself to do it. You're a big boy now, you're as famous as I am. Well, almost.'

'Sorry, uh, Bill, will do.'

But he knew it wouldn't last any more than it ever had before. William Tuskahoma O'Malley, M.D., Ph.D., was a towering figure in skeletal pathology and one of the very few academics who could still intimidate him. He had been one of Gideon's professors at the University of Wisconsin and had served on his dissertation committee. His *Non-traumatic Osteomyelitis of the Post-cranial Skeleton* remained the undisputed giant of the field, even after thirty years in print. A gruff, melodramatic, bugle-voiced genius famously impatient with unpreparedness, inattention, fuzzy thinking, and most other human failings, he had terrified Gideon as a young graduate student.

Gideon had taken O'Malley's courses at a time when, in an effort to make his dissertation deadline, his resources were stretched thin and he was starving for sleep. With most of his professors, he was able to get away with the occasional discreet catnap in class. Not with the eagle-eyed O'Malley, however, who would pounce before he knew himself that he was drifting off. 'Snap out of it, Oliver!' the bulky, bearded figure would bark at about eighty decibels, and Gideon would jerk awake. It happened so often that for a while his friends started referring to him as Snap-Out-of-It-Oliver.

Even now, the occasional back-to-school stress dreams that he had didn't involve discovering he'd studied for the wrong test or being unable to find the right room in which to take an exam. Instead, he would dream that he was peacefully dozing, perhaps on a beach, perhaps in a hammock, and would suddenly hear O'Malley's curt 'Snap out of it, Oliver!' He would awaken (in his dream) to find himself in O'Malley's paleopathology seminar. Totally unprepared, of course.

These days, they were professional colleagues, sometimes serving on the same panels, and Gideon had discovered that, underneath the crust, O'Malley was a pretty good egg. Not quite a heart of gold, no, but not so bad, once you made allowances. Still, some things were hard to get over.

'What can I do for you?' O'Malley asked. 'Where are you calling from?'

'I'm in Italy, and the reason that I'm calling

is that the other day somebody mentioned the Gaetano Pini Institute in Milan, which made me remember that you'd taken your residency there years ago, and that brought to mind — '

'I'm going to go make myself a cup of coffee now, Oliver. You just keep talking away, and maybe by the time I get back, you'll be getting to the point.'

Gideon coughed. 'Well, the point, Pro — uh, Bill, is that I remembered the segment in *Non-traumatic Osteomyelitis* that discusses aseptic necrosis of the epiphysis of the femoral head, and that mentions the possibility of confusing the results of a subcapital or transcervical fracture of the neck of the femur with the aftereffects of certain pathological — '

'Yes, yes, the aftereffects of Perthes disease. When did you get so damned verbose? I don't remember you talking so much.'

'Well, um, anyway, I don't have your book here with me to compare your photographs — '

'What are you saying? You travel without a copy of *Non-traumatic Osteomyelitis of the Post-cranial Skeleton* with you at all times? I'm shocked, shocked!' Gideon could imagine his hand going to his breast, his eyes rolling in mock disbelief.

He laughed politely. ' — so what I'd like to do is fax you a few photos — of the femoral head and surrounding area — from a case I'm working on, and ask you which you think it is, Perthes disease or a fracture. Would that be all right? And if it looks like Perthes to you, I'd appreciate a summary of the disease's incidence, heritability, demographics, that kind of thing. Today, if you can manage.'

'Oh, is that all you want? Well, of course, what else could I possibly have to do today?'

'I know it's an imposition — '

'I'm glad you know it,' he said, then abruptly decided he'd terrorized Gideon enough this time around. 'Well, look, I don't have a fax machine here at home, but I'll be at the university from one o'clock on.' O'Malley was an emeritus professor at Columbia and went to his office most days. 'You can fax it to me there: 212-854-1111. I'll look at it first thing and see what I can do.'

Gideon scrambled for a pen and wrote it down. 'Great, thanks a million.' One P.M., New York time, would be seven in the evening in Stresa. He'd be on the Isola de Grazia at Achille's farewell party. 'And if you come up with anything definitive, I'd really appreciate it if you'd call me right away.' He read him

349

the villa's phone number from a note he'd made earlier.

'You don't expect very much, do you?' O'Malley grumbled, but Gideon heard the scratching of a pen.

'Thank you, professor.'

He was wincing even before the shouted reply: 'Oliver, for crying out — '

'Bill!' Gideon quickly amended. 'Bill, Bill. Thank you very much, Bill. Good-bye, Bill.'

He hung up and with his finger wiped a sheen of sweat from his forehead.

Sheesh. It was as bad as being back in Paleopathology 502.

23

Dr Luzzatto's home and office were on the ground floor of one of the better-kept apartment buildings in Gignese, a few blocks from the village center. The mustard-colored paint on the outside was relatively new, the balconies had hardly any rust, and last night's bedding had already been taken in from the upstairs windowsills. A satellite dish, not a frequent sight in Gignese, was bolted to one of the third-floor balconies. When Gideon arrived, he found Caravale sitting on the low stone wall bordering the driveway, leafing through a pocket-sized, leather-bound notebook and having his afternoon half-cigar.

'OK if I go in?' Gideon said.

'Hm?' Barely looking up, Caravale waved his cigar in the direction of the door. 'Mm.'

But Gideon stopped, caught by Caravale's preoccupation. 'Got something interesting there?'

'Perhaps, if I could figure out what it means.' With a sigh, he snapped the notebook shut and slipped it into his jacket pocket. 'I need to walk around a little, stretch my legs, maybe find a cup of coffee. Do you want to come, or are you in a hurry to get in there?'

'No, I'm not in a hurry. I could use some coffee myself.'

They walked half a block without speaking. Caravale was in a sport coat and blue jeans, so the curious stares they drew from the locals were no more than any strangers in this part of the village would have gotten.

'Your theory of Interconnected Monkey Business?' Caravale finally said pensively. 'It looks as if it's panning out.'

'Oh?' Gideon prompted when it appeared Caravale was going back to smoking and ruminating in silence.

Caravale tapped ash from his cigar. 'The chauffeur, the bodyguard, that was killed in the kidnapping? He was a replacement. Praga, the one that was scheduled to drive the boy that day, called in just before he was due and begged off with an upset stomach, then never showed up again. You see what that means, don't you?'

'Well . . . that the original guy — Praga — was part of the plan and got cold feet at the last minute?'

'That's right. And here's guy number two, Dellochio, who knows nothing about it — '

' — and the kidnappers haven't heard that guy number one won't be driving — '

' — so instead of putting up a fake

352

resistance and letting them get away with it, the way they expected him to, the poor bastard defends Achille with his life and ends up shot to death.'

'An inside job at Aurora,' Gideon murmured. 'Huh. What does that do to the theory that it has to be one of the de Grazias?'

'Nothing. The company drivers occasionally chauffeured family members around in their off-hours. They all knew Praga. Any of them could have approached him with this. Of course, it's worth noting that several of them work at Aurora, so they'd have the easiest access to him and would probably know him best — it's not exactly the sort of thing you ask a stranger to do.'

Gideon nodded. 'Francesca is the CFO and Basilio is something in payroll.'

'And last but not least' — Caravale ran his tongue over his lips — 'let's not forget the boss man . . . Vincenzo.'

Gideon stopped. 'You suspect Vincenzo of kidnapping his own son? Of staging the whole thing? Why would he do that?'

'The money. Five million euros is a lot of money.'

'But he's rich as . . . as . . . ' He groped.

'Croesus?' suggested Caravale around the cigar. He gestured at a bar across the street. 'Let's go get that coffee.' Using the fingers of

353

his left hand, he carefully snuffed out the cigar and stuck the inch and-a-half-long stub behind his ear. 'I'm rationing myself,' he explained.

The Bar Lanterna, as opposed to the distinctly blue-collar Bar Ricci, where Phil and Gideon had met Franco and Gia, appeared to be the meeting place for Gignese's with-it set. A sign advertised evening karaoke, video games, and Internet access, and one of the tables actually had two unaccompanied women at it. The air held only a thin veil of old cigarette smoke. Over a couple of espressos served with slender glasses of water, Gideon picked up where they'd left off.

'Thank you. Croesus. So why would he need the money?'

Caravale smiled tolerantly while he stirred sugar into the tiny cup. 'Well, I tell you, my naïve professor-friend: You'd be surprised at the things rich people do for money. Besides . . . Vincenzo isn't as rich as Croesus. I've been doing some checking, and our Vincenzo, in fact, is having financial difficulties. The money that was raised to ransom Achille? It wasn't his own at all. Raising it took some, shall we say, highly creative accounting practices with the books at Aurora Costruzioni.'

'I don't get this at all. How could he need money? Look at that house he maintains. Look at that whole island. Did you see some of those paintings? The tapestries? If he needed the money, all he had to do was sell off five million euros' worth of paintings and nobody would even notice they were gone. What would he want to rig up something as crazy as this for?'

'Ah, now, his private wealth, that's interesting too. We've had a look at the provisions of the de Grazia legacy, and it turns out the bequest, which is enormous, is strictly entailed for the purpose of keeping Isola de Grazia in the family, in perpetuity. It provides for physical maintenance of the property, for household staff, for death taxes when the generations change, and for the food, clothing, and general upkeep of the family members staying there. I think there's some kind of small allowance for them too. Beyond that, they're expected to fend for themselves. They get nothing, not even Vincenzo.'

'Wow. You've been busy,' Gideon said.

Caravale touched the tip of his tongue to his espresso, then drank. 'Most of them also got an inheritance from Domenico's personal will, but it wasn't all that much, and it's long gone now. And as for selling the art, he can't.

It's expressly prohibited, and the lawyers stay on him like leeches. He can have things restored or cleaned, and the bequest will pay for it, but he can't sell anything. He's more like the custodian of the place, really, than the owner.'

'Well, OK, I understand what you're getting at,' Gideon agreed. 'He has money problems. But to kidnap Achille . . . his own son? He almost got him killed!'

'Ah, but couldn't that have been because of the change in chauffeurs? That's my whole point. If Praga had been there as planned, there wouldn't have been any gunfire, or maybe just a little harmless shooting to make it look good.'

'I see what you mean. Right.'

'Of course, right. Pay attention. In any case, I'm not saying it's Vincenzo. Not for certain. It could still be any one of them.'

'Not Cosimo, surely?'

'Well, he's not at the top of my list,' Caravale said with a smile. 'Neither is your friend Phil, but I think you knew that. But we're getting close to the end here, Gideon. I have good intuition about these things, and I can feel it in my stomach.' He brought the thumb and fingers of his hand together. 'I can sense the closing of the net.'

'Mm,' Gideon said. He drank half the

espresso, savoring the bitter taste, the ashy texture.

'What do you mean, 'Mm'? We've already established it has to be one of the de Grazia crowd, haven't we?'

'Well, yes,' Gideon allowed. 'Big Paolo's being involved in the kidnapping and the attack on me — '

'And in trying to steal Domenico's bones,' Caravale added, jabbing the cigar at him. 'Oh, didn't I tell you about that? One of the nuns identified him as the man she saw sneaking around the hospital courtyard in the middle of the night, how about that? So he was definitely tied in with everything — Domenico's murder, Achille's kidnapping — which means — well, you know.'

Gideon nodded. What it meant, as they'd established earlier, was that at least one of the de Grazias was *also* tied up with everything, because only the de Grazias — no one else — had known that Domenico's bones had been found. Whoever it was, therefore, Big Paolo's presence linked him or her to both Domenico's death and Achille's kidnapping. And since the de Grazias were the only ones who had heard Luzzatto muttering about the mysterious things Domenico had had on his mind the day he was killed, that almost certainly had to mean that one of them was involved in Luzzatto's murder too — assuming that Luzzatto had been murdered.

'Wait a minute, though,' Gideon said. 'Back to Vincenzo for a minute. At the *consiglio* he said he'd told the previous *carabinieri* commander that Domenico was murdered ten years ago, back when it happened.'

'And he did. I looked at the case file.'

'So, does that add up? A man murders his father, then tells the cop in charge — who thinks it's an accident and is inclined to let it go — that he ought to investigate it as a homicide?'

'On the surface, maybe not. But if in that way he establishes a façade of innocence for himself without providing any incriminating information for the police to work with . . . maybe yes.'

Gideon stretched and sighed. 'OK, I grant you, it all makes sense on paper, but it's pretty . . . well, ornate. It'd sure be nice if you could get your hands on Big Paolo and just ask him who hired him. That'd settle it.'

Caravale grinned at him.

'You found him?'

They had indeed. With the help of local police in Sesto San Giovanni, one of the gritty industrial suburbs north of Milan, Big Paolo Tossignani had been located and apprehended. Caravale had not yet had a chance to talk to him, but he was at this moment being transported to Stresa for that purpose. He would arrive by 4 P.M.

'And I'll be there to welcome him with open arms,' Caravale said.

'That's great,' said Gideon, impressed. 'If he cooperates — '

'I doubt if there'll be any problem with that. This young man is in very big trouble. He's been positively identified at the kidnapping, remember, and there's a homicide charge associated with that, let alone the attack on you and everything else he has to worry about. So he can either say nothing and go to prison for the next thirty years while the person that originated the idea and paid him a few euros comes away from it all without a scratch, or he can cooperate by giving us some information that would make the court look more favorably on him.'

'And you think he will?'

'Sure, why wouldn't he? They call him Dumb Paolo, but he can't be that dumb.' He chuckled delightedly. 'And listen to this. The Sesto people faxed me what records they had on him. In the past three years, lo and behold, he's hired on twice as a laborer on Milanese projects, with a regional construction company. Not only that, but Ugo Fogazzaro — the dead kidnapper — was hired for the same jobs, by the same company. Would you care to hazard a guess as to the name of this well-known construction company that is on such familiar terms with these two particular gangsters?'

'Aurora!' said Gideon. 'Damn!'

The links to the de Grazias were piling up too thick and too fast to be shrugged off now. Caravale was getting close to wrapping things up, and it looked as if Paolo was going to provide the ribbon with which to do it. They had finished their coffees but they both had some water left, and Caravale looked so tickled that Gideon raised his water glass for a congratulatory toast.

'To Dumb Paolo,' Caravale said as the glasses clinked.

★　★　★

'Before you go in, look at this and tell me what you think,' Caravale said as they got back to Luzzatto's apartment building. He handed Gideon the leather-bound notebook he'd been reading earlier. 'It's not very long.' From his manner, Gideon could see that he had only that moment decided to let Gideon in on it.

Gideon took it. 'What is it?'

'It's a personal journal. He started keeping

360

it some years ago, one notebook per year. We found them at the back of a drawer in his desk. This is the last one.' He sat down on the stone wall again, plucked the cigar from behind his ear, and stuck it between his lips. 'While you read it, keep in mind what he was saying that day at the *consiglio*.'

'About Domenico having something to ponder the day he was killed?'

'Exactly.' He scratched a wooden match on the mortar between the stones of the wall, lit up, and settled back to watch Gideon read.

Gideon sat down beside him, taking care to keep upwind. The notebook had perhaps a hundred pages, but only the first few had been used. The first entry was dated January 3, 1992. Gideon tried struggling through a sentence or two, but then shook his head and handed the journal to Caravale. 'I'm not used to this kind of handwriting. You'll have to tell me what it says. Something about leukemia?'

'Yes,' Caravale said, spreading the notebook open on his thigh. 'He was diagnosed with advanced acute leukemia on December twenty-eighth, 1991 — '

'Wait a minute. And he was still alive and riding his motorcycle in 2003? That's — '

'Unlikely, yes. The fact is, there was a mistake at the laboratory. His bone marrow sample was confused with someone else's.'

'Some mistake,' Gideon said.

Caravale tapped the notebook. 'It's all in here, but the important thing is that — at the time — Luzzatto believed he had only a few weeks or months to live. Now listen to this. This is January fifth. 'For twenty-seven years',' he read, translating as he went along, ' 'I have kept this secret buried in my heart, unwilling (or unable?) to tell Domenico. Now it can wait no longer. Tomorrow I will speak with him'.' He looked up from the journal. 'Would you like to guess the date of Domenico's death?'

'January sixth?'

'January eighth. Two days after Luzzatto told him.'

'Told him what?'

'That's the question, all right. And the answer, unfortunately, is that I have no idea. There are no entries until the tenth of January.'

'So you can't even be sure he did tell him.'

'No, we can be quite sure. Here is what he had to say on the tenth: 'Dear God, can this terrible thing be my fault? Did I drive this fine, generous man to his death? Even if not, surely I made him wretched for the last few days of his life. And for what? For vanity's sake? To satisfy my egotistical notions of honesty, of candor? For the bitter, self-indulgent pleasure of living my own last few hours on this earth as an 'honest' man? May God forgive me'.'

Caravale blew out a cloud of sour cigar smoke. 'Quite a philosopher, our Dr Luzzatto. After this, he wrote nothing for a week, and then there was a brief entry describing the error in the laboratory tests. After that, apparently he lost his taste for journals.'

'And there's no clue as to what he told Domenico?'

'So far, we've found nothing, not a hint. Fasoli has been going back through the earlier journals.'

'What about the one from — what would twenty-seven years before 1992 be?'

'It would be 1966, and there isn't any. He began keeping them in 1973, on his fiftieth birthday.'

'Well, then, how about his medical records for 1966? Have you looked at those to see if there's something?'

Caravale nodded. 'And 1965 and 1967 as well, just to be sure.'

'You've looked specifically at the de Grazia files?'

'Of course,' Caravale said crossly. 'Do I look stupid to you? There was nothing, nothing. Oh, Cosimo developed bronchitis, Vincenzo broke his finger, Bella complained of recurring gastric pains, that sort of thing. Nothing. But we'll take them all back with us and go through them word by word.'

'Do you mind if I have a look first?'

'Help yourself,' Caravale said. He stood up and with his heel ground out the nubbin of tobacco that was left. 'But you're not going to find anything.'

24

The marble-floored, stucco-ceilinged, gilt-encrusted Villa de Grazia wowed Julie, but the party itself was a dud. The family members were listless and apathetic, seemingly lacking the energy needed for their customary jibes, and the guests were taking their cues from their hosts. Aside from Julie and Gideon, there were only about a dozen guests altogether, most whom seemed to be local dignitaries who had come to celebrate Achille's safe return (or more likely, Phil suggested, his imminent departure).

The predinner reception was being held in the aptly named *salone grande*, the largest, grandest chamber in the house, and no doubt the immensity of the room — it must have once been the ball room, Gideon thought — had something to do with the weight that seemed to hang over the small group of people, almost all of whom were bunched together at one end of the room, near the bar, as if for mutual protection. Only Cosimo and Achille sat apart, side by side and stiffly erect in two of the French Regency chairs lined up along one mirrored wall, occasionally greeting well-wishers. Bacco lay between them, snoring and snuffling in his sleep, with his head under Cosimo's chair and his rear end under Achille's.

There had been some laughter and a little applause earlier, when the family had presented Achille with his going-away presents — a hand-illustrated set of Dante's works from Cosimo, a laptop computer from Bella and Basilio, a membership in Bern's toniest country club (so he wouldn't forget his riding and his golf) from Francesca and Dante — but things had gone downhill after that, and now people had fallen into small groups with those they knew best, where they milled awkwardly about, balancing their drinks and hors d'oeuvres and surreptitiously checking their watches and waiting for the call to dinner.

Gideon, Julie, and Phil had moved off to one side, where they were talking about the ramifications of Phil's new family tree, or rather the lack thereof.

'But how do you feel about it?' Julie asked.

'Happy as a pig in clover. Wouldn't you be?'

Julie's eyes lingered on the princely surroundings. 'Well . . . '

'Have you told Lea?' Gideon asked.

'No, I've got a call in to her. She's down in Naples on one of her consulting gigs. She actually left me all alone with these people. I'll tell her when she gets back.'

'How's she going to feel about it?'

'Are you kidding? She'll love it, same as me. I feel like a new man!' He sipped jubilantly from a glass of red wine. 'I just wish I knew who,' he said, and grinned happily.

Clemente, in white dinner jacket and black tie, entered the room and made his stately way toward Vincenzo, who was talking to Francesca and a couple of the dignitaries' wives, a few feet behind Julie. Despite a bowed spine, he was a tall man and had to bend to speak into his master's ear.

Vincenzo pulled back his head and looked incredulously at him. 'He's here now? Caravale?'

Gideon had earlier told Julie and Phil about Caravale's 'closing of the net,' and now the three of them exchanged eloquent glances.

'Uh-oh,' Phil said.

'With two men,' Clemente informed Vincenzo.

'What?' Vincenzo exclaimed. 'Tell Cesare — '

'Too late,' Clemente said with a shake of his head. 'They're on their way.'

'On their way? What the hell do they — ' He interrupted himself. 'Very well, Clemente, you can show them in. Offer them something to drink. Thank you, Clemente.'

'What do you suppose this is about?' Julie whispered. 'You don't think — '

'Signore?' It was Clemente, back again, but this time for Gideon. 'A telephone call for you. In the Medallion Room. If you'll follow me . . . '

'Hey, you might miss the big scene,' Phil called after Gideon.

Gideon stopped and turned. 'I don't think so.'

*   *   *

My father would be proud of me.

Of all the things to be thinking at a time like this. But there it was, right at the front of his mind as Caravale strode purposefully across the pebbled courtyard and toward the great villa with Fasoli and Lombardo on either side of him. Ordinarily, when he had reached this stage of an investigation, about to make a well-conceived arrest, there would be a tingling mixture of satisfaction and anticipation, and of pride in himself and his staff. Those familiar reactions were there, all right, but they were all taking a backseat to this one unexpected, overwhelming feeling of childish self-justification.

My father would finally be proud of me. I'm about to bring down a great family.

* ★ ★

Leaving his men at the entry of the salon, Caravale approached Vincenzo and Francesca, his uniform cap under his arm. He had primly turned down Clemente's offer of a drink.

'Good evening, Colonel,' Vincenzo said, 'is there a problem?'

'I'm afraid so, signore.'

'This is a private party,' Francesca said reprovingly. 'My brother has his guests to attend to.'

'Of course.' Caravale turned to face her directly. 'But as a matter of fact, it's you that I'm here to see, signora.'

A long second and a half ticked by. 'I?'

'Yes. Perhaps you would be good enough to step outside?' He gestured toward the doorway and the waiting officers.

'What the devil is this about?' Vincenzo snapped.

The two women they'd been talking with exchanged glances and began to sidle away.

'I asked a question,' Vincenzo said, but Caravale was looking at Francesca, waiting for her to respond.

She didn't move. 'Is it really so urgent?'

'It's important,' Caravale told her. 'Now, if you please . . . '

'I think not,' Francesca said. She walked a

369

few steps to place her wine glass on the bar, then returned to face him. Her voice took on a metallic edge. 'Whatever you have to say can be said in front of our guests.'

At which point Caravale's quickly fraying patience, not in great supply in the first place, ran out. If she wanted to do this in front of everybody, he would be happy to oblige her.

'Very well, signora. I am here to arrest you for knowingly providing false information to your insurance company and to the police for the purpose of committing fraud. Also for knowingly obstructing the police in the performance — '

'That's ridiculous!' a flushed Vincenzo interrupted. 'What are you talking about?'

Francesca flung her hand up in disbelief. 'Is the man serious? He has actually come here, uninvited, to a private residence, to accuse us of' — she faltered, but only for a moment — 'of a few balance-sheet irregularities in the effort to recover Achille without harm coming to him — something we successfully accomplished, I need hardly remind anyone here, without the assistance of the colonel and his vaunted regiment.'

Somewhere along the way she had turned it into theater. She was speaking now for the benefit of the onlookers, most of whom had joined the two women in drifting inconspicuously backward, leaving Caravale, Vincenzo, and Francesca all alone on center stage. Theater-in-the-round.

Caravale, normally averse to public performances, went willingly along this time. 'I am not referring to the peculiarities in your company's balance sheet,' he said evenly. 'That is a matter for another officer, another time. I am talking about your contracting to have your nephew kidnapped in an effort to extort money from your insurer.'

That naturally brought a round of gasps and exclamations, almost enough to drown out Francesca's ragged, harsh 'Absurd!'

'Caravale, this is outrageous!' said Vincenzo. The muscles in front of his ears were bunching and knotting under the skin. 'Now you've gone too far. You can expect to hear from my attorney about this before the night is out.'

'Oho, he'll hear from more than our attorney,' Francesca said hotly. 'I'll have your job for this, you stupid little man! You don't know who you're dealing with. To have the nerve to walk into our home with unsubstantiated — '

'In addition, signora, I am also placing you under arrest for contracting for the theft of material evidence in the form of the remains of Domenico de Grazia — '

'How dare you — '

' — and for the assault on Professor Oliver to thwart his examination of said remains so as to prevent — '

Francesca cut him off with a raucous laugh. 'Unbelievable! He's gone completely mad.' She appealed to her audience, arms outspread. 'Is he now accusing us of murdering our own father?'

He could see Lombardo and Fasoli making motions from the doorway: *Enough already, let's go, let's get out of here.* They were right, of course, but that 'stupid little man' rankled and his juices were flowing.

'Not 'us', signora,' he said and paused, relishing the dramatic effect more than he knew he should. 'You. Only you.'

Her body stiffened, and for a second he thought she might stagger or fall, like a heroine in a melodrama. Vincenzo, staring at her with his mouth open, automatically reached out to steady her.

'Francesca . . . ?'

She shook him off and shouted at Caravale: 'What an utterly despicable accusation. Why would I do such an inconceivable thing?'

Caravale was now winding down. Besides, he had yet to come up with the answer to that question. 'We can deal with that later,' he said, speaking more gruffly. 'Now, I think it's time for you to come with me.'

When she again failed to move, he turned toward the doorway. 'Corporal? Sergeant?' He motioned them into the room.

Vincenzo looked as if somebody had hit him over the head with a baseball bat, but Francesca was afire, jerking her hands away when instructed to hold them out for the handcuffs. She was in full fury now, not so far from hysteria, with flashing eyes and high color in her cheeks. If he didn't know better, Caravale might have thought she was enjoying herself. Possibly, she was.

'No, I want to hear why! I want everyone to hear! Don't you all want to know? You can't arrest me without a reason. The law doesn't allow it. Tell me, why did I kill my father?'

Fasoli, holding the cuffs, looked at Caravale for guidance. Caravale sighed. It had been a mistake to let it get this far, and now he was paying for it.

Gideon had appeared at the doorway a short while before, watching quietly like everyone else. Now he came up beside Caravale. 'I think,' he said, 'that I can give you the answer to that.'

He had spoken quietly, but in the electric silence that surrounded them, his words seemed to bounce off the walls and go rattling around the room.

'You?' Francesca threw back her head and

looked down her formidable nose at him. 'The skeleton man? All right, why?'

Vincenzo was trying to shut her up. 'Come, Francesca, let's go with them,' he coaxed. 'I'll come with you. There's no reason to make a scene. We'll easily straighten this all out later. Don't worry,' he said, and threw a fierce, hawkeyed glance at Caravale, 'there will be hell to pay.'

She pushed him away, still watching Gideon. 'I'm waiting. Why?'

Gideon looked at Caravale, who shrugged and wearily waved a hand. *Go ahead, why stop now?*

'Because you wanted to keep your father from disinheriting Vincenzo — '

'Disinheriting Vincenzo?' Vincenzo shouted, his voice cracking. 'Disinheriting . . . '

' — and installing the legitimate heir in his place.'

'Installing the . . . the . . . ' Vincenzo swallowed and made an effort to collect his resources. 'And who, who would that be?'

'That,' Gideon said, and looked along the wall until he found Phil, standing next to Julie, 'would be that man right . . . there.'

'What?' Vincenzo said.

'What?' Caravale said.

'Whoa,' said Phil, doing his best to shrink into the Chinoiserie-tiled wall behind him.

25

The police launch could hold no more than five passengers, and even that took some doing, what with one of them in custody. So, while Gideon went back in it with Caravale, Vincenzo, Francesca, and the two officers, Julie was shuttled back to Stresa with the other guests in the family launches. Phil remained at the villa. Like the rest of the de Grazias, he was thoroughly shell-shocked — which meant that he would probably do what he usually did when events piled up on him: go to bed and sleep it off in hopes that things would be better in the morning. A futile hope in this case, but all things considered, it was probably a good idea.

It was a little after 11 P.M. when a weary Gideon finished making his depositions at *carabinieri* headquarters and was dropped off by Corporal Fasoli at the hotel.

Angela, behind the reception desk, caught him before he reached the elevator. 'Your wife got hungry,' she said. 'I sent her over to the Ristorante Piemontese.' She pointed to her right. 'Next block, Via Mazzini.'

'Thanks, Angela,' Gideon said, turning

back toward the door.

'Try the *risotto alla monzese!*' she shouted after him.

He found Julie plowing vigorously into her meal at a table toward the back of the restaurant, a sedate, invitingly restful place with dark wood decor and low, arched ceilings.

'Sorry,' she said with her mouth full. 'I was starving. I couldn't wait anymore. I started on my *primo piatto. Cotoletta alla milanese* to follow.'

'I don't blame you,' Gideon said, his mouth already watering. Neither of them had had lunch or dinner, and the grilled meat and rich, wine-barrel smells of the restaurant were making his knees weak. 'That looks delicious, what is it?'

'Angela recommended it. It's wonderful. Risotto with sausage, tomato, Marsala — '

'God, I need some of that too.' He signaled the waiter for some for himself, tore off a chunk of the bread in the basket that was on the table, and demolished it in two bites.

'I understand it's better if you chew,' Julie said.

'Too hungry to chew.' He reached for her glass, half-full of red wine from a bottle beside the bread basket. 'Mind?'

'Help yourself. It's local — Barbacalo. Ever hear of it?'

'Nope.' He took a swallow, savored the surprisingly heavy, concentrated heat of it, and then had a second, longer swallow. He could feel it slither all the way down his gullet and sit in a warm, comforting pool in his stomach. 'Hoo, boy, that's better. Red wine and crusty Italian bread, nature's perfect foods.' Grabbing another chunk of bread, he took the time to butter this one, bit gratefully into it, and relaxed with a sigh. 'Well, I imagine you have a few questions.'

'A few thousand is more like it.'

'OK, where do I start? Well, first, the reason we know it was Francesca is that they found Big Paolo, the guy that tried to strangle me and was also one of the kidnappers, and when Caravale interrogated him, Paolo was very clear about who hired him for both jobs: Francesca de Grazia; no one else. Vincenzo was to be kept in the dark. That came as a surprise to Caravale because he'd pretty much settled on Vincenzo in his mind. Me, too, for that matter. But you see, Francesca had been milking money from the company for years — '

'No, no, no, that's all very interesting, but I want to know about Phil! Start with Phil. I mean, the day before yesterday he was simply good old Phil Boyajian, and then yesterday the two of you come back from Gignese with a story that he's the illegitimate son of this bizarre woman who doesn't even know his father's name, and just when I start getting used to that, suddenly tonight, he's the *padrone* of Isola de Grazia?'

'In a word . . . yes.'

'How did you come up with that? Was *that* your 'crazy idea'?'

'That was part of it.'

Without being asked, the waiter had brought another glass, and Gideon poured himself some more wine. He was unwinding by the second. 'But as to how I came up with it . . . you know, it's always hard to trace your thought processes after the fact, but I think it was something like this.' He chewed his bread, sipped his wine, arranged his thoughts. 'Do you remember my mentioning that the Gaetano Pini Institute came up at the *consiglio?* Dr Luzzatto was talking about it.'

'Can't say that I do, no.'

'Well, I probably forgot. There really wasn't any reason to tell you at the time. But it stuck in my mind. Do you know what the Gaetano Pini Institute is?'

'Not a clue.'

'No, I ordered the *risotto alla monzese,*' Gideon said in Italian to the waiter, who had just set an antipasto plate — salami,

378

prosciutto, fried mozzarella, marinated vegetables — in front of him, along with some more bread.

The waiter shrugged. 'The risotto, it takes a little while. You look hungry. You want me to take it back?'

'No!' Gideon said, making a grab for it before the man could follow through. 'And thank you very much.'

He made a start on the sausage before continuing. 'The Gaetano Pini Institute is an orthopedic clinic specializing in ambulatory joint diseases. It's associated with the University of Milan, and the reason that I know about it is that this old professor of mine did a year of postdoc in the rheumatology department there and he had a wonderful set of slides from it that he used to show. Anyway, thinking about old O'Malley made me think about his work on Perthes disease — Legg-Calvé-Perthes disease. You know what Perthes disease is?'

'Gideon, dear,' Julie said with a sweet smile, 'could you possibly just explain without asking me questions you know I don't know the answer to?'

'Was that what I was doing?'

'That's what you always do. I think it's a pedagogical technique. I'm sure it's very effective in class.'

'Sorry about that,' he said, laughing. 'Pedagogical habits die hard. Anyway, one of the things about Perthes disease — which, between us, I had completely forgotten — is that its effects can sometimes be confused with the aftereffects of a broken femoral neck. So what naturally jumped into my mind at that point was that — '

' — the injury you thought you'd found in Domenico's hip — the reason for his walking with a limp — might not be an injury at all, but the result of Perthes disease.'

'Exactly. That's why I wanted to go back and look at the bones again. Well, the bones had been sent off to Rome, but they had a good set of photographs, which I looked at, but I still wasn't positive, so I sent them off to O'Malley for diagnosis.'

'And was it? Perthes disease?'

'Sure enough. The call I got at the villa was from him. Perthes disease for sure. And that settled it. *That* was what Francesca was afraid I'd find. *That* was why they tried to get rid of the bones. That was why they tried to get rid of me. It had nothing at all to do with the cause of death. Ahh,' he said as the steaming plate of risotto was set down in front of him.

The waiter had also brought Julie's veal cutlet. Thoughtfully, while Gideon dug in, she picked up her knife and fork and began to cut off a piece of meat, but then shook her head and put the utensils down. 'No. Wait a minute. *What* did it settle? What does all this have to do with Phil? What does it have to do with anything?'

'Patience,' he counseled between bites. 'There's some pretty intricate deduction involved here. What it has to do with is Phil's limp.'

'His limp? I wouldn't call that a limp. He just has a sort of a . . . snag to his walk.'

'What he has, not that I ever gave it much thought before, is a very mild form of what's known as a Trendelenburg gait, or a gluteus medius lurch, which is what you get with inadequately functioning hip abductors in one leg. The affected leg tends to be held in an externally rotated posture and the joint itself is kept flexed — '

'Are you saying that Phil has Perthes disease too?'

'Yes. The operation apparently corrected it to the point where the limp is barely noticeable. But you're getting ahead of me now. See, hearing that he had an operation when he was five got me thinking about what kind of condition he might have had, and one of the first things that naturally came to mind was Perthes disease.'

'Why 'naturally'?'

'Because, even though it's rare, it is the most common of the osteochondroses, and it usually shows up right around that age — five, six, seven — and unlike most other joint diseases, it's unilateral more often than not — and Phil, like Domenico, is only affected on one side. Umm, this is really good risotto. Now, then: once Perthes disease started knocking around in my brain, it got me thinking about Vincenzo — '

'Vincenzo? Does Vincenzo have it too? I didn't notice any kind of limp.'

'No, he doesn't have one, and that's what struck me.' Sated enough to take a breather now, he put down his own knife and fork, leaned forward, and told her what O'Malley had told him. 'The genetics of Perthes disease are obscure and very complex, but in general it's inherited, and if it shows up twice among close relatives, you can *bet* it's inherited, so — '

'So if anybody had it, it should have been Vincenzo,' Julie said slowly, 'not Phil. Only it's the other way around.'

'Right. Ergo: it's Phil who's Domenico's son, not Vincenzo.'

'Wow.' Mechanically, she started eating again. 'But . . . ' She chewed and swallowed. 'Francesca is Domenico's daughter, isn't she? Why doesn't she have it?'

'Because it doesn't always show up, and when it does, it's five to one in boys as opposed to girls.'

'Oh. No, wait, there's a big problem here. What about that whole story that his so-called father told? About how Vincenzo was really Emma's baby, and Phil was bought from that woman, that Gia, for five hundred dollars as a . . . a consolation prize?'

'The story was true. Only he reversed Phil and Vincenzo. Phil was the baby. Vincenzo was the consolation prize.'

'Gideon, the more you explain, the more confused I get. I am getting really frustrated here. What reason would Franco have to lie like that?'

The waiter came to take Gideon's plate and to ask what he wanted for his second course. 'I'll have another plate of this,' Gideon told him, earning a tolerant shake of the waiter's head. These Americans.

'He wasn't lying, Julie. Emma fooled them both — Franco and Domenico. I'm doing a little surmising here, but what I figure is that her maternal hormones kicked in as she got into her pregnancy, and she didn't want to give her own baby up — her own baby being Phil. So, overcome with remorse, she works out a plan with Gia, who's also at about the same stage: a switch. When the babies are born, she'll give Gia's child — '

'Vincenzo?'

He nodded. 'Vincenzo — to Domenico, leaving her own child — '

'Phil.'

'Yes, Phil — with Gia for the time being. Then she finesses Domenico into suggesting that she adopt a child — and paying for it — and she pretends to adopt Gia's son ... who's really her own, her own and Domenico's.'

'And how do you finesse someone into suggesting that you adopt a child?'

'That I don't know, but I don't doubt it's possible.'

'Well, maybe ... but wouldn't Franco know — '

'Franco wasn't there for the last month.'

'But the mother — the other mother, Gia — *she* seemed to think Phil was hers.'

'Julie, you didn't get to meet this woman. She's so zonked out she'd believe I was her kid if Franco told her so.'

Julie had eaten only half of her *cotoletta*, but with a shake of her head, she pushed the plate aside. 'Well, I suppose it's all *possible*, but 'surmising' is putting it mildly, wouldn't you say? You're taking quite a leap here.'

'No, I don't think so. I haven't told you yet about what happened when I went up to

Gignese this afternoon to look at Luzzatto's records.'

She laughed. 'You've had yourself quite a day, haven't you?' Over his second helping of the risotto Gideon told her about Luzzatto's journal, with its angst-ridden references to the mysterious 'secret buried in my heart' that was kept from Domenico for twenty-seven years, and then finally revealed to him . . . two days before he was killed.

Julie listened, sipping her second glass of wine and nibbling at a cheese tray they'd ordered. 'I think I finally see where you're going. Luzzatto was in on the baby switch too, correct? That Vincenzo wasn't the real son — that was the secret. And when he finally told Domenico, Francesca must have found out too, and to prevent him from disinheriting Vincenzo, she . . . No? I'm not right?' she said when she saw Gideon shaking his head.

'You're almost right. That was the secret, all right, but Luzzatto wasn't in on the switch. He only found out years later.'

'How can you possibly know that, if it wasn't in the journal?'

'Luzzatto told me, or rather his medical records did. See, twenty-seven years ago wouldn't have been when the babies were born. Twenty-seven years ago would have been 1966, five years after that. And in 1966, according to his files, he took five-year-old Filiberto Ungaretti in to the Gaetano Pini Institute for an operation to correct an incipient case of . . . ' He waited.

'Perthes disease!' Julie said. 'And since he was also Domenico's doctor, he already knew that Domenico had it, so he came to the same conclusion you did: Emma had pulled a fast one to keep her own baby. Phil was really his son, not Vincenzo.'

'Now you've got it. He then kept it to himself all those years, but when he thought he was dying, he went to Domenico with it, and Domenico, with his unshakable belief in the importance of good blood, probably would have disinherited Vincenzo — '

'Hold on. So why didn't *Vincenzo* kill him, then? No, I didn't put that right. I meant, why would Francesca be the one to murder him over that? She was still his legitimate daughter, wasn't she? It wouldn't affect her. And for that matter, why was she skimming money? Why would she have had Achille kidnapped? Why did she need so much money anyway?'

'I don't know.'

'Don't know which?'

'Any of it, any of the 'whys'. Neither does

386

Caravale at this point. Francesca's the only one who knows, and she wasn't exactly forthcoming at the police station. She's a pretty tough cookie, Julie. She just might never explain. We might never find out.'

26

They found out the following Sunday, four days later, back home in Port Angeles. Phil had come in from Italy on a red-eye at 7:50 A.M. and had driven straight out to Port Angeles, having promised to fill them in on everything. The idea had been to take a picnic brunch down to Dungeness Spit, the hump-backed, six-mile ribbon of sand and driftwood that angled out into the stormy strait like a sheltering arm, protecting the quiet waters of Dungeness Bay within its curve. It was Phil's favorite spot on the Peninsula, and he thought the salt air, the sense of space, the cries of seals and gulls, and the grand, ever-present backdrop of the Olympics might help him decompress.

But Sunday, like the previous three days, came up rainy and glowering, a typical Pacific Northwest spring morning without a 'sun-break' in sight, and so they'd settled for a brunch of scrambled eggs, lox, bagels, and cream cheese at home instead. Phil had been taciturn and a little grumpy when he'd walked in, and Gideon's greeting of 'How goes it, *padrone?*' hadn't helped matters.

'This is nothing to joke about,' had been the querulous reply.

But a bagel sandwich of lox and cream cheese smeared with cherry jam ('That's the way we Armenians like it,' he'd said defensively. 'You want to make something of it?') had helped him unwind, and with the pouring of his second cup of coffee, he began to open up.

'I had a talk with Francesca, you know,' he said, stirring in sugar. 'Yesterday. They're holding her in Turin. I drove up there to see her.'

'And she talked to you?' Gideon said. 'I'm surprised.'

'So am I, to tell you the truth. But I had to at least ask her some questions — you know, to try to make sense of things. They've got her in a kind of a . . . not really a cell, but like a dorm room, only the door is metal, and it has a window in it. Somebody stood outside and watched us the whole time. They said I couldn't see her at first, but I called Caravale and he got me in.' He was stirring, stirring, his mind 7,000 miles away, back in a dorm-like room in Turin.

'How did she seem?' Julie prompted.

'Like Francesca. Nasty. 'So you've come to gloat, eh? Go ahead, have your fill.' Those were her first words to me.'

He had spent half an hour in her company, he explained, unable to get her to say anything. She had sat on her cot in silence, with her arms folded, and her eyes half-closed, and a distant half-smile on her face, while he pleaded with her to shed some light on what she'd done. And then, when he had already gotten up and was about to leave, he had stopped just before signaling to get out and had said, in bafflement and frustration: 'He was stabbed in the *back*, Francesca! I can't even make myself imagine that. That you would stab Domenico . . . your father . . . in the back — '

She had jumped up from the cot on which she'd been sitting, her dark eyes alight for the first time. 'Yes, in the back, the way he stabbed *me* in the back!'

'She confessed to you?' Gideon said, astounded.

Phil nodded. He'd finally finished stirring his coffee and lifted it to his lips, but it was obvious he hardly knew he was drinking it. 'She got carried away; she couldn't hold it back. I mean, it just poured out of her. It was horrible — this flood of bile, of resentment . . . it was like I wasn't even there. I was, like, paralyzed . . . ' He put the coffee down, stared out at the gray murk, and in a quiet, neutral voice told them what had burst from her with so much passion.

When Dr Luzzatto had finally told Domenico the truth (Francesca said) — that her supposed younger brother Vincenzo was neither her brother nor Domenico's son — but that Phil was — Domenico had made the mistake of coming to her for advice, for guidance — to Francesca, his own natural daughter; Francesca, whose own husband had been banished from the villa. As she had sat there in the kitchen of her gloomy Modena apartment, watching him wring his fine hands and debate with himself about the proper thing to do and the proper way to do it, it had struck her with terrible clarity that his concerns were all about what this might mean to Vincenzo, to the brat Achille, to the de Grazia bloodline. Not for a second did it cross his mind to concern himself with what a change in heirs might mean to *her*.

Until that moment she had never, except in occasional moments of pique, begrudged her father his stiff-necked adherence to the old-fashioned view that the entailed de Grazia estate was properly passed from son to son, with daughters — even elder daughters — given no consideration. That was a tradition. But now, for the first time she understood that to Domenico she counted for nothing at all, she was a woman, a zero, someone who might provide a reasonably intelligent sounding board, but whose views, whose own interest in the matter, were of no concern.

And the fact was, she *did* have an interest in the matter. If Phil actually became *padrone*, a time of unthinkable retribution would descend on her. She would no longer be mistress of the estate, she would be treated like dirt. It was true enough that Phil had many snubs, many disparagements, even many cruelties for which to repay her. She was ready to admit that. But whose fault was it that she had been brought up to look down on the Ungarettis? Couldn't her father see it was his, no one's but his?

No, he couldn't see. Nor, apparently, could he see that the weedy, churlish Phil, regardless of his precious genes, was a *cavone* through and through — a boor, a vulgarian — whose commonplace manners and lack of breeding would mean the end of the house of de Grazia as they knew it.

But as they talked — as *he* talked — it had become increasingly clear that for her father one thing mattered above all else: the de Grazia blood line. There had never been any real doubt in his mind about what course he would pursue. He would convene a *consiglio* as soon as possible, as soon as Phil could fly to Italy; tomorrow, if possible. He would . . .

As he spoke, a reddish cloud had come down in front of her eyes like a blood-tinged cloth. He was so proud of himself, of 'sacrificing' the man he had always thought of as his son — with tears in his eyes he actually compared himself to the Abraham of the Bible, giving up his only begotten son for the greater good — so completely oblivious to Francesca's needs that, in a fit of shuddering, uncontrollable rage, she had snatched a knife from the block on the kitchen counter . . .

'And that's it,' Phil said with a shrug. 'She didn't tell me how she faked the boating accident, but what's the difference?'

'I don't understand,' Gideon said. 'Why would she confess to you when she wouldn't to the police?'

'I'm telling you, it gushed out of her like water. She was white, she was shaking. When she got control of herself, she told me I was obligated — as a de Grazia, no less — to keep it to myself. And if I told anyone, she'd just deny she'd said it anyway, and what proof did I have?'

'And what did you do?'

'I called Caravale first thing, of course. But she's right. What proof of anything do I have? Still, it ought to be useful to him.'

Julie was shaking her head from side to

side. 'My God, the whole thing sounds like an opera.'

'Well, we are Italian,' Phil said with his first smile of the morning.

'What about kidnapping Achille?' Gideon asked. 'And skimming money from the company all those years? What was that all about, do you know?'

'Yeah, more or less. She kind of touched on some of it obliquely and I think I can put the rest together. From what I can tell, she was pretty confident right from the first that she'd gotten away with it — with the murder — but after a while, she started to worry that somehow, somewhere, I'd eventually find out who I really was and I'd come down on Isola de Grazia like Attila the Hun, claiming my birthright, sowing strife and destruction, and making life hell for everybody, but especially her.'

'I don't blame her for being worried,' Julie said. 'Dr Luzzatto could have told you anytime he wanted.'

'No, she was pretty comfortable about that once she saw that he was going to sit by without saying anything and let Vincenzo inherit. Who knows, maybe she talked to him about it.'

'But she *did* kill him in the end.'

'Yes.'

'But only after Luzzatto found out that Domenico's death was murder and started muttering to himself,' Gideon said. 'And that took ten years.'

They carried the dishes into the kitchen and took fresh coffee into the living room. 'Go ahead, Phil,' Gideon said. 'She was afraid you'd find out you were Domenico's son sometime, so . . . '

'So she started skimming in order to be ready to take care of herself when the time came.' He had perked up with the food and coffee and was looking better, despite a little haggardness from the overnight flight. And his new position in life seemed to be having an effect on him, whatever he claimed. He was wearing a nice, new knit shirt, decent trousers, and new oxfords. Gone were the T-shirt, shorts, and sneakers he'd flown out in.

'She was the CFO,' Gideon said. 'It probably wasn't that hard to fudge things.'

'Right. And Vincenzo hated that part of the operation — he'd rather be out drumming up business — so he was glad to leave it to her. She's a smart girl, so she worked out ways of putting money in her pocket, a little at a time, when transactions came through. But when the stock market went south and there weren't so many transactions anymore, that got harder. And she was starting to get nervous anyway; the longer she did that kind of finagling, the more likely she'd make a mistake and get caught.'

'And so she set up Achille's kidnapping?' Julie said. 'Five million euros in one shot, and then no more having to play around with company finances.'

'Yup, that's the way it looks.'

They were in armchairs arranged in front of the big picture window, and for a while they sat quietly and looked out at the view. Ordinarily you could see all the way to Vancouver Island, and sometimes to the mountains of the Canadian mainland, but today they could barely see as far as the ferry dock. If anything, the murk was getting darker, the rain heavier. It was a good day to be inside. Gideon began thinking about building a fire but was too comfortable to get up.

'What about Vincenzo?' Julie asked. 'What are you going to do about him?'

'Nothing,' Phil said, seemingly surprised at the question.

'But you can't leave him there as the *padrone*.'

'Who says?' Phil responded, showing some animation. 'You think I want to take over? I told you, I can't stand that place for more than a couple of days at a time. You think I want to *live* there? Everything'll stay just the way it was. Vincenzo's not perfect, but he's been doing fine. I'll visit once in a while, same as always, that's all.'

'Well, what happens after Vincenzo? Who follows him?'

'Achille, same as before.' He laughed at their expressions. 'Don't look so amazed. I think this kidnap thing has sobered the kid up. He'll be OK, trust me.'

'But is that legal?' Julie asked. 'After all, Vincenzo isn't really a de Grazia.'

'So? Who's gonna sue over it? Me? Not likely.'

Gideon whistled softly. 'Vincenzo must think you're out of your mind.'

'Actually, he's been pretty honorable about it. He offered to pack up and leave, but I told him a little peasant blood was good for the family.'

'I bet he loved that.'

'He'll get over it. He's still getting used to the idea that his father's name is Pietro Somebody . . . or was it Pasquale Somebody, the one with the warts . . . or was it Guglielmo Somebody?' He laughed. 'I happen to think this whole thing will make a better man of him.'

'I happen to think so too,' Gideon said.

Phil leaned forward, his elbows on his knees, slowly turning his mug in his hands. 'Look, the main thing is, I'm the same guy I always was. I'm happy the way I am. I was okay with Emma Ungaretti as my mother, I was OK with crazy Gia as my mother, and I'm OK with this arrangement. I mean, I'm glad Emma really is my mother, but it doesn't have anything to do with *me* . . . if you know what I mean.' He put down his coffee and stood up. 'Thanks a lot, people. You've really been great. Hey, maybe we can get together — '

'Not so fast, pal,' Julie said. 'Let's get down to important matters. How do things stand with you and Lea?'

A slow, shy grin tipped up the corners of his mouth. 'Not too bad. Can you believe this is happening to me? She's been to the States and she likes it here, and with a little language training, her skills would be usable here too. She's a kind of hotel consultant — '

'Slow down. When do you see her next?'

'Well, I'm inviting her to spend a week up in Bellingham. You know, to see the great Pacific Northwest.' The grin spread. 'From there . . . who knows what could happen?'

'Not this month, I hope,' Gideon said as a gust of wind flung a noisy spatter of rain against the window, almost like a handful of pebbles. Just below, a couple of rhododendron bushes, their leaves shiny black with water, swayed and fluttered in the storm. 'She's from sunny Italy. This could be pretty traumatic.'

'True,' Julie said. 'You know, you'd better not make it January or February either.'

'Or March,' Gideon said.

'Or November or December.'

'Or — '

'I was thinking,' said Phil, 'of the third week in July, three months from now.'

Gideon chewed his lip, considering. 'That should work,' he said.

do hope that you have enjoyed reading this large print book.

Did you know that all of our titles are available for purchase?

We publish a wide range of high quality large print books including:
**Romances, Mysteries, Classics
General Fiction
Non Fiction and Westerns**

Special interest titles available in large print are:
**The Little Oxford Dictionary
Music Book
Song Book
Hymn Book
Service Book**

Also available from us courtesy of Oxford University Press:
**Young Readers' Dictionary
(large print edition)
Young Readers' Thesaurus
(large print edition)**

For further information or a free brochure, please contact us at:
**Ulverscroft Large Print Books Ltd.,
The Green, Bradgate Road, Anstey,
Leicester, LE7 7FU, England.
Tel:** (00 44) 0116 236 4325
Fax: (00 44) 0116 234 0205